"This is my wingman."

Michael's enthusiasm spread as he introduced his clearly unenthusiastic friend. "Jet—"

"Broughman." His name fell from Clara's lips before Michael had a chance to say anything. "I thought I recognized you."

And here it was, all uneasiness explained.

Jet Broughman was Clara's one, tentative foray into high-school flirtation gone horribly wrong. They had gone to a small school, and she was friendly with everyone. A lot of guys asked her out, but with all she had going on, and the anxiety she was learning to master, she'd instinctively declined any offers.

Then one bright, early October morning, he'd held the door for her as she entered the school. When she glanced up to say thank you, their eyes met, and that was it. There'd been something about Jet's intelligent, dark gaze and occasional smile that warmed her to the core. She'd had one chance with him and messed it up so irrevocably she still cringed at the memory.

Now the quiet, brilliant, gorgeous boy had grown up. *Wow*.

Dear Reader,

Welcome to Outcrop, Oregon! Nestled between the Cascade Mountains and Crooked River, Outcrop is home to ranchers, small business owners, outdoor adventurers and the Wallace family. These five lovable, flawed siblings have each other's backs, but also push each other's buttons.

In *A Rancher Worth Remembering*, you'll meet Clara Wallace and Jet Broughman. Jet's had a crush on Clara since he first saw her ten years earlier, but he can't bring himself to trust their growing friendship. Both Jet and Clara met with challenges in their youth and responded to adversity by cultivating resilience. While they've created extraordinary lives for themselves, there's still growth ahead as they learn to open up to love. Sometimes, the hardest goal to achieve is the one you want the most: love.

I'm thrilled you have the first book in the Love, Oregon series in your hands. *A Rancher Worth Remembering* is my debut with Harlequin Heartwarming, and I'd love to hear what you think. You can find me on Twitter, Facebook and Instagram.

Happy reading!

Anna

HEARTWARMING

A Rancher Worth Remembering

—

Anna Grace

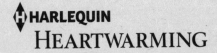

HARLEQUIN®
HEARTWARMING™

Recycling programs
for this product may
not exist in your area.

ISBN-13: 978-1-335-58480-9

A Rancher Worth Remembering

Copyright © 2022 by Anna Grace

For questions and comments about the quality of this book,
please contact us at CustomerService@Harlequin.com.

Harlequin Enterprises ULC
22 Adelaide St. West, 41st Floor
Toronto, Ontario M5H 4E3, Canada
www.Harlequin.com

Printed in U.S.A.

Anna Grace justifies her espresso addiction by writing fun, modern romance novels in the early morning hours. Once the sun comes up, you can find her teaching high school history, or outside with her adventure-loving husband. Anna is a mediocre rock climber, award-winning author, mom of two fun kids and snack enthusiast. She lives rurally in Oregon, and travels to big cities whenever she gets the chance. Anna loves connecting with readers, and you can find her on social media and at her website, anna-grace-author.com.

Twitter: @AnnaEmilyGrace
IG: @annagraceauthor
Facebook: Anna Grace Author

To my parents, Denis and Lynn Grace,
for their steadfast and unwavering support of
this endeavor.

CHAPTER ONE

CLARA DIDN'T MEAN to run over the cowboy. She'd ridden her bicycle around Outcrop for the last ten years without hitting so much as a shrub. But now a grown man lay sprawled out in the parking lot of Eighty Local. Both he and her fender were bent out of shape.

"I'm *so* sorry." Clara hopped off her bike, letting it fall. "Are you okay?"

"I'm fine." He sounded a little winded.

"Really, I feel terrible!" She knelt beside him. "I didn't see you."

"It's not the first time I've been thrown to the ground." The gravel crunched as he rolled to a sitting position. He winced and blew out a sharp breath.

"I was distracted by that old truck." She gestured to a Chevy, trying for humor. "Like, how did someone even get it running?"

He gave a dry laugh. "That's *my* old truck."

Clara pressed her palms against her bike helmet. Exactly how much worse could she make a situation? If her brothers taught her nothing else, it was that men in central Oregon were deeply attached to their trucks.

"I mean, it's nice. It looks, um, refurbished."

"It looks like I pulled it off the field at the Deschutes County demolition derby."

Clara warmed. Not every guy would be so nice after being knocked off his feet by an old, fixed-gear Schwinn.

The man moved slowly, like someone who knew how to check for injury. He straightened his Stetson, dusted his hands across his jeans and looked up at her.

He was gorgeous.

Not gorgeous in an *I should set you up with one of my clients* sort of way. It was more of a *Let's you and I take that Chevy for a long, slow drive as soon as possible* type of handsome.

His broad shoulders were clad in a simple but expensive-looking T-shirt. Long legs were predictably covered in denim. He wore what appeared to be handmade boots, well-worn and dust covered. The deep brown eyes shining beneath his Stetson were Clara's weakness.

A fluttering bloomed in her belly, like a kaleidoscope of butterflies taking flight. She was used to intense nervous reactions; her heart rate amping up, sending what felt like tiny tidal waves of blood through her system. She would normally combat the reaction with one of a myriad strategies she'd learned over the years.

But the interaction didn't feel stressful, it felt good. There was something deeply appealing about this cowboy. Something familiar. She was nervous, sure, but also felt safe. She glanced into his eyes below the rim of his hat. He smiled. The tidal waves turned into tsunamis.

She shook her head to dislodge the image of herself in his truck, tucked up under his arm for a moonlit drive on a country road. She'd just run over the guy, so she probably wasn't his first choice for shotgun.

"I feel terrible for knocking you over," she said.

"It's my fault." He pushed himself to his feet. "I wasn't looking where I was going."

"It was *my* fault. I'm late for a meeting, but even I know better than to go tearing through the Eighty Local lot. This restaurant is always packed."

The man ambled to Clara's bike and righted it, prominent biceps noticeable through the fabric of his T-shirt. She tried to get a good look at his face, but his hat was pulled low.

"I was distracted myself. My best friend's about to make a huge mistake, and I agreed to hang out while he goes through with it." His steady, deep voice set off a hum inside her.

"Sounds like you're a pretty good friend."

"Good friend, good sandwich maker, that's about all I got." He wheeled the bike to her.

"I'll add good sport to that." She took the bike. "Again, I feel terrible."

"Don't feel bad. I'm fine. You okay?" He bent slightly to look into her face.

Clara pulled her helmet off and ran her fingers through her hair. The man's gaze followed the swing of her hair.

Interesting.

She repeated the action. A flush rose up his neck.

Oh. Hmm.

"I'm great." She was fantastic. She was late for a meeting. Her new client was probably furious. But the handsome, easygoing cowboy seemed to like her hair.

Clara reached up to pull off her sunglasses but stopped before she became a total 1980s cliché. She glanced back at his truck.

"It's my grandfather's truck." The man rolled his shoulders. "*Was* my grandfather's truck. I keep meaning to get a new one, but this runs fine. Sometimes I even hit the speed limit."

Oh, yes. Perfect for a slow ride on a back-

country road. My bare feet on his dashboard, his arm around my shoulder...

Clara tore her gaze away from the truck. But then she was staring into the warm brown eyes of a wounded cowboy. Her heart skipped to a funny rhythm, like a mix of disco and champagne bubbles.

A soft breeze danced past them, the scent of juniper peppering the perfect summer day. All signs suggested this man was interested. Despite being a matchmaker, and having a life mission of helping others find love, Clara had never actually asked a man out, or even been in a relationship that lasted more than a few weeks. Convincing others to open up to love was much easier than risking her own heart. It would be just like her to run over the man of her dreams, then run away.

She drew in a deep breath for courage.

Was she really going to do this? Actually ask him out?

She glanced up into those warm brown eyes. *Yes. Definitely.*

"So I have a meeting right now, but I'll be free in about an hour." Clara's pulse rushed in her ears. She took another steadying breath and gestured to her brother's restaurant. "Can I buy you coffee?"

The man pulled his head back, surprised. Then he smiled. "Or I could buy you coffee, for getting in your way."

She laughed. This was going so well. Too well. Like, it could be a great story to tell their grandkids.

But something shifted in his expression as she laughed. He took a step backward.

Cautiously, Clara continued. "When I said buy you coffee, I actually meant make you coffee. This is my brother's restaurant."

The hesitant smile dropped from his face.

"Hunter Wallace is your brother?" he asked, with an edge to his voice.

Clara pulled off her sunglasses. He took another step back. An uncomfortable buzz began to rattle around in her mind. Had she said something wrong?

"Yep," she said, flashing him a smile that generally put people at ease. It had the opposite effect on this man. "I'm Clara Wallace."

OF COURSE IT was Clara Wallace. Who else could knock a man head over boots, then make him grateful for the experience? The minute she'd pulled off her bike helmet he should have known. But he just stood there, mooning around like a lovesick bull. *Idiot.*

This was not how Jet Broughman wanted to run into Clara for the first time since returning to Outcrop. She didn't recognize him. Probably didn't even remember him. He'd come so far, but the sound of her laughter sent him straight back to high school.

"It's the least I can do," she said, her big brown eyes wide.

"Thanks," he said, glancing away. "I, uh, don't know how long this is going to take."

Her face transformed, like an actress in a melodrama wrestling with confusion and hurt. *Because she hadn't inspired those feelings in enough men during her twenty-eight years?*

"This is seriously the best restaurant you'll find anywhere," she said. "If you're a sandwich connoisseur you'll want to check it out."

"Yeah, I know Hunter."

"You do?"

He let his gaze connect with hers and waited.

Nothing. She had absolutely no idea who he was.

But what had he expected? That news of his lucrative run in the tech industry and innovative restoration of his grandfather's ranch would spread like Scotch thistle through this town?

Right.

It didn't matter. It wasn't like he'd worked incredibly hard and done well for himself solely to get Clara's approval. Not at all.

"My friend's waiting." Jet took another step away from Clara. "I'd better get going."

"O-okay. See you around." She ran her fingers through her hair, the strands of brown and blond shifting around her shoulders. She raised both hands to pull her hair back, her eyes on him as he continued to stand there staring.

He cleared his throat. "See you."

Jet moved quickly across the parking lot, away from Clara. Coming back to Outcrop was the right thing to do. He was twenty-nine, educated and successful. He was going to run into people sooner or later. May as well get comfortable with the fact that Clara was still in Outcrop.

And still so beautiful it made it hard to breathe.

Jet pulled himself together, then headed into Eighty Local. In the early afternoon the restaurant was quieter but still home to a cheerful rumble of customer conversation.

"Hey," Hunter called from over the counter.

Jet leveled his shoulders and looked up. He'd never been real comfortable in social situations, but he liked working with Hunter. The two men had a common interest in local food production. And Hunter had at least remembered Jet when he'd contacted him about buying beef from the ranch.

If Jet could solidify a deal to be the main supplier of beef to Eighty Local, he'd be on the way to creating the income stream he needed for the success of the ranching operation. He intended to keep the money he'd earned in Seattle invested, supporting himself with the ranch.

"How's business?" Jet asked.

"Good. Busy. You see the board?" Hunter pointed to the large piece of slate that held the specials.

Jet scanned the day's offerings, not knowing what he was supposed to be looking for. Then it popped out at him. *Burma Mile Burger, Tillamook cheddar, roasted green chilis and 8L Sauce on top of ½ lb. of organic beef, locally sourced from Broughman Ranch.*

"I'm on the board!" Jet said.

"Yeah. I came up with that one for hungry climbers and hikers, but it's about all anyone's ordered all day."

This was a great first step. But what he wanted was his ranch's name in the printed menu. He hoped that in the near future, every burger served at Eighty Local was organic, grass-fed, free-range Broughman beef.

"I'm going to step in the back for a minute," Hunter said. "Holler if you need anything."

"Thanks."

If Clara saw this, would it register that she'd been in school with a kid named Jet Broughman? Or had she forgotten him completely? In high school she and her twin sister Piper had been the popular, outgoing cheerleaders everyone loved to love. The other girls would do whatever Clara and Piper did, and the boys would follow wherever they went. Piper had been more aloof, but Clara would sparkle at you for four weeks straight, then walk past you on the fifth as though you'd never existed.

Jet still cringed when he remembered his awkward attempt to ask her out. Somehow, he'd thought he had a chance with her. There'd been something in the way she smiled and pulled him into conversations that convinced his lonely, awkward, high school self that she could see past the disconnected foster kid to the man he aspired to be. Jet had worked for weeks to save up the money and plan a date worthy of Clara. Her rejection was swift and clear. For a boy with a lifetime of abandonment behind him, it had been devastating.

Over the years he'd realized her rejection was an effective kick in the behind to get himself out of Outcrop and on the path to the financial freedom he now enjoyed. He couldn't be abandoned, or rejected, if he was self-sufficient. If everyone who fell in love with Clara had a similar reaction, the world would be full of motivated, successful, still slightly heartbroken men.

"Jet!" Michael waved at him from a corner booth along the front window. "Hey, man." Jet felt better as he approached his old friend.

"What happened out there?" Michael gestured out the window.

I was knocked flat on my behind by the most beautiful, inconsiderate woman in Outcrop.

"Nothing."

Michael shifted in his seat, a huge grin splitting his face. "Something's about to happen here. Time to meet the matchmaker!"

"This is a terrible idea." Jet tried not to laugh at his friend's enthusiasm. "You can't hire someone to help you fall in love. It doesn't work that way."

"But if it does work, I will be laughing at you from the altar."

"And if it doesn't?"

"Then, we can joke about it when we're old men sitting in front of the hardware store."

Jet shook his head at Michael's optimism. "Don't say I didn't warn you."

"I have it on the record. Jet Broughman thinks middle-aged doctors should not hire professional matchmakers. You happy now?"

"You're not middle-aged—"

"Jet, I'm a doctor. I know how old I am."

"You're thirty-two. That's not middle-aged."

"I'm in my mid-thirties. And I want a family."

Jet grunted in response. He should be more supportive. Michael was his oldest friend, and he'd taken a job in central Oregon in part because Jet was returning to his grandfather's ranch. Jet had underestimated how much his friend wanted to be married and how difficult finding the right woman could be in a rural community.

"Why don't you just—"

"Just what? I cannot meet a woman, Jet, you know that. I've tried it all. Online dating, barhopping, church, singles skiing."

"Have you tried a gym membership?"

"And possibly meet a woman who thinks I'm going to work out with her? Forget it."

Jet laughed. "Good point. If you have to go through with this, I'm here for you."

"I appreciate it. You can tell the matchmaker what a catch I am."

Jet shook his head. Michael was as excited as a kid in a carnival bouncy house. Objectively, this wasn't the worst way to get your heart broken in central Oregon, not by a long shot. Even a misguided matchmaker couldn't cause as much trouble as Clara Wallace.

CHAPTER TWO

CLARA PUSHED HER bike across the gravel parking lot of her brother's restaurant, embarrassment and disappointment spiking in her chest. It was literally the first time she'd gone out on a limb to ask someone out, and that limb had snapped seconds later.

Wow. Could the morning get any worse?

She checked the time. Apparently, it could.

At most first-meets Clara was waiting, composed and professional, at the fifth booth along the front window at Eighty Local. But now she'd be running in at the last minute, trying to work in a fog of anxiety and foolishness.

"You're not late yet," her brother said, emerging out the back door.

"Is he here?" Clara grabbed her leather-bound notebook from her basket.

"He'll be fine."

"I hate being late." She balanced and readjusted a strap on her espadrilles. "I couldn't get out of the house. A distressed client called, right in the middle of planning my outfits for the week." Hunter's lips twitched. Clara glared. "Don't laugh. I'm not in the mood today."

"I'm not laughing."

"Your eyes are mirthful."

"No, they're not." Hunter opened the door. "I have no mirth. You gonna lock your bike up?"

Clara glanced back at her cream-colored cruiser, then up at her brother. "Zero bike thieves are interested in the Schwinn."

Hunter studied her ancient, beloved bicycle. "That's for sure."

Clara stopped inside the back door. She placed a hand on the wall and drew in three deep breaths. Hunter rubbed her back.

"You okay?"

She opened her mouth to tell him about the man in the parking lot, but nothing came out. What was she going to say to her brother? *I ran over a man out there, then was stupid enough to ask him out.*

No, Hunter already knew the truth about her. She was an excellent matchmaker and a terrible match.

She allowed herself a moment to bask in her brother's concern. Clara was ridiculously lucky when it came to family: two wonderful parents, two sets of twins and a bossy oldest brother who kept them all in line.

But it was Hunter she depended on when she had a rough day. Her twin, Piper, was her best friend, and unconditionally supportive, but she ran a branch of their matchmaking business from Portland and wasn't home half as much as Clara would have liked. Hunter's twin, Bowman, was fantastic, but his work as a firefighter kept him busy. And Ash, their oldest sibling, was more inclined to give a lecture than a hug.

Clara was deeply grateful for Hunter. Not that she would actually tell him any of this, but still.

She shook her hair back and adjusted her pale green sundress. "How awful do I look right now?"

"You look fine," Hunter said.

"Thank you. And this place smells amazing." She scanned the back room of Hunter's restaurant. With its piles of fresh, local vegetables, reclaimed fixtures and natural light, this room was one of her favorite places on earth. *And when Hunter's trying out a new recipe? Even better.* "What are you making?"

"A new summer vegetable soup. Can you stay after your meeting and try it?"

"I will try all the soups. I'm also happy to try

the sweet potato fries again, should that sacrifice be necessary."

"We've established the viability of sweet potato fries," Hunter said. "Since you *try* them every time you stop by."

He glanced up at the clock. Clara followed his gaze, then headed toward the dining room.

"Who you got today?"

She pulled out the file on her newest Potential.

"Thirty-two-year-old Michael Williams: pediatric surgeon, self-described extrovert, lives and works in Redmond."

"Go hook him up," Hunter said.

"When do I get to match you up?" Clara asked, still studying the file.

"When do you get yourself matched up?"

She glared at her brother. Then she hit him with the file.

"I'm glad we have this settled," he said. "Soup's waiting for you when you finish."

Clara paused at the entrance to the dining room, uneasiness weighing on her chest. *What was it about that guy in the parking lot?*

Besides the obvious.

She needed to take time to think. Why was she so bothered by the interaction, and what had inspired her to ask him out in the first place? But there was no time for reflection. She rounded the counter into the dining room.

"The usual spot." Hunter gestured to the table Clara always claimed for meetings.

Her client was sitting at the edge of the booth with his back to her: dark, close-cropped hair, broad shoulders, triceps visible through the fabric of a nice T-shirt. A Stetson hung on the hook at the end of the booth.

Clara stopped. She zeroed in on the triceps. *Oh, no.*

She rested one hand on the counter and deliberately pulled in three deep breaths. She could hear Hunter's concerned approach, and she shook her head to keep him from speaking. Clara readjusted her necklace, squared her shoulders and approached the booth.

"Hello," Clara said cheerfully. "Sorry I'm late—"

"Hi!" A sweet-faced man popped out of the other side of the booth. Time stuttered as she realigned her expectations. The man was so eager Clara could feel the hope pouring off him.

Oh, wait. This *was the friend. Did that make her services the huge mistake?* Clara turned and locked eyes with the cowboy. He met her gaze with unconcealed horror and shock.

"You must be Clara," her client said, eyes wide behind heavily framed glasses.

She took both his hands in hers and clasped them. "Yes, Clara Wallace. I am so happy to meet you, Michael." She turned to the other occupant of the booth. His brown eyes were no longer warm. "And your friend?"

"This is my wingman." Michael's enthusiasm spread as he introduced his clearly unenthusiastic friend. "Jet—"

"Broughman." His name fell from Clara's lips before Michael had a chance to say anything. "I thought I recognized you."

And here it was, all uneasiness explained.

Jet Broughman was Clara's one, tentative foray into high school flirtation gone horribly wrong. They had gone to a small school, and she was friendly with everyone. A lot of guys asked her out, but with all she had going on, and the anxiety she was learning to master, she'd instinctively declined any offers.

Then one bright, early October morning, he'd held the door for her as she entered the school. When she glanced up to say thank you, their eyes met, and that was it. There'd been something about Jet's intelligent, dark gaze and occasional smile that warmed her to the core. She'd had one chance with him and messed it up so irrevocably that she still cringed at the memory.

Now the quiet, brilliant, gorgeous boy had grown up. *Wow.*

He was taller, his shoulders filled out, his jawline more prominent, but that was no excuse for not recognizing him, even under the Stetson. She had, however, recognized the way he'd made her feel: both safe and excited.

Until she introduced herself. At that point he seemed to remember what a mess she'd been in high school. He got himself out of her sight as quickly as possible.

This first-meet with a new client was not optimum, but she could do it. Michael seemed like a good guy, and he wanted to find love. She might be completely incapable of a relationship, but her superpower was helping other people achieve what she could not.

"Welcome back to Outcrop." She gave Jet a bright smile, as she would have done with any old high school acquaintance. Jet held eye contact and nodded coolly.

And that was Jet Broughman, illuminating her every failing.

JET COULDN'T BELIEVE this was happening. Of all the women profiting off the hope of love, his friend *had* to choose Clara Wallace? Match-making was exactly the sort of potentially heartbreaking venture Clara would go for.

"Did Jet tell you I ran him down in the parking lot?" she asked Michael.

Michael laughed. "The pretty ones always go for Jet."

"I didn't know you were back in town," she said to Jet.

"I am."

"Are you running your grandfather's ranch?" Somehow a chair appeared as though she'd summoned it. Clara sat down at the end of the booth, rather than share a bench with either of them.

"Yep."

"The burger you ate last Saturday came from his place," Hunter called from over the counter.

"Oh, seriously?" Clara widened her eyes. "It was delicious."

"I bought half a steer from Jet," Michael said sheepishly. "Then I had to buy a freezer to put it in."

Clara laughed, her adorable dimples flexing. "Let's see if we can find you a woman to grill those steaks with." She opened a soft leather notebook. "But before we begin—" she glanced at Jet "—we're only here for Michael, correct? Jet, are you interested—"

"No. Absolutely not. I'm here for Michael."

"You felt you needed some backup?" she asked Michael.

Michael looked across the table at him. The guy needed help, all right.

"I did. I've made a lot of mistakes with women before. Jet knows me. He'll keep me out of trouble."

"All right, then. Hunter?" she called over her shoulder. Hunter appeared with two beers and a suspiciously small pour of red wine. Michael, unsuspicious and unaware, picked up one of the beers and drank. No curiosity about what kind it was or who was paying or why it was placed in front of him.

"I love Deschutes Amber Ale!" Michael sputtered after one gulp.

"I know. I read your portfolio." Clara winked.

"What's this?" Jet asked Hunter.

"That's a new stout from Three Creeks Brewing," Hunter said. "Clara takes care of her clients. I brought the stout for you. You'll like it."

Jet's eyes jumped from Hunter to Clara. He wanted to supply Eighty Local with beef. That meant he had to stay in the good graces of Clara's protective family. So he should probably just drink the beer rather than grab his best friend and shove him out the door.

"Thanks."

"Thank you, bro." Clara refocused on Michael. "Okay, let's get down to business. Michael, tell me why you want to find love."

Michael spilled his heart out, succumbing to the charm of Clara Wallace. She and her sister had held this power over the boys in high school. One-and-a-half smiles and you were in love with one of the Wallace twins, sure as anything. Jet had been too quiet to receive many of those smiles: too quiet, too studious, too from-a-broken-home.

Until he wasn't. He'd never really understood why Clara had turned her charm on him in October of his senior year. He'd been as smitten with her as the rest of the guys, sneaking glances from beneath his ball cap. Then one day, Clara came drifting down the hall right toward him, nearly stopping his heart with her radiant smile. Jet remembered looking over his shoulder to see who she was smiling at, then realizing it had to be him. By the time he'd gotten his head back around she had passed. He'd lain awake on the lumpy sofa in his grandfather's house, listening to the wind slice through the window casings, contemplating her smile late into the night.

The next day she did it again. Jet had no idea

how to respond or even if he should. Clara was beautiful, popular and friendly. He was awkward and disconnected. But something in her smile warmed him from the center of his heart outward. Somewhere around the fourth or fifth time, he got up the nerve to say hi. The walk to AP Biology became his favorite part of the day. He would stop the flow of traffic as she approached, and they'd talk until the bell rang. It was her dad's class in which he ran up the tardy slips, but Mr. Wallace never seemed upset about it. It took a few weeks and one incredibly lucky catch at a Friday night football game before he finally got the nerve to ask her out.

She'd said no. Her sister came over and hustled her away from him as quickly as possible. At the time it had felt like someone ripped the sun out of the sky and expected everyone to carry on as normal. Clara might have tried to smile at him in the hall again, but his eighteen-year-old self knew what abandonment looked like. His mom always acted sorry as he climbed into the car of yet another social worker, but he could see the relief on her face when she closed the door.

He'd been an idiot thinking a girl like Clara would ever go out with him. Jet found another route through school to his science class and avoided any place he might run into her. A few weeks later Mr. Wallace had encouraged him to apply for a lucrative scholarship. After graduation, Jet left Outcrop for a full ride at the University of Washington. He and Clara had never spoken again. Or not until she laid him flat with her bicycle, anyway.

He shifted in his seat. He'd come a long way since high school. There was no reason to feel uncomfortable around Clara now. *No reason at all.*

"Talk to me about your interests," she was saying to Michael. "On the application, rather than listing interests you say you are up for anything."

"I am." Michael nodded. "I'm easy to please."

"Right, but when you have the choice, what do you like to do?"

Michael deferred again. "It doesn't have to be all about me."

Clara pressed on. "That is a wonderful characteristic. It's going to make your dating life a lot easier, and it's going to make the rest of your life a lot more fun. But I need to know what you like."

Jet interrupted. "Why can't you take him at his word? I've known Michael since we were in undergrad. He's up for anything."

Clara's pretty mouth shot into a straight line. "Thanks, Jet." She turned to Michael. "It's Saturday morning, you're not on call, and your laundry is finished. What do you want to do?"

Michael pondered the question. Jet was about to interject with one of a hundred things the two of them had done on a Saturday when Michael said, "Look at the birds."

"Birds?"

Michael studied his beer. "I like birds. And the squirrels. And the chipmunks."

"I love chipmunks," Clara exclaimed.

"I can't get enough of it." Michael gestured out the window. "I grew up in the city, and I've never seen a place like this. In my town house they come right up on the porch, the deer and raccoons and everything. I could watch the birds and the critters all day. Even Jet's cattle or the emus."

Jet groaned inwardly. *Why did Michael have to bring up the emus?*

Clara slowly turned to face him and arched her brows. "You have emus?"

"A few." He glanced over the end of the booth, hoping to avoid this line of conversation. The six curious emus were a ranching experiment that wasn't working out so well.

She grinned. "How many?"

"Too many."

"Not nearly enough!" Michael enthused. "They're a riot. They're really young, like teenagers in bird years, always getting into trouble. I love those emus."

Jet planted his face in his palm. No wonder his friend had to resort to a matchmaker to get a date.

Clara reached over and tapped his hand off his face. Jet sat up in shock at the intimacy of the gesture.

"There is nothing wrong with bird-watching. Or squirrel-gazing." She sent Jet a look.

"But you probably don't want to advertise it," Michael admitted.

"That's where you're wrong. You are a nice, enthusiastic man with a good job who likes birds and fuzzy critters. What's not to love?" She bent over and took a few more notes, tucking her perfect hair behind her ear.

Michael beamed. Jet guessed that Michael would marry Clara on the spot if she'd have him.

"Okay. I want you to think more on this topic and get back to me. What do *you* enjoy? But for now, let's talk about what you don't like."

Michael gave the predictable list of bad life choices he didn't want to deal with. Clara didn't take notes. She watched Michael, like she was waiting for the real issues to spill.

His phone pinged, and Michael lunged for it. "I'm sorry," he said to Clara, studying the message. "This woman I used to date is having a really hard time with her fiancé, and I've been helping her through it."

"Do not answer that text," Jet said.

"It'll just take a second. She needs to know I'm here for her." Michael stood and adjusted his pants. "Be right back."

"Michael, we've talked about this." Jet turned in the booth, speaking as Michael walked away. "She's not going to leave that hockey player, and if she does, it's not going to be for—" But his friend was already gone, down the rabbit hole of another insecure ex who'd left him for a jerk.

Jet closed his eyes and leaned back in the booth. This was a disaster.

"You know I'm going to help him."

Jet opened one eye. Clara's deceptively beautiful smile shone. He'd learned a long time ago not to trust that smile. He rested his arms on the table and leaned toward her.

"I don't believe you."

She started to protest, but he interrupted. "I'm not saying you have bad intentions, but I know my friend. You're going to take his money and trot him out in front of a line of women. They'll be real interested when they hear he's a doctor, but the minute he turns out to be—"

"An incredibly nice man with zero fashion sense and a weakness for manipulative women?" Clara finished for him.

Jet met her eyes and willed himself to keep from smiling. She hit that nail on the head.

"Yeah. That. Then I clean up the mess."

"I don't know what you think my business is." She pressed her lips together and glanced out the window. Her fingers drifted up to her necklace. "I don't know what your problem with me is. I'm sorry about the parking lot but—"

"I don't have a problem with you."

She flexed her brow.

"What I object to is you getting his hopes up, charging him money to introduce him to someone he could probably bump into at Thriftway if he were patient enough."

She readjusted the wineglass in front of her, which seemed to be purely ornamental at this point. "Has the Thriftway in Redmond seen an upswing in romantic connections?"

"I'm just saying—"

"No, really. Does Thriftway have any statistics on their match success rate? Because I do. Since my sister and I started Love, Oregon four years ago, we have made hundreds of successful matches. Your friend hired me. This is my job." She shifted her binder and readjusted several sticky notes. "Why are you even here?"

Right. He was unwanted. Unnecessary. Like always in this town.

"I'm looking out for my friend."

Michael came bounding back to the table, scrolling through messages on his phone.

"Michael, may I see your phone?" Clara held out her hand. Michael obediently dropped the phone into it. "What was that woman's name?"

"Lauren Bickenhall. She's a really good person, but right now she's struggling."

Clara studied Lauren's picture in Michael's contacts, then held the phone out to him. "Please block her."

"W-what?"

"Block Lauren. Should you decide to disengage my services, you're free to do as you like. For the duration of this contract, you are not to speak to her. Am I clear?"

She lifted her chin and leveled a gaze on Michael.

"Okay." Michael blinked, then nodded. "Okay. Thank you. Lauren has been...distracting me."

Michael's fingers shook as he obeyed Clara's command.

Jet stared, dumbfounded. He'd had this conversation with Michael a hundred times, and Clara had shut it down in less than thirty seconds. It was almost enough to make him think hiring her might be a good idea.

But that was Clara. Just when you thought she was the answer to all your dreams, she crushed those dreams beneath the heel of her pretty summer sandal.

Clara's smile broke out, bathing Michael in her charm. "This is a good time to mention that you're not allowed to check your phone on dates."

Michael furrowed his brow. "But I—"

"Do not check your phone when you're on a date."

"You're overstepping here," Jet interrupted, leaning toward Clara. The faint trace of her scent, orange and ginger, caught him in its grasp and pulled him closer. Jet stopped speaking for a moment, then forced himself to sit back. "He's a doctor. He has to answer his phone."

Clara ignored him, turning all her attention on Michael. "Your early dates won't last more than two hours. If you're on call, use a pager.

Turn your phone off, and focus when you're with your Potential."

"My *Potential*," Michael repeated the word cautiously. "Like a potential girlfriend?"

"Like a potential *wife*."

The huge grin returned to Michael's face.

"Hold up." Jet set his hand over Clara's paperwork. "You need to think this through."

"I don't need to think it through. Potential wife!"

"This woman is mandating when and how you can use your phone."

"This woman is an expert."

Jet snorted. Clara pinned him with a look that could take down a bull. Then she let her smile shine on Michael.

"I *am* an expert," she said. "And I can't wait to get started finding you the love of your life."

"Did I do something?" Clara asked.

"Nothing outside of the ordinary," Hunter said, sliding a fragrant bowl of soup across the counter to her. "You were bossy, smug. Typical."

Clara glared at Hunter. "Not in the mood, bro."

"Try the soup."

"Seriously, I'm helping his friend." Clara glanced out to the parking lot. Jet and Michael were still there, having some sort of deep discussion. Jet gestured to Clara's bike, his biceps flexing.

"He's just keeping an eye on his friend."

"His friend hired me. I'm not forcing my business on anyone."

"Try the soup."

Clara drew her spoon through the bowl. Dark greens floated in a light cream and bone broth base. She wasn't particularly hungry. But she knew her brother well enough to know that the minute she tried whatever he served her, she'd feel hungry.

"I don't think it's fair to be rude to someone who is just doing her job."

She glanced out the window again. Jet had his fingers laced behind his head and was exhaling in what appeared to be frustration at something Michael said. Michael laughed. Jet shook his head, then began laughing, too.

Great. He's even more attractive when he's having fun.

"Clara, I'm not feeding you out of the goodness of my heart. I need you to try the soup."

She lifted the spoon to her lips. Savory and rich flavors gave way to sweet, followed by a snap of spice. The complex taste melded and transformed in her mouth. "Oh, wow."

"Yeah?" he asked, a smile growing across his face.

"You are the master of all things broth-based."

"Can you taste the fennel?"

Clara savored another mouthful.

"I don't even know what fennel is, but I can taste the delicious."

There was no limit to the amount of pride Clara took in her brother. Hunter's road to success, and in fact his entire road, had been bumpy. He'd scraped together the money to buy the rundown restaurant in their hometown and transformed it into a modern, stylish, ethically sourced destination that drew customers from all over the state.

The name Eighty Local had been inspired by Hunter's practice of sourcing at least eighty percent of everything he served from Oregon, from the vegetables trucked in from the Willamette Valley to the microbrews from Bend. Meat was supplied by local ranchers, and some even came from the bows and arrows of local hunters. Business had been so strong Hunter was breaking ground on an addition. He would have an events venue up and running by the holiday season.

Hunter was hands down the best brother anyone could ask for. But it would be awesome if he'd stop being such a good guy for a second and agree with her that Jet was being ridiculous.

"It's good to have Jet back in town," Hunter said.

Clara dropped her spoon. "Seriously?"

Hunter reached across the counter and ruffled her hair. "Sis, not everyone is going to like you all the time."

Clara smoothed her hair. "I know that."

He rested his elbows on the counter and leaned toward her. "Sometimes, your anxiety disorder can make things seem—"

"It's not a disorder."

Hunter raised his brow.

"It's not. For my anxiety to qualify as a disorder, it would need to be a harmful dysfunction that's maladaptive, unjustifiable, disturbing and atypical." Her family all knew the technical definition of a psychological disorder by now, but Clara still liked to remind them and herself. "Yes, I'm wired a little more tightly than most folks, but I manage it."

"You do an incredible job of managing. I'm impressed, we all are, with the healthy habits, the breathing techniques, but you can't outrun your chemistry."

Clara turned on her brother. "I have no interest in outrunning my chemistry. I love my chemistry. I like having something inside me that drives me to do my best at everything I set out to do. I benefit from the healthy habits that keep the anxiety in check. I'm glad I was born like this."

She *was* glad. Her anxiety had been hard to manage in high school, and occasionally it kept her from moving forward in her life as she would like to. But she'd never seen it as a disability. Well-managed perfectionism came in handy when running a business that involved a lot of messy emotions from other people.

And so what if she'd made it to twenty-eight without actually experiencing any of those messy emotions herself? She'd fall in love when she met the right guy. Hopefully.

Concern shadowed her brother's eyes. "I'm just saying it's a fine line between wanting to do things well and the cycles of perfectionism you used to fall into."

"It's a sturdy, thick line, and I am firmly on the safe side of it." Clara placed her fingers on the pendants in her necklace, then checked to make sure the clasp was at the nape of her neck. It was.

Hunter held his hands up in surrender. "Okay. My original point was that Jet's a good guy, even if he's not fully supportive of your business. You're going to step on a few toes once in a while. Don't let it get you down."

In the parking lot, Jet slapped Michael on the back as the two men shared another joke. Sure, he was a good guy. A good guy who had experienced her worst behavior in high school and would always remind her of how miserably she'd failed at the one thing that really mattered to her. *Love.*

Clara's heart beat hard as she studied Michael. She was going to knock this one out of the park. She'd find the perfect woman for him, and they would be so happy they'd be toasting her at their fiftieth wedding anniversary. It might not cure her problems, but it would teach Jet Broughman.

CHAPTER THREE

"You need to disengage her services and cancel your check immediately," Jet said, shouldering past a customer in the aisle on his way to the fencing supplies. He glanced back to find Michael lagging behind.

"You need to back off," Michael said cheerfully, stopping at a rack of rain gear.

"I didn't invite you here to back off. We're having this conversation so I can talk some sense into you."

"Oh, look. Should I get this hat?"

"No." Jet took the rain hat out of Michael's hands and put it back on the rack. Michael grabbed a similar hat in a different color and placed it on his head. Jet should have known better than to meet Michael at Outcrop Hardware, Tack and Feed. The guy couldn't walk into OHTAF without buying half a dozen things he had no use for.

Jet shook his head. "You asked me for my advice."

"It's just a hat."

"I'm talking about Clara Wallace."

Jet breathed in deeply, the combined scents of wood shavings, alfalfa and leather drawing out memories of his youth. He lowered his voice. "Michael, please trust me. You don't want Clara anywhere near your love life."

Michael's eyes lit up beneath the floppy hat. "I wouldn't mind Clara Wallace right at the center of my love life."

Jet felt the blood rush to his face. His vision blurred, and he clamped his jaw shut to keep from lashing out at his best friend.

"Whoa," Michael said, gently distancing himself. "That's quite the physiological response, my friend."

Jet unclenched his fists and shook his shoulders loose. He glanced up at the rafters. *Settle down, man.* He knew he had a tendency to overreact where Clara was involved. But that didn't mean that she wouldn't hurt Michael.

"That's what I'm talking about," Jet said. "That's the effect she has on everyone."

Michael put his hand on Jet's back and started walking. Jet straightened. They were here for hardware and a friendly conversation. OHTAF was one of his favorite places on earth. Founded by Mr. Fareas over forty years ago, the store carried the goods necessary for life in central Oregon: work boots, gardening supplies, horse tack, pine tar soap, you name it. If a farmer requested a certain type of chicken feed once, Mr. Fareas made sure to have it in stock every time that customer returned. When Outcrop became a destination for outdoor adventurers, he began stocking camping equipment and climbing gear.

But along with his ability to change with the times, Mr. Fareas kept some things the same. The hundred-year-old building was still painted brick red, and the ancient, wide-plank fir flooring would always have a hollow-sounding thunk as you walked across it. Chessboards were set up on the porch in the summer and around the woodstove in the winter. As a teenager Jet had tagged along behind his grandfather, dreaming of the day he had enough money to buy whatever he wanted.

Right now, he wanted fencing. Then maybe lunch at Eighty Local. And somewhere in the course of all this he'd get his friend to fire Clara. Jet and Michael liked to joke about the day they would join the ranks of older men playing chess at OHTAF. That wasn't going to happen if Clara sank her hooks into Michael, broke his heart with this matchmaking scheme and ran him back into the big city.

They moved into the gardening section. Michael paused to look at a selection of books.

"I did ask for your help. And there's a part of me that wants to take you at your word. But Clara is competent."

Jet snorted.

"She seems very sweet—"

"She's not sweet. That's an act. It gets her what she wants, and what she wants is your money."

Michael eyed him from beneath the rain hat. "What'd she do to you?"

"Nothing."

Michael turned his intelligent gaze on Jet. It was the same look that could get a kid to confess to swallowing a piece of Lego.

"Nothing," Jet lied again. "We barely knew each other in high school. I'm surprised she even remembered me."

"You must have been some kind of academic superstar, Rural Scholar Program and all that."

"In this town I was nothing more than Hal Broughman's poor grandson."

It was hard to shake off a high school memory of Clara as they approached a galvanized-steel stock tank where Mr. Fareas had baby chicks for sale. She'd been leaning over the tank, trying to convince her parents that October was the perfect time to get chickens. Mr. and Mrs. Wallace, Jet's two favorite teachers and owners of a profitable horse-breeding operation, were patiently explaining that in their busy lives there was never going to be time for chickens.

Clara had glanced up and seen him, then flashed her brilliant smile. He'd come to a full stop, just gazing at her and smiling back. It was like being struck by some really pleasant lightning. "There's Jet," she'd proclaimed, turning to her dad. "You said he's the smartest kid you've ever had in class. Jet, convince my parents we have to get chickens!"

Jet had shored up the courage he'd been working on for weeks and joined Clara at the stock tank. He hadn't even been aware of her parents drifting away, leaving him and Clara to pick up the fluffy chicks and craft arguments she could use on her parents. He couldn't remember two words of their conversation but would never forget the way her laugh made him feel: like coming home to a warm fire, after a lifetime of being cold. While Jet knew nothing of girls, and less of dating, he understood what was happening. Clara had patiently walked the ball over to his side of the court and handed it to him. As he watched Clara leave with her parents, he resolved to ask her out, and soon.

Then his grandfather's heavy hand landed on his back. "Best not get your hopes up, son. A girl like Clara Wallace doesn't go out with a Broughman."

His grandfather didn't mean to be discouraging, just realistic. And as angry as it had made Jet at the time, the man turned out to be right. Mr. Fareas, on the other hand, saw things differently. He'd offered Jet a few days' work stocking feed in the back, grumbled at him the entire time, then overpaid him, adding the admonishment, "Take her someplace nice."

Jet had invited Clara on the most impressive, creative and thrilling date his eighteen-year-old self could come up with. She'd responded by stammering out her rejection and running away. And while Jet had long since worked through the humiliation and had ten successful years of dating since then, he still couldn't help but wonder how he had gotten it all so terribly wrong.

He stalked by the tank of baby chicks, Michael close on his heels.

"Jet, let's walk through the information. In high school you were awkward and didn't fit in. Welcome to the club. But you've grown and changed. You got out. You worked hard. You made… How much money *did* you make?"

"Enough."

"*Enough.* Great word. You made enough money. In high school, Clara was, what? Mean?"

"No, not mean."

"Unaware? Cute, I'm assuming. Whatever it was, she had you turning red and clenching your fists back there. She hurt you. Is it possible that she has grown and changed, too?"

Jet turned to glower at Michael, but caught himself. He didn't need Michael judging his *physiological reactions.*

"Look, I want to trust you. But if you'd seen Clara's website, you'd understand why I have to give this a try. I read through page after page of testimonials." Michael looked wistful. "Hundreds of pictures of couples, all grateful to Clara and Love, Oregon. She can help me."

"What if she doesn't?" Jet asked. "What if she takes your money and leaves you with nothing?"

"Well," Michael smiled cheerfully, "she won't be the first woman to do that."

"Please, Ash!" Clara begged, following her oldest brother into OHTAF.

"I am already giving you the use of the ranch,

fourteen horses and the help of my son. There's no way I can join your clients on this group date." His voice had a finality to it that would have made any of their other siblings drop the request and apologize for asking.

Clara squared her shoulders.

"Please. I only have six men, and you *know* I can't run it a man short."

"I don't *know* the first thing about your business," Ash said, walking directly to the hardware section. He didn't even stop to look at the fun socks. "You may be a man short—"

Clara started to explain, but Ash spoke over her.

"I will support you unconditionally. But I will not help you by joining your clients on this date."

Clara lifted her foot to stomp it, then set it lightly on the painted wood floor. This group date had to go well. Michael Williams needed to have so much fun he couldn't stop telling his best friend about it.

"Group dates are Love, Oregon's signature service." Ash kept walking as Clara spoke. She followed him closely. "They bring clients together for an activity where everyone can shine in a stress-free environment. I can't invite more women than men. Uneven numbers reinforce false stereotypes and a scarcity mindset."

"Then, invite one less woman."

"You don't understand. I need another man for this group date. Someone who isn't looking for a match, someone to defuse the feelings of expectation."

Ash stopped walking and gave her a bored look. It made her want to pull out a few of her favorite kickboxing moves.

"I'm not going to try to set you up. I promise."

"Right," Ash grumbled, continuing through the maze of OHTAF. Clara scampered after him.

The truth was she *did* want to set up her oldest brother. Okay, fine. She wanted to set up all her brothers and everyone else on earth.

But Ash was a special project. He hadn't been the same since he returned home after his last deployment with the National Guard. All she knew was that it had been difficult, and his wife had left him because of something that happened at that time. Their parents had asked Ash to take over the day-to-day operation of Wallace Ranch, and suggested he and his son move into the family home. Their excuse had been that it would allow them to travel more, and they'd be happier in the apartment over the garage. But Clara suspected there was more to it than simple convenience. They were worried.

Ash was still committed to the family, their ranch and his son, and he was still an active member of the community, but something was missing. Clara absently reached out and tugged at his sleeve. His expression softened ever so slightly.

Until they were interrupted by an enthusiastic, "Clara!"

She looked up at the voice. It was Michael Williams, with a floppy rain hat on his head, the *Farmer's Almanac* under his arm and an adorable chick in his hands.

"Michael," she said, smiling and trying to keep her eyes off the stock tank behind him. "How nice to see you. Ash, this is my latest client, Michael Williams."

Ash walked forward, hand extended. Michael started to juggle the chick and the almanac.

Clara scooped the fluffy bird from his hands as she spoke. "Michael, this is my oldest brother, Ash. You already met Hunter at the restaurant. Now you know two-thirds of my brothers, and we met less than twenty-four hours ago. Well done, you."

Michael beamed. "Nice to meet you."

"Michael is one of the people you have the

opportunity to help this weekend." Clara turned to Michael and explained. "We're one man short for the group date, so I've asked Ash to join us."

Ash drew his brows together.

"I'm happy to go to a party with more women than men," Michael said. "Clara might have more luck if I were the only man."

Clara laughed. "You are going to be just fine."

"You're in good hands," Ash told him. "I returned to Oregon two years ago to find out my sisters had matched up half the state." He turned to Clara. "I'd be of no help at all."

The clunk of boots sounded on the wooden floor as a deep, steady voice said, "Michael, I'm done."

Clara froze.

"Four hundred and ninety-five yards of fencing ordered to keep the emus in."

Jet looked up from his list and stopped.

Thoughts of snuggling up under his arm in the cab of his truck popped unbidden into Clara's head. *Like that's ever going to happen.*

She narrowed her eyes.

"Hi, Jet," she said, cuddling the chick like she'd come here for no other reason.

"Clara." He nodded stiffly.

The hum of customer chatter dimmed. Clara lifted her chin. OHTAF was her favorite store.

This was her town. If Jet thought he could just walk in and glower at her for no good reason, he needed to think again.

Clara shifted her posture. Jet folded his arm across his chest.

"Jet Broughman," her brother broke the silence, extending his hand. "I'm Ash Wallace, Clara's older brother. Welcome back to Outcrop."

Jet startled at Ash's words. He paused, then shook his hand. "Thank you. Glad to be back."

"I was sorry to hear about your grandfather. Hal was a good man."

Jet stared down at the floor. His jaw flexed. His expression looked pained and hard-fought, like he had a system for keeping his emotions in check.

"I hope…" Jet stopped, then looked up. "I hope to honor his memory by keeping the ranch running."

Clara watched Jet carefully. He was clearly uncomfortable. Like this relatively simple social interaction was difficult for him.

Interesting.

Ash continued. "To hear Hunter tell it, you're producing a great product."

"He said that?"

"Yep. Told me that Outcrop's Exterminator

was back in town, with a new source of free-range beef."

A flush crept up Jet's neck.

"Exterminator?" Michael asked.

"It's a football thing," Jet said. His gaze connected with Clara's, then shifted away.

Did he remember?

Seriously, is my humiliation what he remembers about that night?

"Some night in October." Clara rolled her eyes at Michael, looking as bored as she could muster. "Young men were footballing."

"It was the night we beat the Swarm and made it to the state semifinals," Ash said, like it was the sort of thing that mattered at all, ever.

"A ball was involved," Clara told Michael. "Points were scored. Winning, you know."

Michael laughed, then turned to Jet. "You never told me you were a football hero."

"It was one catch," Jet said.

"He was a solid, four-year varsity player," Ash told Michael. "And fast. Coach Kessler's still talking about him."

Jet's expression relaxed, his face broke into a real smile, like the one that had lit the stadium when he'd made that catch all those years ago. His eyes brightened, and the suspicion that seemed to hang on him shrugged off. "Is Coach still in town?"

"He is. My son will be playing for him this fall."

Jet seemed to think this was the greatest piece of information possible. He and Ash started laughing and talking about Coach Kessler and Eagle football. Ash—her terse, bossy, near-silent brother—was chatting it up with Jet like they'd been friends forever.

And that sent Clara over the edge. Jet did not get to be all friendly with Hunter and friendly to Ash and mean to her.

An uncomfortable buzzing filled her head. She stared at the chick in her hands, fighting back the urge to check her necklace. Slowly, she inhaled three deep breaths.

Ash looked at her sharply. "You okay?"

"Fine," she snapped.

He dropped a hand on her shoulder. "Let's get our shopping done, then go grab lunch at Hunter's place."

Clara nodded. She was mad at herself for letting Jet get to her and mad at her brother for noticing.

"You're going to have lunch at Eighty Local?" Jet asked or, rather, accused.

"Yes," Clara said, stroking the baby chicken.

"My brother and I often support Hunter by eating at his amazing restaurant. We're a supportive family."

Jet turned away.

Because what's more offensive than a supportive family?

"Nice to see you, Jet." Ash nodded. "Nice to meet you, Michael."

"See you later, Michael," Clara said, pointedly not including Jet in people she might see later.

Jet looked at Clara, then at Michael. "Maybe."

"Maybe?" Clara asked. She turned to Michael. "You have a group date on Saturday. I'll be in touch later this week about what you should expect."

"He might decide this isn't for him," Jet said.

"Or someone might try to convince him to back out," Clara said.

"Someone might listen to reason." Jet focused on Michael.

"No one is going to convince me of anything," Michael said. "A group date with too many women? I'm in. Should I wear this hat?"

"No," Clara and Jet said in unison.

A funny sound intruded on the buzzing in Clara's head. She looked up to find her brother laughing. She glared at him, then gave Michael her brightest smile.

"I can't wait to match you up with a wonderful woman. You're going to be so happy."

Clara turned to Jet and took his hand. She could feel his reaction to her touch. The move had him baffled. *Good.*

She placed the baby chick in his palm.

"Good luck with your emus. Maybe all the fencing in OHTAF can keep this little guy penned up, too. Nothing's too difficult for the Exterminator."

JET SLAMMED THE door to his truck and started the engine. A quick glance at the side mirror told him that Clara was still on the porch of OHTAF with her brother and Michael. They didn't show any signs of leaving.

The clutch protested as he put the truck in reverse. He'd planned to buy fencing, then have a decent meal at Eighty Local. It was important to him to cultivate a strong working relationship with Hunter. And he was getting tired of eating at home, alone.

But once again, Clara Wallace.

She'd invited Michael to join her and Ash for lunch, commandeering his friend *and* his lunch spot. It was fine. Jet had plenty of sandwich fixings at home. Unfortunately, the reason he was such a good sandwich maker was that it was the only thing he knew how to make. Baloney sandwiches had been the primary food group of the Broughman household growing up, with the occasional side of dry cereal. As Jet broadened his horizons, his sandwiches had improved, but he still hadn't really learned how to cook. Preparing real meals for one person felt too lonely to attempt.

Jet pulled out of the gravel lot. He needed to settle down. He'd been uncomfortable a lot of times in life. This was no different. He just needed to put his head down and get through.

An image of Clara's face appeared, condescending as she said, *Yes, my brother and I often support Hunter by eating at his amazing restaurant. We're a supportive family.*

Like he needed a reminder. The Wallaces were a perfect, happy, loving family. And he was headed home to eat another sandwich by himself.

The truck picked up speed along the highway. Jet ran through the figures on a projected sale to Eighty Local. If Hunter sourced nothing more than hamburger, what could that look like in real money? He ran the entire operation on his own, except for processing, which he sourced to an operation in Redmond. Jet calculated hanging weight, price per pound, processing fees.

It was good money. He had a solid product.

Only one thing could throw the deal. One *supportive* family member who could convince anyone of anything. If Clara didn't want Hunter to buy from Jet, Eighty Local would not be serving Broughman beef. He couldn't let down his grandfather's memory by letting the ranch fail.

Hal Broughman had been an exceptional rancher, if a stern and stoic guardian. Jet had learned a lot from him in the years after the social worker had dropped him off at the ranch. He'd learned perseverance, self-reliance and the ability to work through fatigue. This set of skills served him well at the University of Washington and in the cubical warrens of the software industry afterward.

The hard deadlines of the business world held few horrors after a man had helped cows give birth until three in the morning, then finished his math homework on the way to school.

His grandfather might have never expressed love, or even a mild affection, for Jet, but he'd given him a stable home and the grit to make it in a tough world.

A familiar stand of pine trees flashed past, and his property came into view. This was what mattered. His ranch, caring for the land his grandfather had left him. Someday Jet would raise his kids here, in a stable, two-parent home. Over time, his family would fit in. He'd spent eleven hard years in Seattle to finance his return to the ranch. This is where he would put down roots and create the family he'd always dreamed of. He didn't kid himself into thinking he'd experience the love he witnessed in other families. If his dating history was any indicator, it was unlikely he was capable of all-encompassing love. But he was steady and dependable and would do his best for his family.

A soft peep from the passenger seat distracted him from his thoughts. He glanced into the cardboard box Mr. Fareas had provided for him. He was as bad at picking up stray animals as Michael was at collecting needy ex-girlfriends. Clara had placed the chick in his hand, and he couldn't make himself put it back in that stock tank.

"I hope you get along with emus," he told the chick.

The bird fluffed her feathers in contentment and settled into a corner of the box. He wouldn't be entirely alone at home. There were six emus, two hundred head of cattle, a horse he'd accepted from an elderly neighbor who could no longer care for it and now this little one.

No, he had plenty of creatures counting on him; now it was time to start helping people. He'd made a promise to himself his senior year in high school that he'd return to Outcrop and give kids the same confidence that his teachers and coaches had given him. If Kessler was still head coach for the Eagles, this would be a chance to pay him back and help the community. Coach Kessler, along with Mr. and Mrs. Wallace, had been one of the most important influences in his life. *Maybe I could do the same for one of these kids?*

He needed to keep his head in the game and make good on his promise. It shouldn't matter if Clara had grown from the prettiest girl in Outcrop into a stunningly beautiful woman. He'd managed to protect his heart for most of high school, and he could do it again.

CHAPTER FOUR

THE GROUP DATE was going to be a disaster.

Michael's first real impression of her services would be terrible, and then he'd fire her, and Jet would be there to witness her failure.

Clara stood up and paced toward the living room, then back to the kitchen. She picked up her master list from where it lay on the table. Rows of client folders were spread out before her, color-coded by age and interest. There had to be a seventh man she could invite. Ash was out, mainly because she was still mad at him for being all chatty-friendly with Jet.

Also, because he'd said no.

Clara headed to her file cabinet. She had to be overlooking someone.

She pulled out the second drawer, which was full of men. Well, profiles of men. She pawed through the folders, her chest tight and breath shallow. There was no one she could possibly invite. Maybe Piper had a client in Portland who might want to join them? But that was an awfully long drive just for a trail ride. Her fingers moved faster, bending a file, and she accidentally ripped off the label. Clara slammed the file drawer shut.

Okaaay. Time to settle down.

Clara rested her head against the filing cabinet and drew in a deep breath, then two more. She closed her eyes.

This wasn't a crisis. Jet was one man whose opinion about her didn't matter in the grand scheme of life. He'd seen her at her worst in high school; it was no wonder he didn't trust her with his best friend.

Michael, on the other hand, was going to have only the best experiences with her, starting with this group date. All she needed was one more nice, reasonably normal, single man.

Clara's phone buzzed. It was Hunter.

Hunter, a nice, reasonably normal, single man.

"Hey," she sang into the phone.

"Hey, I hate to ask, but can you come down and pull espresso for a few hours?"

"Absolutely. Two o'clock okay? I've got an appointment there at four, anyway."

"I need you to come now." Clara was surprised by her brother's tone. Hunter had been under a fair amount of stress recently. She could hear the poorly masked panic in his voice as he said, "Please. Janet's sick, and Caleb has worked the last six nights."

Clara glanced at her notes, then back at the phone. She had a weakness for the espresso machine. The day Hunter installed the vintage Italian beauty, Clara wasn't sure she'd ever be able to leave Eighty Local again. Learning to make a cappuccino was as exciting as learning how to drive, but without all the speeches about horrible accidents that really didn't sit well with someone prone to anxiety. Plus, everyone loved you when you controlled the town's caffeine delivery system.

And if she dropped everything to help her brother, there's no way he could say no to the group date.

"Of course," she said. "Let me get changed."

"Thank you. I owe you."

"Yes, you do." Clara disconnected the call.

With a wicked grin, she finished off her guest list with Hunter's name.

"THAT'S THE LAST of it." Jet deposited a final box of hamburger into the back room of Eighty Local. Hunter stood at the worktable, deftly slicing through a bunch of kale.

"Thanks." He didn't look up. Jet shifted.

"You want me to put it in the freezer?"

"Nah."

Sweat prickled at the back of Jet's neck. Did Hunter not want this beef? Had Clara said something?

Hunter swept the kale into a large bowl, then dropped the knife. He looked exhausted. A smile broke out when he saw the boxes.

"Burger sales went up last week when I led advertising with a local rancher supplying the meat."

Jet readjusted his ball cap. "People like a good burger."

"Yes and no. People drive past your cattle on the way to the restaurant, they see it's a humane operation. The old-timers are happy to see your granddad's place up and functioning. All I have to do is mention my beef comes from Broughman Ranch and the burger's sold."

"I'm happy to sell to you." Jet tried to keep the note of pride from his voice. This was good. He was on the road, shoring up a deal to supply a local restaurateur with beef. First stop, Eighty Local. Second stop, every other restaurant in the Pacific Northwest.

"My dad's going to be stoked to hear you've got the ranch running," Hunter said.

Jet looked up sharply. "How a-are your parents?" he asked, annoyed at the disfluency in his speech.

"Great. They're out of the country right now. Ever since they retired from teaching and Ash took over the horses, they've been traveling nonstop."

Jet swallowed and nodded.

"You a fan?" Hunter asked.

"Probably their biggest," Jet admitted. "I didn't have a lot of support at that time. Your parents…" He cleared his throat, trying to put words to his thoughts.

Mr. and Mrs. Wallace, his science and geography teachers respectively, had been an encouraging presence throughout his bleak adolescent years. Their classroom doors were always open, their conversations and interest were given freely.

His grandfather had done the best he could, but Jet had been raised by the community. From the teachers and coaches who actively helped him to townspeople who offered him the occasional odd job or kind word, Outcrop had made him.

But it was to Mr. and Mrs. Wallace that he owed his biggest debt.

"Your parents had a big impact on me."

"Yeah, I remember Dad talking about you.

I don't think he's ever been more excited than when you got the Rural Scholar award." Hunter focused on the floor in front of him. "Bowman and I were such academic disappointments."

"You look like you're doing okay now."

He shook his head. "Amazing what a man can achieve when he doesn't have to sit at a desk all day. Come in and have some coffee before you go."

"Thanks."

Jet's shoulders dropped, his lungs filled as they left the topic of Mr. and Mrs. Wallace. Did the Wallace kids know how good they'd had it? In high school, Clara would drift in and out of her parents' classrooms, getting gum out of her mom's desk, asking her dad for five dollars. They would always drop whatever they were doing and fuss over her. Had she eaten her whole lunch? Was her phone still off and at the bottom of her backpack? There'd never been a single person in Jet's life who cared whether or not he even had lunch, much less finished it.

Jet followed Hunter through the back of the restaurant into the dining room, narrowly missing a table.

"Hey, Clara, make my friend a cappuccino," Hunter called out.

Jet looked up sharply to see Clara behind the

espresso machine. She wore fitted jeans and an Eighty Local tank top that showed off soft skin and toned arms. Her hair was up in a ponytail, pulling attention to the sparkly diamond stud earrings and a gold chain around her throat that held two small pendants.

Jet ran into the next table.

"Not if he's going to be mean to me." She didn't look up.

Jet straightened, then righted the salt and pepper shakers he'd knocked over. "I wasn't being mean. I was being honest."

"Honestly mean," she countered, tamping fresh-ground espresso into the portafilter and fitting it into the machine.

"Whatever. You two work it out," Hunter said, a note of laughter in his voice. "I've got payroll."

"Knock that mirthful glint out of your eye right now, Hunter Wallace," Clara called after him.

Hunter turned his back to her, raising his hands in surrender. "I have no mirth."

The hiss and hum of the espresso machine commanded silence while Jet stood awkwardly at the counter. Clara gave him a prim glare as she steamed milk. It would all have been so much simpler if she wasn't inconceivably beautiful.

The door opened, and a couple in their mid-fifties walked in. Clara's demeanor changed. She raised a brow at Jet, then welcomed the couple with a broad smile.

"Linda and Dean! It's so lovely to see you. How are the wedding plans coming?"

"Perfect!" Linda said. "We've settled on a date. All the kids can make it. We're letting the resort take care of the rest of the details."

"The kids finally accepted our relationship when they learned they got a free trip to Hawaii out of the deal," Dean said dryly.

"It can be hard for adult children to see their parents as real people who also long for love and companionship," Clara said sagely, pouring Jet's espresso into a cup. "The trip to Hawaii for a destination wedding is nice. But all they really need is to see how happy you are."

The couple turned to gaze at each other. Clara took the moment to level Jet a superior glance.

"Seat yourself," Hunter said from over the counter. "The usual?"

"Yup," Dean confirmed as the couple took a table by the window.

Clara grabbed a saucer and set the cup on it.

"I'm sorry, but I think any good relationship is just dumb luck," Jet said.

"Dumb luck they both happened to see my ad on social media, engaged my services and took a chance on meeting each other." Clara spoke without looking up.

"My theory is if a relationship is meant to be, it will be."

"My theory," she said as she focused on the design she was making in the cappuccino, "is if you ask, you will receive."

"For ten thousand dollars?" he exclaimed, loud enough that several of the restaurant's patrons looked his way.

"Worth every penny," Dean replied from his table, not taking his eyes off his fiancée.

Jet shook his head. Clara slid the coffee across the bar to him. She glanced out the front window.

"Hunter?" she called. "My appointment's here. I'll only be about twenty minutes. Do you mind?"

"Sure," he said. "Just don't order an espresso."

Clara stepped around the counter and brushed past Jet. "Enjoy your coffee!"

He glanced down at the cup where a skillfully created frowny-face of foam and espresso glowered up at him.

CLARA WAS DETERMINED to focus on her client. *The broad shoulders and blue jeans four feet away on a stool at the counter? No conse-*

quence. Completely ignorable. Her eyes flitted over to Jet despite her stern self-admonishment not to.

Focus! This client had a long way to go before she was ready to find the man of her dreams, and Clara was enacting a plan to help her confidence grow.

"This is for three hundred dollars." Clara slid a gift card to her favorite shop across the table. "I want you to completely reoutfit your lingerie. Bras, panties, camisoles, everything. Buy high quality, in colors you love. The saleswomen there are brilliant. They'll help you find the right fit."

"I can't possibly…" Pam Martin, a thirty-five-year-old school nurse waved away the gift card from the other side of the table.

"You can, and you will. This will put a swagger in your step."

"You don't have to pay for it—"

Clara cut her off. "Would you go and spend three hundred dollars on yourself?" Pam looked sheepish. "You would not. And I need you feeling beautiful from the inside out for this to work." Clara pulled a gift certificate from her leather notebook. "This is for a massage."

"Oh, no, this is too much."

Clara pinned her with a glance. "Tell me you don't need a massage."

Pam reddened, then broke into laughter. "Fine. Yes, you're right. I need a massage."

"All those sick children all day long?"

Pam grinned, her lovely smile lighting up the room.

"A massage sounds wonderful. But you don't have to pay for all this." She gestured at the gift cards. "It's too much."

Clara snapped her folder shut. "Pam, you are paying me ten thousand dollars to find you the love of your life. You would not have put down that kind of money if you weren't serious."

Pam swallowed, her eyes traveling to the window. The wonderful, kind woman had been waiting so long for Mr. Right.

"I can't find someone to treat you like a queen until you start treating yourself like one."

Pam nodded. Jet shifted on the stool behind her, and Clara strained to keep her eyes on her client. *Hasn't he finished his coffee yet?*

"Did you…" Pam pressed her lips together, then finished her question "…did you ask Daniel if he wanted my number?"

Clara reached across the table and took Pam's hand. The gesture answered the question, but

Clara pressed on. "Pam, what is Love Rule Number One?"

Pam studied the tabletop.

"*Never waste time on someone who isn't into you*," she muttered.

"Because you are amazing." Clara leaned across the table. "You are beautiful, thoughtful, kind and creative. Honestly, you're too smart for Daniel." Pam started to protest, but Clara cut her off. "It's not a knock against him or praise for you. It's a fact. I'm glad you two got a chance to chat at the last group date, but Daniel is not a strong match for you. He wants a woman to binge-watch reality television with. You need a man to road trip to the Oregon Shakespeare Festival with you."

Hope spilled from Pam's eyes along with a few tears. "That would be so great."

"Then, let's make it happen." Clara sat up and pointed to the paperwork in front of her. "Last week we were discussing your list of nonnegotiables. Have you thought of anything you'd like to add?"

Getting Pam to come up with a list of things she had to have in a relationship had been tough. Intellectually, she knew she deserved a good man. Emotionally, she took what was offered, which hadn't been great. Clara had seen it a million times, unworthy people preying on those with low self-esteem.

"I did." Pam sat up straight. "I don't want a man who is too into how he looks. He can be handsome, no problem." Clara laughed with her at this. "But I don't want a guy… I don't want a guy who needs the world to think he's handsome. Does that make sense?"

Clara fought to keep herself from looking at the particularly handsome man in a ball cap and T-shirt at the counter. A man who should have finished his coffee and left by now.

"Perfect sense," Clara said. "What else?"

Pam wrestled out her next request. "I want someone…" Her voice dropped and she cleared her throat. Jet turned slightly in his seat. "I want someone who likes *me*. Someone who really likes me, not just my looks, or my job, or some list of attributes, but someone who thinks I am…" her voice trailed off to a whisper as she dropped the final word "…wonderful."

Clara swept her notebook aside and took Pam's hands again.

"We will find him," she promised. "He is out there, and we will find him."

Pam stared down at their hands as Clara continued. "In the meantime, I want you to remember you *are* wonderful. Go treat yourself."

A rueful smile spread across Pam's face. "I guess I could get a massage."

"Great idea." Clara grinned, gratified to watch her scoop up the gift cards. This was the best job in the world, no matter what some people thought.

JET HESITATED AFTER Clara's client left. Then he shifted on his stool at the counter and looked at her. She was too pretty, arranging papers in her file, slipping sticky notes onto separate pages.

Huh. Since when were organizational tasks so attractive?

"Mr. Broughman, any insulting commentary you'd like to make?" she asked without looking up.

Jet shook his head. "You thinking about her for Michael?"

"Absolutely not."

"No? She's a health-care professional who works with children. She seems nice."

"She is." Clara looked over at him. Jet found himself moving to her booth, sitting down across from her.

"Michael is too eager. I could put any woman in front of him right now, and he would accept her on my word. And since you've been listening in on my conversation for the last half hour, you know Pam needs to learn to love herself. So long as she feels unworthy, she can't really love anyone. Michael and Pam would be miserable together. Miserable."

Jet leaned back and put his arm on the top of the booth. Clara wasn't just helping people find love, she was helping her clients find themselves. And apparently buying them underwear.

"You buy all your clients lingerie?" he asked.

"I'm not buying Michael any, so no."

Jet laughed. Clara graced him with a grin, and he felt better. He just had to remember to look away before her smile got to him.

"I buy my clients what they need," she explained. "I budget four hundred dollars for everyone, but some need more. Some don't need anything."

"What will you get for Michael?"

"I doubt I will buy Michael anything. He's ready to commit to a good woman. My job is to find the right one." Jet could see the wheels in her mind turning, as though mentally walking through her client list. "Although, if you want to encourage him to ditch the short-sleeve dress shirts, I would be grateful."

"Already tried. Several times."

"It's no matter." She waved the problem

away. "Michael's light is on. I'd say it's a matter of weeks, not months, before he's settled."

Jet shook his head. "His light is on?"

"His light is on. He's ready to commit, get married, have kids. When a man's light is on, he will literally marry anyone who happens to be standing in front of him. This makes my job tougher in some respects. I need to make sure Michael doesn't find himself standing in front of the wrong woman."

"Seriously?"

"Seriously."

Jet pulled his hat off and pressed the bill in. "Is my…" he stopped, returned the hat to his head, then pushed on "…is my light on?"

"No."

"Phew." Jet slumped back in the booth. His relief was short-lived.

"I don't think you have a light."

"What?" He sat up. "What do you mean I don't have a light? I'll get married. Someday."

A startled expression passed over her face. "Of course you'll get married. Probably."

"Not probably. Look, if you think I'm going to stay single because my parents divorced and my grandfather never remarried after—"

"Oh, Jet, no. This isn't about your family." Clara reached across the table and touched his arm. Jet stared down at her fingers. Her touch was so light, it settled him against his intense reaction. She didn't know about his mom or that he'd been in and out of foster care. She had no inkling of the cold, silent shack he'd shared with his grandfather in high school. She didn't know her parents and Coach Kessler were the closest thing he'd had to a real family.

She wasn't judging him, because she had no idea how close she was to the frightening truth. He might never have the family he'd always wanted.

"If you want to get married, you'll get married," she said. "I only meant you're different than Michael."

"No kidding." Jet glanced out the window.

"Look, this is just one woman's opinion," she said, then muttered, "One woman who has helped well over a hundred men find love." She cleared her throat and continued. "I think, from the entire seventy-five minutes we have spent in each other's company since high school, that you are the type of man who falls in love hard, fast and once. When you fall in love, which might be in twenty years or twenty minutes, you will be in love with her until the day you die. Michael could fall in love tomorrow, get his heart broken Wednesday and be back in love the following week. You, I think, will be pickier. But when you do fall in love, watch out."

Clara met his eyes, a faint blush rising in her cheeks. Jet had to remind himself to breathe. Then he reminded himself that he had a long history of misreading Clara's signals.

He leaned back, pondering her words. He had never been in love. Relationships, yes, but not love. His mom's self-destructive behaviors had landed him in and out of foster care, where the shuffling of homes and broken promises of love made him wary. His grandfather's self-sufficiency and mistrust of emotion kept him that way. The only time he'd felt anything like what was described as love had been standing over the stock tank holding baby chickens with Clara his senior year in high school. But that couldn't have been love, just a bad crush gone wrong. It was time he got over it and accepted that Clara probably knew what she was talking about when it came to relationships.

"When is Michael's first date?" he asked.

"Technically, Saturday."

"Thank you," Jet managed. "I know I was a jerk about this, but I appreciate what you're trying to do for my friend. He's a good guy."

Clara looked into his eyes. She seemed surprised and gratified. "Michael is a gem. I'll take care of him."

Jet nodded, then drew his gaze away.

"I'm planning a group date," Clara said, "for a trail ride and picnic out at the family place—"

"I'm not going," Hunter interjected from behind the counter.

Clara had a full-body reaction to her brother's comment, dramatically clutching the booth and table as though the world was spinning off its axis. "Please?"

"Nope. Bowman and I are fishing early, then Abe's guys are here to lay the foundation for the addition."

"Do you have to be here for that? Hunter, I'm a man short, and you know Ash won't come."

"Sorry, sis. I love you, but I can't put my business on hold so a handful of desperate people will feel slightly less desperate."

"My clients aren't desperate."

Jet laughed at the look Hunter gave his sister.

"You're talking about his best friend," Clara said, pulling Jet into the argument.

She was so cute it was hard to remember he didn't want to take sides. "Michael's a little desperate," he admitted.

She turned a scowl on him, then wrinkled her nose.

"Okay, he does read as desperate sometimes." She held his gaze, and Jet found himself smiling with her. "But I'm going to find him the perfect woman. And I need another guy to lift some of the pressure on Saturday."

Hunter set down his clipboard and rubbed his eyes. Concern flooded Clara's face.

"It's okay," she said. "I know you've got a lot going on."

"It's just with the local business fair on Friday, on top of everything else."

"Really, Hunter. I'll find someone else."

"What's a group date?" Jet asked, hoping to ease the tension.

Clara turned to him. Her posture shifted, her eyes sparkled. Jet felt like one of the unwitting fish Hunter and Bowman would be catching this weekend.

"A group date is a casual get-together of my clients. Low stakes, good company and engaging activity. It gives them a social outing where they can flex their dating muscles without risk of failure. It's also an opportunity for Potentials to scout out prospective dates. I'm a man down for Saturday." Her smile sliced through him. "Would you like to join us?"

Jet groaned.

"You walked into that one, man," Hunter said sympathetically.

"Please!" Clara clasped her hands and leaned across the table toward him.

He shook his head.

"For Michael?" she asked, her smile growing impossibly sweeter. Jet started laughing.

"You're trapped, dude," Hunter told him.

"Fine, I'll go. For Michael. Just don't try to set me up."

"I promise." She jumped up. "I will not accidentally introduce you to the one woman you are destined to love forever."

She bustled around the table and placed her hand on the booth behind him. Scents of orange and ginger floated from her skin, and he was enveloped in her fragrance. She leaned toward him, hesitated, then brushed her lips across his cheek in an unexpected kiss.

Magic seemed to ripple out from the kiss like rings on a pond.

Her face lingered next to his for a fraction of a second before she pulled back sharply. She placed her fingers over her mouth, her eyes wide with confusion, like she hadn't meant to kiss him.

Then she started to talk, fast. "Okay, great! See you Saturday! Awesome!" She pulled in a deep breath. "Thanks," she sang and raced out the door.

Jet reached up and rubbed his cheek where she had kissed him, watching as she hopped on her bike and pedaled out onto the road.

"Welcome," he replied.

CHAPTER FIVE

JET WRESTLED THE fencing into place, straining against the pull of the wire. A squawk from the nearby barn urged him to hurry. After the latest emu break that morning he'd locked the birds in the barn. He glanced up at the fading sun, hoping they didn't completely destroy his barn from the inside out. The damage six curious birds could do was astounding.

Plus, there was nothing like hard work to keep a man from thinking about an unexpected kiss from a pretty woman.

Except when that man's best friend was there, getting in his way and constantly bringing up the woman in question.

"Clara said the group date will be casual, so I shouldn't be nervous."

"Then, don't be nervous." Jet was nervous enough for both of them. *Why did I agree to go?* "You weren't nervous when she invited you, back at OHTAF."

"It seemed so far off." Michael paused. "Speaking of OHTAF, last time we were there, you and Clara were at each other's throats. How'd she rope you into going?"

That kiss meant nothing. Clara was friendly and vivacious, and she wanted Jet to come on her group date to balance the numbers. If he thought he saw anything in her eyes that suggested something more, it was imagination on his part. There had to be men in every corner of this county having the exact same thoughts about Clara, probably at this very minute.

"She asked."

Michael leaned against a fence post, his intelligent gaze burning into Jet.

"I'm doing this for you." Jet crossed his arms, volleying the unspoken challenge back.

Michael flexed his brow, giving Jet a sidelong glance.

"You gonna help with this fence or just get in my way?" Jet asked.

Michael raised his hands in protest. "I'm just here to help make a nice pasture for your emus."

Jet passed his friend a nine-pound hammer and gestured to the post. "You sure? 'Cause with the way you're working, I'm beginning to suspect you're on the emus' side."

"I'm working, I'm working." Michael took a

few swings with the hammer, then said, "I'm glad you're going to be there Saturday."

"It'll be fun," Jet forced himself to say. It *would* be fun—for Michael and Clara's other clients. They were taking steps toward their goal of finding relationships. Jet was the only one who didn't belong.

He glanced up at the sky again. He needed to get this finished, then run into town for groceries. He had nothing to eat and Hunter had said something about Eighty Local being closed tonight, which was fine. He'd been finding a few too many excuses to drop by ever since running into Clara there. He had to snap out of this. The kiss, and inviting him on this group date, would amount to the same thing her flirtation back in high school did: nothing.

It was one thing to be rejected by a thoughtless young woman as a teenager. Putting his heart on the line as an adult was completely out of the question. The years of broken promises from his mom and the foster families who'd pledged forever then changed their mind a month later had made him wary. It would be better to find a partner who didn't spark the same kind of intense feelings Clara inspired.

You can't be rejected if you're never really attached.

"That's what Melissa said."

Jet looked up from the fencing at the mention of yet another of Michael's manipulative ex-girlfriends. "You called Melissa?"

"She called me." Michael surveyed the front pasture, specifically not meeting Jet's eyes. "She's been really upset lately, and I'm one of the few people she has to talk to."

Jet clamped down harder than necessary on the wire cutters. Clara had made Michael delete Lauren's contact info the first day, and he'd assumed Michael would do the same for the other women who continued to use him for free therapy.

"What's your matchmaker have to say about this?"

Michael gestured to the north. "What's that building over there?"

Jet set the wire cutters on top of a fence post and leaned against it, crossing his arms. "Clara doesn't know?" he guessed, trying to steer Michael back to the issue of manipulative ex-girlfriends.

Michael studied the shack in the distance. "Is that where you lived with your grandfather?"

Jet shifted so he couldn't see the eyesore Michael was trying to redirect the conversation toward. The memory of his first night in that shack bloomed fresh. The cramp in his leg as he climbed out of the car into the cold evening air. The faint blue glow of the television flickering. The first look at his grandfather's face, knowing that the man was taking him in out of duty, not any interest in parenting.

A swift shake of his head had Jet's focus back on topic. "Clara told you on day one to stop being everyone's pillow to cry on."

"I'm helping Melissa!"

"Are you?"

The guilty flash in Michael's eye gave way to an intelligent gleam. "I'm not taking advice about women from you. You've broken up with more intelligent, successful women since we've been friends than I can count."

"You can't count to eight?" Jet asked dryly. "How'd you get through med school?"

"You get the point. Consider yourself the glass house, and the unwanted dating advice you're lobbing my way, stones."

Jet glared at Michael. Michael volleyed back a knowing glower.

If this continued one minute longer, Michael might start asking questions about one particularly intelligent, successful woman that Jet really should not be thinking about. He glanced at the old shack. Unbidden, his grandfather's words came back to him. *A girl like Clara Wallace doesn't go out with a Broughman.*

Jet shook off the uncomfortable feeling. "Yeah, that's where I grew up with my grandfather. Not much to look at."

Michael, satisfied that he'd won this round, took a few steps toward the cabin. "It's rustic. Let's go check it out."

"Nah." Jet shook his head. The smell in that place always put him right back to his lonely teenage years.

"I'm serious. It's a cool cabin. You could fix it up and rent it out."

What to do with that old house? Jet had built a custom home on the far side of the property, overlooking the creek with views all the way to the Cascade Mountains. Most days he succeeded in ignoring this little shack on the edge of the highway where he'd spent his high school years. He wanted to get rid of it, but structurally it was in good shape. Like his grandfather, the cabin could weather any storm. A red tin roof kept the old, timber-framed structure safe. He'd thought about bulldozing the place, but that felt wasteful. Waste of any kind was disrespectful to his grandfather's memory. And Michael was right: it was kind of cool-looking. With some landscaping and a fresh coat of stain, it could look pretty good. On the outside, anyway.

"The inside is a different story," Jet said. "Hal wasn't the best of housekeepers on a good day, and when I was away in Seattle the place went south, fast."

Michael, his relentless optimism leading the way, trotted up to the front door.

"Watch out for cobwebs," Jet cautioned.

Michael swatted in front of him, stirring up dust as he reached for the doorknob. The smell hit Jet even in the yard. Musty furniture, and the lingering scent of baloney sandwiches.

"Whoa." Michael got two feet into the main room and stopped.

Jet knew what he saw. Walking into that room for the first time as a fourteen-year-old, he'd immediately noticed the grime, the sparse furnishings and dust swirling in the air. Wind rattled through the old window casings. Light came from single bulbs suspended from the wood-beamed ceiling. There were only two chairs—his grandfather's kitchen chair and his grandfather's so-called good chair, a second-hand recliner that he watched television in. Not long after Jet had moved in, Hal had picked up a sofa from the giveaway pile at a garage sale for Jet to sleep on. The aggressive yellow flowers faded against the blue and pink background over time, but the lumps never did soften up.

The gift of a dumpster-bound sofa defined his grandfather. Hal was hardworking and conscientious but miserly to a fault. He took Jet in, despite the fact that he hadn't known what to do with a kid the first time around, let alone the homeless son of his irresponsible daughter. It wouldn't occur to Hal to clean out the back room and make a bedroom for Jet, just as it wouldn't have occurred to Jet to ask for anything more than was offered.

"Yeah, I know. It's—"

"Incredible! This place is so cool." Michael poked his head back out the front door. "We have to fix this up. Or you have to fix it up, and I have to come over and get in your way by trying to help."

"You've had a lot of crazy ideas, man, but this is certifiable."

"You could rent this place out to tourists. Or a writer or artist."

"Stephen King maybe…"

Jet shook out his shoulders and followed Michael into the house where he was hit with the smell, the mess and the memories. Michael pointed out the wide-plank flooring, the stone fireplace, the built-in bookcases and open floor plan. He was in and out of the bedroom, the loft, the kitchen and back room, not unlike the occasional mouse that used to infiltrate the premises.

"Can you explain the economics of this to me again?" Michael asked, finally coming to a standstill in the center of a room filled with ancient paperwork. The back room had been Hal's office, where he'd kept every scrap of paper he'd ever come into contact with. Michael shifted a massive box of old receipts, exposing a large, divided light window with an excellent view of the mountains. "It seems like your grandfather was barely hanging on financially and, from what you say, worked himself to death ranching. But you gave up a lucrative job to come back here and do it all over again."

Jet nodded. "That was always the plan to come back here." He gazed at the stacks of paper Hal would never consider letting anyone help him with. "Like a lot of the old ranchers, Hal grew up in one economic climate, then kept trying to make the same living in a changing landscape. He sold to big companies, which is one way to go. But he was getting the same price per pound for organic, free-range, grass-fed beef that guys were getting for feedlot stock. Any money he made he kept in the bank, rather than investing it, which he thought was gambling."

Michael chuckled. Jet shifted uncomfortably. "I don't mean to make fun of him. He was a good man and did his best in this world. I was fortunate enough to go to college and get a wider worldview. I made enough in Seattle to keep me comfortable, and I want to keep that money invested. I own the land free and clear thanks to all this." Jet waved at the stacks of paper. "I want to spend my time ranching rather than marketing. So for me, the best option is to contract with local businesses to supply beef."

"Like Eighty Local?"

"Like Eighty Local."

"So that's why you have to be nice to Clara."

"Right," Jet said quickly. "I gotta keep on Hunter's good side. They're a close family."

"All makes sense now." Michael had a sly grin on his face as he moved a second box of papers to reveal more built-in bookshelves. "I was starting to think you liked her."

Jet glared at Michael, but his friend had already shot back out to the kitchen and was making noises about the old slate countertop.

Jet *did* need to keep on Hunter's good side. He wanted to be there, too. He wanted Mr. and Mrs. Wallace to continue thinking he was a good guy. Getting himself mixed up with Clara was a surefire way to ruin all of that. The best way to keep himself from falling back in love with her was to avoid her altogether. But he'd agreed to the group date, and he wasn't going to back out now.

A thought came to him. If he could get Michael interested in saving this house, rather than saving half a dozen women with self-esteem issues, that could be a win for Clara. And if Clara, or anyone else from town, ever did happen to drop by the property, they'd never see this pathetic shack in its original state and know how humble his roots really were.

He glanced back at Michael. Maybe his friend just needed to try Hal Broughman's prescription for everything: good old-fashioned hard work. It certainly got Jet's mind off any number of issues. And right now, he was in need of a distraction himself.

STRINGS OF LIGHTS glittered across Main Street. Music drifted over the crowd in the warm, summer night air. Clara hopped off her bike. The whole town seemed to have turned out for Outcrop Outside, the local business fair, and she was determined not to run anyone over this evening.

Clara loved these nights, where every business in town opened their doors or set up booths along the main block. The event was held quarterly and always had a seasonal theme. It didn't matter to Clara if the evening was scented with pumpkin spice, crowded with holly boughs, celebrating the return of spring or, like tonight, warm and lively with the mouthwatering scent of her brother's barbecue drawing in the crowds. She loved Outcrop Outside and was looking forward to supporting her favorite local shops. She planned to be particularly supportive of the new chocolate shop that had opened last month.

This was the perfect distraction. She wouldn't spend another minute wondering what had possessed her to kiss Jet.

"Clara!"

She glanced up to see her favorite history teacher and Outcrop's beloved football coach waving at her.

"Coach Kessler, how are you?"

"Can't complain." He held up a pulled pork sandwich. "If I did, I'd have to stop eating."

Clara laughed. "Hunter's food has that effect on people."

"The whole town's lined up for a sandwich." He gestured at the long line snaking from Hunter's booth on the edge of the town square.

"I'm proud of my brother. He's a local hero."

"I always knew he'd turn out all right." Coach

fell in next to Clara and walked along with her. "Your mother used to worry, but I knew he'd come around."

Clara studied the ground. She'd been too absorbed with her own problems in high school to even realize it had been hard for Hunter. Her anxiety attacks had engulfed everything. It wasn't until she was in college that she realized how difficult school had been for him. Yet in the midst of his own struggle, he'd always taken the time to care for her.

She was ridiculously lucky when it came to family.

"How are your parents?" Coach asked. "I don't see them as much now that they're retired."

"You don't see them because they're always traveling. You take a man who spent his whole life teaching biology and a woman who taught geography, give 'em a little free time, and they're off like a rocket."

Coach laughed. "I'm happy for them."

"They're happy for themselves, too. There are a lot of birds and plants and old ruined buildings they need to look at."

"Well, they deserve it," Coach said. "Two of the best teachers I've ever known."

"Two of the three best teachers," Clara corrected. "High school would not have been half as fun without your history class."

Coach deftly caught a piece of barbecue as it slipped from the sandwich. "You still hold the high score on the US history final exam at Outcrop High."

"I worked hard for that record." Clara maneuvered her bike past Mrs. Fareas, who was balancing two sandwiches and some of Hunter's town-famous kale slaw.

"If only I could have gotten you to pay as much attention to the football games you were supposed to be cheering for."

Clara stopped walking and rolled her eyes. "Okay, I tried."

"Did you, though?" Coach teased her.

"That game is baffling." Clara threw up her hands.

"The Spanish–American War is baffling, and you seemed to have mastered that all right."

"All the stopping and starting and horns blowing." Clara shuddered. Trying out for the cheerleading team had been one of Piper's schemes to help Clara acclimate to high school. It had worked, and Clara enjoyed absolutely every aspect of cheer. Except trying to figure out what all the crunching and jostling was about in a football game.

"Speaking of football, Jet Broughman is back in town," Coach said. "He offered to help with the team."

Clara's heart launched itself into her throat, as though trying to make an escape. She closed her eyes briefly. Football. Jet Broughman. One chilly night in late October. Embarrassment washed over her as she remembered.

"I never will forget that playoff game." Coach chuckled.

Clara nodded. She wouldn't forget it either and still cringed with humiliation every time anyone brought it up. Which was all the time, because heaven forbid a small town stop rehashing a football game that happened twelve years ago.

"He just came out of nowhere. That kid was fast."

Clara tucked her hair behind her ear. "Sure was."

It was in the last few minutes of a particularly painful game that Clara had almost given up trying to watch. The Crest High Swarm was up by three points, and it looked like Outcrop was going to lose a spot in the semifinals, again.

Everyone else in town loved to discuss Jet's catch, his speed, the various shuffling and blocking from the team that made it possible for him to sail across the line and score. What Clara remembered was what happened after number thirty-five took off his helmet.

A rare smile lit Jet's face, brightening the entire stadium like a flash of lightning. His brown hair was attractively mussed, getting messier by the minute as teammates would not stop hurling themselves at him. Clara was unaware of anything except for the gorgeous boy jogging off the field. A nudge from her sister brought her back to reality.

"He's kinda cute," Piper had said.

Kinda didn't come close to covering it.

Dating had never been high on Clara's to-do list. With everything she had going on, it wasn't worth the risk. But there was something about Jet's smile that overrode her concerns and had her floating among the stars that October evening.

Jet had inspired Clara to stretch way past her comfort zone, smiling at him in the halls and talking with him when she got the chance. If the way he responded to her was any sign, he was interested in her, too. Clara decided that night: she would start dating, if dating meant spending time with Jet Broughman.

The blast of a horn signaled the end of the game, and the student body flooded the field. Clara pulled in three deep breaths, then headed toward Jet. He was scanning the field, looking over the heads of his well-wishers. When his eyes met hers, his smile reemerged. Without an apology to the people he'd been speaking with, Jet headed straight for her.

Clara's heart beat hard as she offered her hands up in a double high five and Jet pressed his palms to hers, his fingers briefly curling around hers.

"Congratulations!" she'd said. A flush colored his neck. Clara drew in another breath. She could do this. "We should celebrate."

His dark eyes sparkled as they met hers. He nodded, the flush on his neck deepening. He looked away, then back at her. "I was just going to ask you about that. I wanted to ask you earlier this week but…" Clara remembered a conversation in the hall, where Jet had seemed to have something to say but couldn't quite get it out. "A-are you busy Sunday afternoon?"

It was happening! He was asking her out. With the intensity of her anxiety, she worried she'd never go on an actual date. But here they were, standing on the football field, and he wanted to know if she was free on Sunday. "I'm not busy at all. I'm totally free on Sunday. Zero plans."

Okay, maybe that had been a little clearer than she needed to be.

Then it was his turn to draw in a deep breath. "That's great! That's great because I wanted to ask you…" His words trailed off, and he looked into her eyes. "I mean, I have two tickets and hoped that you would go with me."

He was clearly about as proficient at asking someone out as she was. Clara smiled encouragingly. "Go where?"

He'd brightened, offering the lit-fused bomb that it was. "Zip-lining!"

Zip-lining? Flying through the trees on a probably-going-to-break cable, strapped into a who-knows-how-frayed harness? Clara's breath shortened, then stopped. The field and all the people surrounding them started to spin.

Jet, normally so quiet, kept talking. "They just installed one, over near Bend. It should be fun. I wouldn't have gone ahead and gotten the tickets without asking you, but they're booked out for months, and they had just two open tickets—" His words continued to flow and pool around her, but she had slipped underwater. She hadn't had an anxiety attack in over a year, she'd gotten so good at dealing with her chemistry.

But this? "N-no," she managed to say but wasn't able to continue with an excuse or alternate suggestion. Just a stuttered *no* which must have sounded so lame. Searing shame washed through her as she tried to speak. She was losing it, in front of the one guy she desperately wanted to impress.

Confusion flooded his face. Clara opened her mouth, but nothing came out. Her vision blurred. Then next thing she knew, Piper was at her side, slipping an arm around her shoulders, pulling her away.

The following week played out even worse than Clara's anxious brain could have predicted. She'd tried to message him on social media over the weekend, but he was nowhere to be found. Unable to contact him, she played and replayed the awful scenario in her head, feeling worse each time. By the time Monday came around she could barely shoot him a smile as he passed her in the hall. He walked straight by, as if she wasn't even there. Each day she manipulated her route through school so she'd be sure to pass Jet and shot him her best smile given the circumstances. Each day, he walked straight past her.

It felt so clear at the time. Jet wasn't interested in even getting to know a mess like her. That's what had hurt the most, losing someone who had made her feel like she could be something beyond her disorder.

By Thursday Clara had to face facts: Jet was

not that into her. Piper encouraged her to keep trying, but Clara refused. She wrote out and ratified Love Rule Number One: *Never waste time on someone who isn't into you.* It was disappointing, but ignoring the fact wouldn't change anything. The next day when she passed Jet in the hall, she deliberately looked away.

That's what happens when you get a crush on Jet, Clara reminded herself now. You finally decide you can do this messy, unpredictable thing called a romantic relationship and then crumble just when everything's looking up. But that was a long time ago. She'd grown up, mastered her anxiety and created a great life for herself.

"You still with me?" Coach waved a hand in front of her face. Clara shook off her memory.

"Yeah, Jet's back," Clara responded to Coach Kessler, glancing across the street.

"I heard he had a good run in Seattle."

"I'm sure he did." Clara swallowed hard, casting around for a change of subject. "Oh, hey. Second Chance Cowgirl." She slowed to check out the display her favorite store had set up on the sidewalk.

"What's this?" Coach asked, examining the elegant storefront.

"How do you not know about Second Chance

Cowgirl?" Clara reached out to touch the collar on a delicate white blouse.

"I think I must have missed the First Chance Cowgirl."

Clara laughed. "The owner, Christy Jones, has been in town for three years now. She's got the chic women of Bend and Portland rolling into Outcrop in their Teslas to drop big money on vintage boots and turquoise jewelry. This luxe resale shop is all the rage."

"Is it?"

"If you had a wife, you'd know this."

A pained look crossed his face. "I just never found the right one."

"You know I could help you with that."

Coach waved the offer away. "I'm not good enough for any woman I'd be interested in."

"Okay, that is not true—"

"Will you look at that?" Coach held up the empty wrapper to his pulled pork sandwich. "My sandwich is gone. Guess I'd better go see Hunter again."

"Incorrigible," Clara stated.

"I'll leave you here. I'm not much for—" He broke off abruptly, staring through the window.

Clara turned and followed his gaze. Christy Jones was stunning. Tall and slender, with a pale Norse beauty. Add to that business savvy and an extraordinary eye for style. Clara looked back at Coach. He had probably been very handsome in his youth.

But now? Well… He was a really good guy.

Clara glanced at Christy. Coach Kessler was one of the best men on earth, but Christy was ethereal. She was several leagues out of his league. If Christy was in the league where you got fitted for Super Bowl rings on the regular, Coach Kessler was in the league that, well, made it to the semifinals in the state playoffs.

This could be an interesting challenge.

Coach sighed, then glanced across the street. "Nice seeing you, Clara. Give my best to your folks."

"I will."

"And if you happen to run into Jet, ask him about practice. He's a natural at coaching."

"Why would you think I'd—"

Coach held up his empty sandwich wrapper. "Gotta go!"

"—run into Jet?" Clara finished to herself as he walked away.

She brushed her fingers over her lips. Heat flushed across her face at the memory of the kiss. *What was I thinking?*

She shook her head. It made no sense to keep

running one kiss through the hamster wheel of her brain.

Through the picture window, Clara watched Christy smooth her hand over a vintage sweater. She was alone in her store, as everyone else was outside. Coach Kessler was headed back to the Eighty Local line, stopping to chat with former students and old friends.

Coach and Christy might not be the most obvious match, but if she could pull it off, Jet would have to admit her business was legit and she was a genius.

JET COULD HEAR music and smell barbecue as he turned off the highway. What was going on? Whatever it was had to be a lot more interesting than the trip to the grocery store he'd planned.

He pulled up next to the town square and wrestled the truck into Park. People were everywhere. A cover band played an old Eagles song, and Jet was pretty sure he saw his ninth-grade health teacher singing along. All the shops had their doors open, and some businesses had set up booths. Sparkling lights hung across Main Street.

Clara probably loves those lights.

Jet stopped walking and shook his head. There

was no reason to speculate whether Clara did or did not like an outdoor decoration.

He glanced back at the lights. They sparkled at him, like Clara had that brief period during high school.

Jet exhaled and headed into the crowd. That was all the reminder he needed. Clara's charm could turn on and off, just like those lights.

"Broughman!"

Jet looked up, then held a hand in salute. "Hey."

He trotted toward the Eighty Local booth. Two of Hunter's employees were taking orders and cash, while Hunter and Bowman put together sandwiches. A line of hungry people ran down the block.

"Welcome to Outcrop Outside."

"I didn't even know this was happening."

Bowman looked up at Jet. "I'd blame the business fair on one of my sisters, but for once there's something going on around here that neither of them orchestrated."

Jet laughed. He wasn't the only one wary of Clara.

"Thanks, by the way," Bowman said.

"Yeah, thank you." Hunter nodded at him as his hands flew, assembling a sandwich.

"You're welcome?"

"For taking one for the team," Bowman clarified. "You're going on that group date tomorrow."

Jet shuddered.

"It really is going to be that bad," Hunter confirmed. "Here's how it goes down. You show up to balance the numbers—"

"Which is what she always says," Bowman interrupted.

"But you'll get there, and then she just wants you to go talk to one woman for five minutes."

"N-no," Jet said. "I told Clara not to set me up with anyone. She promised."

The two brothers exchanged a glance.

This was going to be even worse than he thought. He could deal with Clara and keep himself from falling for her again. But there was no way he could handle her setting him up with someone.

"Here, man, take this."

Jet refocused on the brothers to see Bowman holding out a sandwich. Jet reached for the basket, but Hunter grabbed it first.

"Take three sandwiches," he said, dropping two more in the basket. "You're gonna need your strength."

Jet laughed, but inwardly his stomach churned. Tomorrow was going to be the most awkward day on record, and he had a long history of not fitting in to compete with.

He headed down Main Street. The town was significantly nicer than when he'd left twelve years ago. Small businesses had popped up in what had been abandoned buildings. Young people were able to find good work and stay in town, raising their families here. Outcrop had long catered to the outdoor enthusiasts who skied, hiked and climbed in the mountains and canyons nearby. But now the town was self-sustaining with its own businesses. They could profit off tourism but no longer relied on it.

A young couple walked past, with a baby in a front carrier and a toddler in a backpack. Jet recognized them from school, but they would have no idea who he was. He nodded but didn't stop to talk. That was a trick he'd learned from his grandfather: be polite but not friendly.

It wasn't until he saw a woman in a yellow sundress, pushing a cream-colored Schwinn through the crowd that he stopped in his tracks.

Jet's phone buzzed in his pocket. He started to reach for it, but then Clara turned from the storefront she'd been studying and saw him.

"Hey!" She smiled and waved.

Jet looked over his shoulder to see who she was waving at.

"I'm not going to run you down this time, I promise."

Right. She's talking to me. Unless there is someone else in the crowd she's mowed down recently? Which is a possibility.

"Hi, Clara."

She advanced on him, smiling. Jet forced himself to remember that he was doing her a favor the next day, and that's why she was being nice.

"Do you have enough sandwiches?" she asked, nodding at the basket.

Sandwiches? Jet glanced down.

"Um…no," he deadpanned. She laughed, so Jet kept talking. "I don't think there *are* enough sandwiches."

Clara widened her eyes. "I agree. How long did you have to wait in line?"

"I didn't. Hunter set me up at the back." Jet's phone buzzed again in his pocket.

"Seriously?" Clara raised her brow. "You got the family special, then. Someone else's messed up order."

Jet glanced down at the basket. It hadn't been a messed up order. Bowman and Hunter consciously had everyone in line wait even longer as they made these sandwiches for him, for free. They must *really* hate group dates.

Before he could think about what he was doing, Jet held the basket out to Clara. "Have one."

"Really?"

"Please."

Clara reached in and took a sandwich. She balanced her bike with one hand and took a bite. Her eyes closed as she savored the barbecue.

Jet would have liked to slap himself for staring at her, but he was still holding two sandwiches.

"I'm going to say that this is my favorite thing Hunter makes. But I know the minute I eat something else of his, that's going to be my favorite."

"Lucky to have a chef in the family." Jet pulled a sandwich from the basket and took a bite. He'd always been more of an enthusiast than a connoisseur of food, but even he could tell this was no ordinary barbecue.

"You have no idea."

His phone buzzed again.

"Are you going to get that?" Clara asked, gesturing at his pocket.

"Nah. It's my old boss."

"What's he want?"

"Ken? He wants me to solve one more problem for him."

Clara nodded. "And one more problem will lead to one more problem after that?"

"Just like Michael and his ex-girlfriends," Jet said.

Clara laughed. The festive lights gave off a soft glow as the sky darkened. Never in his life would he have expected to be sharing sandwiches with Clara at a town festival in Outcrop.

"What did you do in Seattle? I remember you got the big scholarship, then decided on University of Washington. Did you get the job straight out of college?"

Jet nodded. He didn't want to boast, but the job had gotten him, while he was still in school. The work he'd done in DevOps was grueling, detail-oriented, math-based work that took long, focused hours. Few people had both the brains and the grit to get it done.

"Yeah. I worked in programming, finding and solving problems."

"That sounds…interesting?" she guessed.

"Not at all."

Clara laughed again. In high school, he'd always been distracted by her laugh. Whether she was surrounded by friends or her siblings or parents, that laugh had felt like the antithesis of everything in his life back then. But right now, she was laughing at his jokes.

"Did you at least like Seattle?"

"Seattle's a great city, but Outcrop…"

Jet stopped himself from oversharing. He'd only had four years in Outcrop, but the mountain air scented with juniper and the vast expanse of his grandfather's ranch were the closest thing to home he'd ever known. Seattle was full of opportunity and new experiences, but he'd found it hard to breathe in the city.

"Outcrop has OHTAF, this business fair and these sandwiches," she said, holding up her pulled pork.

Jet looked down into Clara's wide brown eyes. There were so many good things in Outcrop.

"Right. It's hard for Seattle or anywhere to compete."

"Dad always said you'd be back. And he's pretty good at predicting how his students will turn out."

Jet jumped on the opportunity to change the subject. "Do your parents still run Canadian horses?"

Clara tilted her head. "Yes and no. Yes, there is still a large herd of Canadians at the ranch. That's where we're riding tomorrow. But with Mom and Dad traveling so much, the care falls on Ash, Hunter and Bowman."

"I always thought it was incredible that they could teach full-time and breed and sell horses."

"And put up with five kids."

Jet laughed. He raised his arm to rest it around Clara's shoulders, then stopped himself. What the heck? This was *not* a date. This was running into someone he knew and having a conversation. Just because it was not possible within the laws of physics to be more beautiful than Clara didn't mean he could get carried away. Everyone was smitten with Clara.

"Do you know about this?" Clara asked. "Three Sisters Chocolatier?" She gestured to the shop behind her. "It's the most amazing thing to pop up in this town since the Outcrop Bakery."

Jet glanced in the window at the rows of chocolates in the glass case, then back at Clara. "It's tempting."

"It's downright dangerous. Come on." She propped her bike up against a streetlamp and tugged at his arm. "You can save me if I go into a sugar coma."

He paused at the door. Following Clara anywhere was a bad idea.

"You have to support the local businesses. If this chocolate shop failed, could you live with yourself?"

Jet laughed, trying to keep his eyes on the storefront, the lights overhead or anywhere but Clara.

"I should really—" Jet gestured in the vague direction of his truck. Clara's brown eyes widened as she blinked up at him. Jet opened the door for her. "Okay, what's the cutoff? Ten chocolates?"

"Ten? That will barely get us started." She tugged at his arm again.

Despite every good intention, Jet found himself, once again, heading for a heartache in the form of Clara Wallace.

CHAPTER SIX

THE AXE RIPPED through the tight grain of the juniper log, sending the split pieces skittering across his patio. Jet dropped the head of the axe. He rolled his shoulders, then grabbed another chunk of wood.

He glanced up at the sky, then to the west where the Cascade Mountain range spanned the horizon. Nothing but miles and miles of clear blue sky, on the one day he needed a storm. He'd been nervous enough about this group date, and that was before he'd spent half the previous night running after Clara in what he'd justified as *supporting Outcrop small business*.

Jet slammed the axe through another log.

Where was bad weather when you needed it? Growing up, it seemed like there was always a storm blowing in, canceling everything. But today? Nothing.

Jet walked to the log pile and grabbed another chunk of juniper. The day was warm, and the air laced with scents of sage. Chopping wood was a satisfying chore. It could have been a perfect morning.

But in less than an hour he was headed to Wallace Ranch, ready for an awkward afternoon of watching other people fall in love. All under the gaze of the one woman he needed to avoid. Last night he'd effectively followed her around like a duckling, incapable of doing anything except try to make her laugh. Then Bowman saw the two of them walking out of a yarn shop together and tapped Hunter to point it out. That's what it took for Jet to finally force himself back into his truck and onto the highway home.

A yarn shop? What was I thinking?

Jet slammed the axe down, missing the log and wedging the axe deep into the chopping block.

"Forget it," he muttered, mad at the wood, the axe and his inability to keep his mind off Clara. He didn't want to admit it, but running around with Clara had felt so easy and fun, like the conversations they'd shared in the hallway outside his science class as teenagers. The difference was now he was old enough to know better.

Aware of eyes on him, Jet looked up. Every emu he owned was lined up along the fence of the east pasture, watching him in stupefied wonder.

"What are you birds looking at?"

The pack jostled together, tripping over their adolescent feet, excited and baffled.

Jet shook his head. Leaving the axe in the block, he crossed to his patio. Sun shone on the outdoor cooking area, reminding him that he had yet to fire up either of the grills. He entered the kitchen and left the doors open. A breeze blowing through his home might take some of his nervous energy with it. He swung through the laundry room to check on the chick, who was still peeping happily in her new home in a newspaper-lined utility sink. In a few more weeks he'd mix her in with the emus.

"Hello?" Jet heard Michael call. His stomach dropped.

Jet checked his phone as he walked through his dining room and into the great room beyond. No message from Clara calling off the trail ride. No dire emergency that would serve as an excuse for not going. Just another text from Ken, asking Jet to reconsider taking his old job back, at twice the salary this time. This morning it was almost tempting.

"Hey," Jet said, moving toward the entryway where Michael had let himself in. "Are we really going to do this?"

"Ride horses with beautiful women? Yes."

"I have a very bad feeling about this."

"Bad feelings make for great stories." Michael ambled down the steps into the great room. "Has anyone ever told you your house looks like an advertisement for a fancy vacation rental?"

"Aside from the women who decorated it, you're the only person who's ever been in it."

Michael stood with his hands on his hips and surveyed the room. Jet's goal had been to build a house that made him as comfortable indoors as he was outside. To that end, vaulted wood ceilings reflected light from the massive windows and shone on the natural materials used throughout. The design was vast and open, a dream house. The decorators had brought in the wood and leather furnishings, a big painting of horses and a bowl that Jet remembered as being ridiculously expensive and with no purpose. The bowl did absolutely nothing. It just sat there.

Michael slapped Jet's back. "This house is incredible. You just need to fill it up with a family."

"I know."

"You should hire a matchmaker," Michael said.

Jet snorted. He snuck another look at his phone. Still no dangerous weather patterns. No imminent evacuation of Deschutes County pending.

Michael sat on the leather sofa, then jumped

up and walked to the window. "I'm nervous," he said. "What if I meet my future wife today? What if she's there?"

"I've got your back."

Michael looked at him. "You'll probably know everyone. You grew up here."

"I won't know anyone."

"That's not possible," said Michael, the man who could make friends while shopping for athlete's foot medication. "This is a small town. I thought the whole point of small towns is that you're all friends for life."

"This is a small town. The social worker dropped me off with my grandfather when I was fourteen. That's a little bit late to get in on the friends for life."

Michael scoffed.

Jet continued. "You know I'm not comfortable in a lot of social situations, and at fourteen I was socially paralyzed."

"I don't believe that. Rural Scholar award, football star—"

"I wasn't a star."

"No one found you the slightest bit interesting?"

"No one." Unless you counted Clara, for those bright October days his senior year.

"Then, why'd you come back?"

Jet glanced out the window at a familiar stand of pine. "This land is my home."

Michael nodded. The moment stretched out, more serious than Jet had intended. He needed to shift the mood. "And how else am I going to fulfill my life's goal of being an old man on the front porch of OHTAF?"

Michael laughed. "That's why I moved here."

Jet checked the time on his phone. "We should head out, get this over with."

"If you insist." Michael bounded out the door and down the front steps. Jet's legs felt like lead as he followed.

Movement beyond Michael caught his eye. "Oh, no."

Two of the most ridiculous birds trotted at about twenty miles an hour down his driveway toward the backyard of his house.

"Are your emus out again?"

"Must be mine. No one else around here is stupid enough to try to raise them."

"Can we round 'em up?" Michael's eyes shone at the prospect.

"Gonna have to." Jet backed up a few steps toward his house. "Let me grab my—" He stopped.

A noise behind him sent a chill down his spine. A cross between a grunt and a coo, with a soft trill to it. He spun around to see the maniacal smile and amber eyes of a five-month-old emu, standing on his coffee table. The creature tilted his head, trying to figure out why either of them was there. Then it squawked, like Jet was the intruder.

He lunged for the bird.

The emu leaped from the table, missing the bowl by inches. Its scaled feet scrambled for purchase on the hardwood floor as it took off down the hall.

"How can I help?" Michael asked.

"Herd him down that way, into the laundry room," Jet called, motioning for Michael to follow the bird. "I'll go through the kitchen and cut him off. Don't let him go up the back stairs!"

Michael followed the bird, hooting and hollering like a rodeo champion. Jet sped through the living room, across the dining room and made it to the kitchen.

Five skinny-legged, molting-feathered, adolescent degenerates stood staring back at him.

Every curse word he had ever taken the time to learn came spewing out of his mouth. The birds jostled together, then began popping out the back door onto Jet's patio. The first emu came sliding around the corner from the laundry room, feet skidding on the varnished cork flooring, Michael in hot pursuit.

"We can trap them by the grill," Jet said, shooing the last bird out of his house.

The U-shaped outdoor kitchen was an extraordinary work of masonry. A gas grill, a charcoal grill, a sink and a pizza oven he'd imagined using for his future children's birthday parties, all seemed to stare back at him. The fixtures were indignant as six of the stupidest birds to ever sprout feathers clustered among them.

Jet and Michael slowly approached the opening, trying not to startle the creatures. This was not easy, as the emus got startled by anything, even their own feet.

"Keep them here," Jet said quietly. "Try to look big and menacing, but don't rile them up. I'll be right back."

Jet took three slow steps across his patio, then ducked around the side of his house and ran to the garage.

Dang if this wasn't going to make them late for Clara's group date. He should have declined in the first place. But Clara had just blinked her big brown eyes at him, and he had said yes. Showing up late might make her think he was backing out at the last minute.

He stopped, wondering if this constituted enough of an emergency to back out.

Right. *I'm sorry, Clara. We couldn't make it*

because I'm an incompetent rancher who can't keep six birds in a pasture.

Jet swung into the utility shed on the side of his garage. Michael shouldn't have to be late. He'd set down good money for Clara's match-making talents and was now running all over Jet's property chasing emus.

Less than a minute later Jet returned to hear Michael telling the emus about a particularly horrible class he'd had in med school.

"Is that your recycle bin?" Michael asked, glancing over his shoulder.

"Yes." Jet set upright the wheeled bin he'd dragged around back along with his trash container.

"You're going to recycle them? That's the plan?"

"I wish. But I don't think the county recycling program accepts large birds."

Jet advanced slowly, holding his arms out so no birds would consider trying to make a run past him. With a quick jab born of practice, he grabbed the closest emu by the neck. He slipped an arm around its middle as it squawked in surprise, then anger.

"You don't want to get picked up?" he asked the struggling bird. "Then, stay in your pen."

The emu strained against Jet's grip, but Jet

managed to get it into the recycling bin. The minute the lid slammed down the bird silenced.

"Do they like being in the bins?" Michael asked.

"No, it's just dark, so he thinks it's nighttime."

"These really are dumb birds."

"The dumbest."

In under fifteen minutes Jet had all six escapees, some of his junk mail and an empty milk carton dumped into his barn. He'd lock them in for now, and he would figure out where they had escaped from the pasture when he got home. A quick text to Michael's house cleaner assured him that, for the right sum, all evidence of the emu invasion into his home could be erased by six o'clock in the evening.

"How late are we?" Jet asked as he jumped in the passenger seat.

"Not very," Michael said. "I texted Clara and let her know."

Jet's blood flowed cold. "You told her about the emus?"

"Yeah. It's a funny story."

Jet shifted in his seat.

"What?" Michael asked.

"I just…" Jet started, then stopped. He tried again. "Look, I appreciate that Clara is a competet matchmaker, and I apologize for my earlier comments."

"But?"

Jet looked out the window. On the other side of his drive was a stand of pine trees. His cattle were placid in the field beyond. And farther still, at the edge of his property, the dilapidated shack he'd shared with his grandfather stood reproachfully. *A girl like Clara Wallace doesn't go out with a Broughman.*

Jet didn't need to worry about Clara Wallace thinking poorly of him, because Clara Wallace didn't think about him at all.

"But nothing. Let's get this over with."

Clara allowed her nerves to sharpen her focus. Her family's riding arena was full of Potentials. Jet and Michael would be here any minute, and she wanted all her clients to be having a fantastic time when they showed up. Jet would walk in, take one look at the scene and realize she ran an extraordinary business.

Right?

Clara gripped the rail and pressed her forehead against the pine pole framing.

Ugh. Why couldn't I just leave it at the chocolate shop last night?

She knew why. The minute he'd held the door

for her, it was like being transported back to the days when their friendship was bright and new.

But they weren't teenagers. They were adults, and she'd pestered him into spending the evening with her because he made her laugh, and she loved seeing their hometown through his eyes. Heat flooded her face as she thought about how she'd coerced him in and out of every business in Outcrop.

Oof.

Clara shook off her nervousness. This was a good time to employ calm thoughts. The day was glorious, a perfect seventy-two degrees of sunshine. Soft breezes bussed the occasional cloud through the sky, casting shadows over the land. Her nephew Jackson, literally the best nephew ever in the entire history of nephews, was leading horses out of their stalls into the arena.

And Jet and Michael were late because of some problem with Jet's emus, which was a really good reason to be late. Plus, it was kind of funny. What did an emu break even look like?

Probably like this barn full of fidgeting Potentials who didn't know what to do with themselves. She needed to get to work.

"Danton?" She flagged a gentleman who was recently retired from the Deschutes County

Mounted Posse. He was a new client, and this was a great place to showcase his skills. "Can you check everyone's saddles and stirrups?"

The silver fox nodded and headed straight for Sylvia's horse first. Perfect.

"Evie, take my camera." Clara placed the strap of her Nikon around the neck of a vivacious, artistic heiress. "I need a ton of pictures, so don't hold back." Taking pictures would allow Evie to interact with everyone, spreading her lively conversation throughout the group.

How else can I get people talking?

Penny sat off to one side, her shoulders slumped as she studied the ground. Another client kept fussing about her outfit.

An uncomfortable buzzing started. Clara steadied herself on the side of the arena and drew in three deep breaths. The group date was going to be fine. The world wouldn't spontaneously combust if things didn't go perfectly.

A gentle snort and restrained stomp came from behind her. Clara turned and addressed the horse.

"I'm fine, Shelby," she said, rubbing the silky ears of the Canadian. He leaned his nose down and nudged her shoulder. "We'll be moving soon." She scratched under his mane, relishing the earthy smell of her favorite animal on the planet. Like most of his brethren, Shelby was a dark, glossy brown, well-muscled and full of personality. At sixteen hands, he was on the tall side but sweet as could be. Canadians were a gentle, intuitive breed but also determined. Shelby sniffed, trying to get his nose into her pocket. "If you think you're getting a treat, you're going to need to think again."

Her horse shifted away and attempted to look disinterested.

"Faker," she said.

Clara glanced up at the sound of a car door slamming. Michael came bounding out of a Subaru.

"Hello!" His eyes scanned the assembled group.

"Michael, nice to see you." She waved him over. "You are going to be on Pepper here."

"Oh! Pepper!" He immediately transferred his enthusiasm to the horse.

Her gaze drifted to the car, but she forced it back to the arena. Jet would get out of the Subaru in his own time. She would play it cool with him today.

A new wave of embarrassment washed through her as she remembered how *not* cool she'd been last night. The yarn shop had clearly been the last straw. He'd practically run to his truck when they got out of the door.

A yarn shop? Seriously, what was I thinking?

Clara's gaze drifted to the car again. Jet gripped the doorframe and pulled his tall, strong body from the passenger side. He caught her eye and tipped his Stetson. Clara gave him a big wave and a smile.

"Hey," he said.

"Hey." She waved a second time. *Like he might have missed the first one?*

He walked slowly, glancing around like he'd rather be anywhere else on earth right now.

"Coach Broughman!" her nephew Jackson called out.

Coach Broughman? Clara looked from her nephew to Jet and back again. Jet smiled and looked about a billion times more comfortable.

"Hey, Jackson." Jet trotted into the arena. "Nice job in drills yesterday. Good focus."

"Thanks. I'm hoping Coach Kessler will let me have some time on offence as well as defense."

Jet seemed to pause for a fraction of a second, then, sounding a lot like Coach Kessler, he said, "Keep working like that and it'll pay off."

"I heard you were helping out with the team," Clara said.

Jet nodded, then smiled at her. "Yep. I called

Coach, offered my time and got a deeply inspiring speech on how to give inspiring speeches. I've been helping out this week. It's a great group of kids."

Her brow furrowed. "But it's only June. Aren't kids supposed to be on break?"

Jackson and Jet looked at her in horror, then answered at almost the same time, "Eagle football never stops."

Clara laughed. It was fun to see Jet in this coaching role. Her nephew would be in good hands.

"I'm glad you're coaching. You'll be great at helping those kids move that ball down the field." Clara nodded.

"No," Jet explained, "I'll be working with defense."

Clara tilted her head in confusion. Wasn't that moving the ball?

Jackson groaned. "Aunt Clara, you have to start paying attention when I explain football to you."

"I'm really trying, sweetie."

Her nephew sighed, speaking patiently as he gestured to Jet. "Coach Broughman is a defense legend. This is the guy who intercepted what would have been the winning touchdown for the Swarm—"

Both Jet and Clara spoke over Jackson, arms waving, voices rising as he started to describe a night they both remembered and didn't relish rehashing together.

"It was just one catch—" Jet started as Clara said, "I know who Jet is. I remember that night—"

At her words Jet turned from Jackson and looked down at her. Something about his gaze managed to shelter both of them, blocking out the noise and confusion of the barn. His words seemed to come out unbidden. "Do you? Remember?"

Clara nodded, trying to convey the apology she'd never gotten to make all those years ago. "Of course."

He didn't look away, and she hoped he could feel her apology. She might never be able to tell him about the anxiety she'd experienced in her youth but hoped he could understand that her rejection of his zip-lining offer had nothing to do with how much she'd liked him.

Jackson interrupted her silent attempt at communication. "Then, have some respect, Aunt Clara. Coach Broughman is the Exterminator. Uncle Bowman told me you dragged him into a yarn shop last night and—"

"Okay." Clara clapped her hands, signaling

her clients and cutting off her nephew. "That's enough. Let's get moving here. Jackson, Danton, can you help people saddle up?"

Before the anxious hamsters of her brain could start chanting *yarn shop* again, Clara marshaled her attention to the task at hand. She had to get thirteen nervous Potentials to introduce themselves to the group, onto horses, and somewhere near the people she believed they would best hit it off with.

"I don't think I wore the right shoes," Denise, a woman in her early forties said, worried.

"I never wear the right anything," Michael said.

"Those are fine," Clara assured her.

"I wear orthopedic inserts at the hospital," Michael babbled.

Jet moved to step in. Clara blocked his path.

"Don't," she said quietly, steering Jet toward his mount. "You can't intercept this one."

"But," Jet gestured toward his friend, "*orthopedic inserts*? I thought we were supposed to be helping him."

Clara placed her hand on Jet's arm. *Mistake.* "I am helping him. By getting you on the other side of the barn."

"I could change the subject." Jet trained his eyes on Michael.

"You need to trust me here."

He shook his head and groaned. "Now he'll start talking about his plantar fasciitis."

Clara angled Jet away from his friend and toward Shelby, who was still trying to snub his favorite human.

"Today's goals for Michael are to get comfortable and learn to be more selective. Denise is not on my radar for Michael. And even if she were, you would not help the situation."

"How do you know that?"

Michael was now gesturing to the soles of his feet with far too much enthusiasm.

"Think about it," Clara whispered. "You're a woman, being talked at by a nervous man who has to wear nerd shoes to work. Then suddenly, a tough, good-looking rancher guy comes sauntering over to redirect the conversation? How could you possibly be helpful to Michael?"

Jet stopped abruptly and looked into Clara's eyes. "I'm *a tough, good-looking rancher guy*?"

Did she say that out loud? Clara cleared her throat. "That's how you read, yes."

A flush crept up his neck, and Clara wondered

if it was possible to kick herself without anyone noticing. Nothing for it now but to lean in.

"What I really need is for you to be tough and good-looking over by that woman in the yellow top. Would you mind hopping on Shelby here and going to talk to her?"

Jet sputtered. "A-are you kidding me?"

This was just going from bad to worse. Clara rounded on Jet. "This is my favorite horse. I put you on him specifically because—"

"No, sorry I didn't mean I wouldn't get on the horse." He turned to Shelby. "Hey. Good to meet you."

Shelby was not impressed. Jet grabbed the horn, swung up on the saddle and patted the horse's neck. Shelby ignored him.

Jet started to speak, then stopped. Finally, he came out with "I didn't know you wanted me to be social at this thing. I'm…I'm not really good at talking to new people."

Clara glanced up at him. *How in heaven's name can he think there is a woman on earth who wouldn't want to talk to him?*

"Jet, this is a group date. People talk on dates."

He laughed. "I know. I just thought I was here—"

"As eye candy?"

This time the flush spread across his entire face. *Interesting.* Did Jet really not know how handsome he was?

Clara took pity on him. "Here's the deal. If you go talk to her, the man with the beard over there will feel the competition and get moving in her direction. It's called drawing focus. When other men see you're interested in her, they'll get interested, too."

"So I just go over to her and say anything?"

"It literally does not matter what you say. She's smitten with the bearded guy, and he likes her, too. My guess is it won't take more than three sentences before he gets moving in her direction."

Jet observed the man, who was carefully *not* looking at the woman in yellow. His eyes danced through the rest of the Potentials in the barn, finally coming to rest on her.

"You have this all figured out, don't you?" It was a sincere question, with a hint of...was it respect?

"I've done some planning. Now, get!"

Jet ambled his mount over to Penny, where she sat morosely on her horse, in all likelihood trying to figure out why the man she'd had a great time with on Thursday was now half a barn away, looking distracted. Clara watched as Penny glanced up, surprised and pleased at Jet's appearance.

Had she really called him *a tough, good-looking rancher* to his face? So much for playing it cool.

CHAPTER SEVEN

THE GROUP DATE was even more uncomfortable than Jet had feared, and his horse wasn't helping matters. From the minute the group departed from the riding arena, Shelby wasn't happy anywhere except right next to Clara. This was a problem, as Jet wanted to keep himself as far from her as possible.

"Whoa." Jet leaned closer to the horse's ear, as if the animal's hearing was the problem.

Shelby flattened his ears and muscled past two of the horses in between him and Clara. Jet was a confident rider, but he wasn't going to commit to a power struggle in front of everyone, and the horse knew it. He pressed his right heel into the horse's flank, keeping steady tension in his leg. Shelby swished his tail in annoyance.

They were coming up on Clara, and Jet had no idea what to say to her now. *What did that look she'd given him in the arena mean?* He'd been pretty sure she didn't even remember their connection in high school and certainly didn't think about the night he'd asked her out. But there was something in her eyes suggesting she regretted the way that evening had turned out, too.

To this day, Jet hadn't forgiven himself for the way he'd reacted after her rejection. At the time, he'd sensed there was more to the situation than just a girl turning a boy down. The way the color had drained from her face and her sister swept her away indicated that something was wrong. But Jet had been too wrapped up in his own disappointment to ask. She tried to connect with him in the weeks after, but he was too attached to his own suffering. He'd never let himself consider the idea that Clara could have had a good reason for saying no and maybe still wanted to be friends.

As an adult, he wanted to apologize for being a jerk. But that was a long time ago. No, for the time being, he just needed to keep out of her way. His horse, however, had other ideas.

Jet gave the reins an authoritative tug to the right. Shelby shook his dark glossy mane and headed left.

"You realize that all these people want to be right next to Clara?" he asked the horse. The horse, apparently, didn't care.

Jet leaned back in his saddle and let Shelby try to maneuver his way up the line. Everybody else was competing for the same spot, so he had his work cut out for him.

Clara led the group down a gentle green slope toward a series of ponds. The stately farmhouse stood behind them at the crest of the hill, Clara's childhood home. A massive garden stretched out past the lawn, with irrigation ditches and water collection systems set up throughout. Creamy, crushed gravel roads connected the outbuildings: bunkhouse, barns, stable and riding arena.

This was Wallace Ranch, famous for the Canadian horses they bred. Mr. and Mrs. Wallace had built the place, working hard to fund their dream. Jet could understand why Clara and Piper were matchmakers. Their parents were an inspiring couple. But what he couldn't figure out was why Clara was still single. She valued relationships and could have her pick of anyone.

Jet scanned the crowd to see what webs Clara was spinning now. Everyone was nervous, despite her calm and happy presence weaving in and among them. A beautiful woman in her late sixties, Sylvia, was actively afraid of her horse, so Danton had to help her the whole time. Some guy in a red pearl-snap shirt was flirting with Clara nonstop. The whole group date was chaos.

The worst was Michael. Jet had seen his friend botch dates before, but here he was botching five dates at once. He babbled on about anything and everything, bouncing in the saddle like an animated gummy bear. When did women get to see the skilled surgeon? The brilliant diagnostician? The kind and gentle doctor who made gravely sick children laugh and their parents smile for the first time since learning of their child's condition? All these women saw was a nervous dweeb on a talking jag.

No, scratch that. Michael was bad, but his horse was worse. The animal nipped one of his brothers on the butt and sent him skittering. Shelby moved confidently into his place next to Clara as they rode into a grove of aspen trees.

Clara turned to Jet like she'd been expecting him.

"You know, if you watch Michael like a hawk this whole time, people are going to feel your disapproval of him."

"But—"

"Shhh. Has it occurred to you that your friend Michael is class A dad material?"

A breeze blew past, lifting Clara's hair from her shoulders. Jet cleared his throat. "Class A?"

"Women who are looking to have a family don't necessarily want a smooth, mysterious man. They want a nice guy, a good guy."

"Michael's been nice and good for the last ten years. It hasn't been working for him."

"Sure, some women are drawn to men who treat them poorly. But not these women. Part of my work is to provide enough guidance so they learn to be attracted to what they want, rather than some ridiculous notion of a tough, brooding, hard-to-get hunk."

"No one would ever mistake Michael for brooding," Jet admitted.

"Or hard to get," she added with a little grin. "That's going to be my challenge here. Michael needs to be more selective."

Aspen leaves fluttered overhead, dappling the sunlight playing across her face. A family of chickadees scuttled through the branches.

A chipmunk raced out into the path, then braced its front feet and chittered at them. The horses moved on, unperturbed.

"Look, a squirrel!" Michael said. "Or a chipmunk! It's fuzzy."

Jet groaned as quietly as possible. At least the guy was consistent—he got just as excited about critters back in Seattle. Clara met his gaze, then blinked slowly and shook her head as they both tried not to laugh. She sighed and patted his back, her hand warm through his shirt. Jet's heart kicked up, rattling out some message about how maybe this time with Clara would be different.

Which meant it was past time to get away from her. He leaned back in the saddle and looked over his shoulder. "Is there anyone else you need me to talk to?"

"Actually, me." She glanced around. "Alex," she said, nodding to the man who had been flirting with her, "won't start talking to other women so long as he thinks he can come talk to me. He's shy."

Jet snorted.

"What? He is shy."

"He's into you. He's barely taken his eyes off you."

She glanced at the man with disinterest. "They all fall a little bit in love with me."

Jealousy coursed through him. Shelby stopped abruptly and uttered a neigh of discontent. This was probably because Jet had a death grip on the reins. He forced his hands to relax, inhaling a deep breath.

"All your customers?" he asked.

"A lot. It's an occupational hazard. They get over it, and I don't let it bother me."

Jet let this news settle. Everyone fell in love with Clara. She knew it, and she didn't care.

"You ever go out with any of your clients?" he asked, hoping to sound casual.

"No! That'd be weird and wrong. And honestly, I'm not tempted. I like my clients a lot. I have to. But it's pretty easy to decide not to be attracted to someone."

Jet glanced down at Clara. She sat relaxed and confident in the saddle, wavy hair shining in the sunlight, lively brown eyes surveying her clients. Jet's lungs tightened.

"You can't decide who you're attracted to."

Her eyes met his. "Sure you can."

Jet shook his head. "You're telling me that if you met a man you thought was a good match for you, but there weren't any..." Jet fished around for the right word, while Clara smiled at him, setting off a string of illegal fireworks in his respiratory system "...sparks, you think you could will yourself to be attracted to him?"

She considered this a moment. "No, it's more like I could keep myself from being attracted to someone who wasn't right for me."

That must be nice. Jet was working overtime to keep his attraction for Clara at bay and his heart firmly closed off. Clara, apparently, just made a well-informed decision based on facts, then marshaled her emotions in line. Jet would give anything for that sort of power over his feelings.

"Handy skill."

Clara glanced at him, then her eyes darted away. "For the most part, anyway."

The group moved into a clearing at the center of the aspen grove. Picnic baskets were waiting under a tree, along with folding chairs and a table. Danton helped people down from their horses and lined the animals up along a hitching post. Clara directed some people to set up tables, others to lay the food out. She pointed out the butter pecan cookies made by one of the group members. Everyone was pitching in. Jet moved to help set up a table. Clara stopped him with the briefest shake of her head.

He sauntered over to where she stood. "Can't I help?"

"Not right now," she said quietly. Her hand came to rest on his arm while she continued to survey the group, her palm soft against his skin.

Jet watched, trying to pick up on whatever Clara had in play. The group was setting up a picnic that could easily have been prepared before their arrival. The bearded man took a basket from Penny and helped her unpack it. Evie, a vivacious lady was showing another woman pictures she'd taken with Clara's camera. Even

Michael mellowed, now that he had something specific to do by doling out hand sanitizer.

Jet looked back at Clara. "You set them up to help each other, didn't you?"

She nodded, her eyes tracking the beautiful older woman who'd had so much trouble on the ride. The woman glanced back at the man who'd been helping with the horses. The air in the aspen grove shifted. Silvery leaves shimmered in the breeze, their movements echoing a fluttering heartbeat. Clara let out a breath.

"It's all part of the plan."

Of course it was part of the plan. But it was working. Maybe Michael was right. Clara had changed in the last twelve years. She still bent the world to her will, but her will now included helping people find love, and it was hard to argue with that.

"Good plan."

Her dazzling grin took him by surprise. She bit her lip. "Thank you."

"At the beginning of this group date, I would not have expected this." Jet gestured to the jovial picnic she'd manifested. "You always get what you want, don't you?"

"If I set reasonable expectations and put solid plans into motion, then yes. I can meet my goals."

"Anyone ever disappoint you?"

She blinked, startled. Sadness flickered across her face, then she cleared her expression. Her eyes met his. "Yes, Jet. I've been disappointed a time or two."

Had he said something wrong? "I didn't mean—"

Clara shook her head. Then she looked up at Jet and grinned, like she'd never felt a moment's discomfort in her life.

"But I am not going to be disappointed by this group of Potentials. A year from now, every one of them will be in a happily committed relationship."

Jet followed her lead and smiled back. "Even Michael?"

"Especially Michael." Clara took a step away from him and dusted off her jeans. "Okay, now that everyone is relaxed, and Danton is flirting with Sylvia, I need your help again."

"What should I do?"

"Make sure no one messes with any of the tack, and when they finish eating, help everyone get back on the right horse."

"You got it."

Clara took a few steps toward the line of horses, then looked back at him with a grin.

"That's what tough, good-looking rancher guys are for, right?"

Jet touched the tips of his fingers to his hat, lowering his head so she couldn't see the rush of blood to his face. He had to remember that he was a means to an end for Clara right now. And that was okay if the end was all these people happy and in love. He was on board with helping. He just needed to make sure he didn't wind up miserable and in love.

"Wait." Clara stopped mid-stride and spun around. "You haven't had lunch."

"I'm good."

"No. You have to eat lunch."

"What about you? You haven't eaten."

Clara glanced around, then walked up close to him. The scent of orange blossom and ginger drifted from her skin.

"I get pretty nervous on these things." She gestured to the crowd. "This matters to me. Once we're back and everything has gone okay, I'll run up to the house and eat the leftovers, but right now I couldn't swallow a thing."

Jet's hand reached out and rested on her shoulder, which was incredible, because he had absolutely no intention of touching her. But she'd opened up about being nervous. She was vulnerable. And he was irrationally touched by the fact that she cared whether or not he had lunch. "Is there anything I can do to make it easier?"

"Eat your lunch," she said, smiling like she hadn't just revealed something personal.

Jet glanced over at the table. He was hungry, and lunch looked fantastic.

"Look, I know you're some kind of fantastic sandwich maker." Clara waved her hands in mock praise.

Jet laughed. "How do you know about my sandwiches? Which are fantastic, by the way."

"You told me. 'Good friend, good sandwich maker,' remember?"

The air washed out of his lungs as he stared at Clara. She remembered that brief sentence from their collision outside of Eighty Local? He shook his head. It didn't mean anything. Clara was smart. If he'd learned anything in the last week, it was that she had a way of making everyone feel like she cared. *They all fall a little bit in love with me.*

"Hunter's no slouch sandwich maker himself. I'll go check it out."

"Then the horses?" Clara asked.

"Then the horses."

Jet strode off toward the table but couldn't help taking one last glance over his shoulder. Faded blue jeans, well-used and well-kept boots, a pale blue plaid top: she was so beautiful and completely at ease as she shared a secret with the horse he'd ridden.

Clara might be able to decide who she was and wasn't attracted to, but he, apparently, had no control whatsoever.

THE HORSES PICKED up the pace as they headed to the arena, tails flipping in the breeze. Jackson opened the gate, and all the horses trotted toward him.

Clara lingered at the back of the pack, enjoying the shifting afternoon light and the steady conversation of her clients. The picnic had been a success. Once Michael relaxed, his fun, goofy side kicked in, inspiring others to joke and enjoy themselves. Conversation started to flow, and she could recede further into the background. Then Jet and Danton got everyone saddled up and took the lead heading back, with Sylvia riding between them.

A burst of laughter erupted from the head of the group. Jet had said something that had Sylvia and Danton in stitches. Jet might not think he was particularly social, but she'd seen enough of him by now to call his bluff. He drew people to him with his steady competence. He subtly moved into leadership positions, naturally, quietly taking charge. As he got more comfortable, his sense of humor emerged. She understood why her brothers, Coach Kessler and everyone else seemed so happy to have him back in town.

She pressed her knee gently to her horse's flank and trotted up to join Jet as he entered the arena.

"Thank you so much," Clara said, drawing up her reins.

"Thanks for inviting me." Jet grabbed the horn of his saddle to dismount, his face partially obscured by his hat. "This was… Well, I learned a lot today."

He looked up at Clara and offered his hand to help her dismount. Clara rested her fingers in Jet's as she climbed off the horse, warmth racing up her arm at the touch.

"Such as?"

"Such as Canadian horses can be real characters."

She laughed, then ran her hand along Shelby's neck. He bent his head so she could rub the crescent on his forehead.

"I love these horses," Denise interrupted.

"They did great," Jet said as he took the reins from her and led the horse to the railing.

Denise sent Jet an appraising glance as he

walked away, then raised her brow in a question to Clara. Clara gave a sharp shake of her head.

The cowboy is off-limits.

Denise gave a comical pout. Clara could commiserate. She found herself wishing she could spend more time with him, too. Instead, she redirected the conversation, loudly. "These horses are super lovable. Canadians are the best."

"I'd never heard of them before today," Michael said.

Clara opened her mouth to give the family pitch about why you should buy a Canadian, despite the fact that none of these people were in the market for a horse right now. But before she could speak, Jet jumped in.

"Canadians were originally bred for work in the cold, northern climate of eastern Canada. They're hardy, hardworking." He pulled the saddle off Shelby. Shelby gave him a cool glance, implying he wasn't interested in compliments from someone who did not have apple slices in his pockets. Jet gave him a pat anyway. "They tend to have a lot of personality."

"Where'd you learn so much about Canadians?" Clara asked.

Jet handed the saddle to Jackson, then started to unbuckle the girth on Pepper. "Your dad."

Clara nodded. "Right. You had my dad for

AP Biology. He did that whole genetics project with horses."

"That was the best science class I've ever had. He used to talk about how Canadian horses were close to going extinct." Jet kept his eyes on Pepper. "It's impressive how your parents saw the potential for this breed."

What was impressive was that Jet recalled these details. He would have learned all this over a decade ago, yet he still remembered. But that was just Jet. He was brilliant, Rural Scholar and everything else. She was *not* going to read anything into his interest in her family's horses.

He glanced over at her as he pulled the saddle from Pepper. "I've always been curious about your family's ranch."

Okay, fine, she was going to read a little bit into it.

Clara shook her head to force herself to stop staring at Jet. She was here to help these people fall in love and had done a pretty good job of that today. She scanned the group, addressing her clients. "I'm so glad you all could make it. I hope you had a good time."

"I had a fantastic time," Danton said, keeping his eyes on Sylvia. Sylvia returned the look as she pulled her long silver hair over one shoulder.

The rest of Clara's clients circled around,

thanking her for the day and exchanging contact information with one another. Jackson led their horses to their stables. As soon as she cleared the arena of people, she'd help her nephew put the tack away. Then she'd sneak him a generous tip when her brother Ash wasn't looking.

"This was great!" Michael said, enthusiastically. "Are all the group dates this fun?"

"The activities vary, but they're always full of good people." Clara grinned at Michael, then let her gaze dart past him to Jet. Jet smiled back at her. His dark brown eyes warmed her. The inhabitants of the barn, and even the barn itself, seemed to vanish.

Then something started buzzing. It wasn't her anxious brain, it was…his pocket? Yes, Jet's pocket was definitely buzzing and rattling, like a small animal had gotten trapped in it. Jet grimaced and pulled out his phone.

Judging from the expression on Jet's face, she had a pretty good idea of who was calling again.

"Ken?" she guessed.

"Who else?" Jet grumbled, silencing his phone.

"They must really want you back in Seattle." Clara was starting to dislike this Ken. The guy needed to solve his own problems.

"Don't go, man," Michael clutched his chest like a bad actor. "Don't let the dark side get to you." The group laughed at Michael's dramatics. Someday, his dad jokes were going to be legendary.

"Wait a minute." Denise looked from Clara to Jet. "You're not supposed to have your phone on dates."

"Yeah," Alex said, still looking a little silly in his red pearl-snap shirt. "You're supposed to pay attention to people, not pixels."

Jet froze. "I'm sorry, I—" Judging from his expression, he was trying to think fast, but this was not a situation in which he had much experience. "I...I'm not—" He stopped, his eyes pleading for help.

"Jet's not a client," Clara cut in.

"Then, why are you here?" Alex asked.

Jet studied the ground, probably trying to figure out the answer to that question himself.

"Jet's helping out," she said.

Denise looked from Jet to Clara, then back again. "Are you two dating?"

The innocent question hung between them. The entire group went silent.

"No!" Clara yelped.

"No," Jet said emphatically.

Okay, way too much reaction for a relatively

simple question. Now everyone was uncomfortable, except for Jackson, who was clearly trying not to laugh.

Waves of panic washed over her. This all felt so out of control: first the kiss, then dragging him all over town and now acting like a crushed-out middle schooler in front of her clients. It had to stop.

She got to decide who she was attracted to.

She set her goals and took steps to achieve them.

The problem was she didn't really know what she wanted here. Everything with Jet was so murky, so different from anything she'd felt before. *Could you have a nice, platonic acquaintance with a guy and still appreciate his biceps?*

Jet shifted his posture and straightened, like he did when he was preparing to defend himself. "I'm a rancher," he said, as though it explained everything. Everyone continued to stare at him. He nodded, ready to try again. "I'm a rancher, and I've been wanting to check out the Wallace operation." He gestured to the barn.

"Do you have horses, too?" Sylvia asked.

"Uh, a couple. Cattle mostly."

"And emus," Michael enthused. "You can't forget the emus."

"I'd like to forget the emus," he muttered. Jet

shook his head, then looked up and met Clara's gaze as he explained to the group. "Clara and I are…friends?"

Clara met his gaze. This was Jet: steady, competent, quietly taking charge. He had the answer. It was simple.

"Friends," she confirmed.

And so long as they remained friends, and just friends, this was all going to be okay.

CHAPTER EIGHT

"And I don't want to sound shallow, but it's important to me that she's good-looking."

Flexing her fingers did nothing to ease the ache in Clara's hand. How many requirements could one guy have? She glanced up at the clock her brother had hanging next to the cash register. Her newest Potential had been talking for ten minutes straight, but it felt like she'd been trapped in this booth at Eighty Local for an hour.

The guy was such a contrast to her wonderful weekend. The trail ride had been a huge success, with one couple matched and others connecting with new interests. And she'd had a wonderful time with Jet.

Friends.

Clara's heart rate picked up. Then she glanced across the table again. Her heart returned to its previous plod.

"And *good-looking* means…?" she asked.

"You know." The man on the other side of the booth had his hands out and might have made the universal gesture for large breasts had Clara not cleared her throat. He dropped his hands on the table. "Beautiful. Slim, nice hair, makeup, nice clothes."

Clara studied the man. He might place third in a male beauty contest. If he had a bath, a decent haircut and a full-time personal trainer. And his mom was the judge.

"As long as I'm paying, I figure I should be honest. I want to be married to a beautiful woman. Like you." He gestured to her with a nervous laugh. Clara did not react.

"You want an educated, professional woman, who spends a lot of time on her physical appearance—"

"Who is into outdoor activity. I see us mountain biking, skiing, rafting. Being outside is important to me."

Clara set down her pen and stared at the potential client. "So you're looking for Outdoor Barbie with a PhD?"

The man blinked. "Oh, I didn't mean…"

Clara glanced back down at the paperwork to remind her of the man's name. "Ryan, I don't think you're ready for my services."

"No, no, no!" He waved his hands in front of her. "She doesn't have to be Barbie, but—"

Clara interrupted. "You are asking for a woman

who spends significant time on her personal appearance. There's nothing wrong with that. We all have a type. But you seem…less inclined to spend any time on your appearance. You seek an educated, professional woman, yet you've stated clearly you don't like to read books and your primary pastime is fantasy football."

"But—"

"When was the last time you went mountain biking?"

Ryan fell silent. In the past, Clara had felt bad about painful conversations like this. Not anymore. She pushed his check back across the table.

"I want you to go home and think about who you are and what you want. If you want to mountain bike, mountain bike. If you want to play fantasy football, play fantasy football. Find yourself, and then I can find you a partner."

His face closed, and Clara was certain that not a word of what she had said penetrated his skull. He would justify his desire for the imaginary woman he thought he could buy from her for ten thousand dollars. He stood, uncertainly.

"You're serious?" he asked. "You're not going to take my business?"

"You're not ready."

He stood up and pulled out his wallet and

stuffed the check back into it with shaking hands. Clara glanced over at the counter where her brother was happily chatting with customers. Some sweet potato fries would make this day so much better.

Clara felt Ryan's eyes on her.

"You want to help me get ready?" he asked.

Clara looked up, her confusion quickly diffusing into confirmation as a hopeful flush spread across the man's face. He stood over her, blocking her exit from the booth.

"We could go out," he suggested. "I could buy you dinner."

Clara dug deep for civility.

"No, thank you." She opened her leather binder and moved Ryan's paperwork to a tab marked *Recycle*.

"I thought maybe that's why you won't take my money." He placed his hand on the top of the booth just behind her head, too close to her face. She leaned back, her eyes instinctively searching for her brother. Annoyed with herself, she sat up and started to speak. Ryan spoke over her.

"Because you're exactly what I'm looking for." He gestured to her. "And... Oh, hey." Ryan's tone changed. Clara glanced up to see Jet moving toward her.

Jet glanced from Ryan to her to Ryan's hand and back again. He seemed to make some sort of decision, then said, "Hey…babe."

Clara stifled a laugh, his words were so forced. And so incredibly sweet to help get rid of this guy. She looked at Jet gratefully. "Hello, sweetheart."

Jet shifted his posture, putting his hands on his hips and squaring his shoulders. Ryan lifted his hand so quickly you'd think the back of the booth had just caught fire.

"New client?" Jet asked.

"U-uh…" Ryan stuttered.

Jet pulled his Stetson from his head and reached in front of Ryan to place it on the hook at the end of the booth, effectively inserting himself between him and Clara. Ryan couldn't see it, but Jet shot her a conspiratorial grin as he said, "I was hoping to get one of those frownyface coffees."

"I think that barista is off duty," she said, gesturing for Jet to sit down.

"I guess I should…" Ryan pointed to the door.

"Yeah. Good call." Jet kept his focus on Clara.

"Well, see you."

"Goodbye," Clara returned, not taking her eyes off Jet.

When she heard the bells jingling on the door signifying Ryan's exit, she breathed out deeply.

"That was impressive," Jet said. "I just caught the end, when you told him to go…find himself."

Clara laughed and tried to shake off the ick lingering from Ryan.

"I hope you don't mind me pretending… Well, that I implied we were—"

"No. Not at all. That was perfect. Efficient."

And honestly a really fun thirty seconds.

"Good. I mean, you had it covered. You gave it to him straight," Jet said. "I think most people would be tempted to lie, tell guys like that your schedule is full or something."

A frisson of discomfort ran down her spine. "I don't lie."

"You never lie?"

"Not to my clients. It doesn't serve them, and it stresses me out. That man needs to hear the truth. The woman he's looking for doesn't exist. And if she did, it's unlikely I would pair her with him."

"What will he do now?" Jet asked.

"Probably go back to online dating, which in his case is a terrible idea. It can work for some people, but he will always be looking for his laundry list of attributes, always searching for someone a little more successful, a little prettier."

"That's so sad."

"Yeah. Or maybe he heard every word I said, and he'll go home and grow up and find the love of his life tomorrow—"

"At the Thriftway in Redmond," Jet finished.

Clara laughed, relaxing. "Thank you again for Saturday."

Jet had been remarkably helpful, directing attention when she'd needed him to and hanging back when she asked. Then choosing to be her friend again, after all these years.

"No problem. Michael had a great time. He's been talking about it all week. What's up next?"

"This week's lesson for Michael is selectivity. He's got several dates, and the goal is for him to get picky."

He grinned at her. "Good luck with that."

"I'll accept the good luck, but I think it's going to take a few tough conversations, too. This is the last big hurdle for Michael. He deserves to be happy."

The last traces of distaste from her appointment evaporated. Clara found herself staring into warm brown eyes for what may have been an inappropriate amount of time, but she didn't feel like caring.

"What about you?" she asked, trying to curtail the flood of pheromones she was pretty sure were flying through her skin at the moment. "What are you up to today?"

"Well, the emus are safely confined to their pen, freeing up my time considerably."

Clara laughed. "Are you going to sell emus to Hunter?"

Jet tilted his head to one side. "That had been the original plan. Emu is low in fat, high in iron and vitamin C. You can use it like red meat."

Something about his tone suggested that he didn't feel quite right about that plan. Clara was getting to know Jet well enough that she was able to take an educated guess as to what the problem was.

"They're awfully cute, aren't they?"

Jet glanced up at the ceiling. "They have no social skills."

"But much adorableness."

Jet laughed. "It's not very *tough, good-looking rancher* of me, but yeah, I'm ready to admit it. The emus are very friendly, no common sense. Spend five minutes in the company of any one of them and you'll find yourself with a new pet."

"Aww! I want to meet your pet emus!"

"I could use your help naming them. I've got six birds, and there were only three Stooges."

Clara giggled. She glanced over at her brother. "I bet Hunter was bummed. He's always looking for a creative local product to sell."

"Actually, that's why I'm here." Jet stood. "To see your brother about a new cut of beef he might find helpful. I call it the Fit Burger."

"That sounds like just the thing for his clientele."

"I hope so. Because if not, I'll have two hundred pounds of Fit Burgers in my freezer."

Clara watched Jet head back to the kitchen, where Hunter greeted him with a bro nod and a big smile. He was a perfect supplier for her brother, with his ethical ranching practices and innovative ideas. He was a great coach for her nephew and a good friend for her.

Jet's Stetson still hung at the end of the booth. She pulled it down and held it in her hands, turning it as she ran her fingers along the brim. A spark raced through her as she remembered him touching his fingers to the hat as he agreed to her requests on the group date.

Friends, she reminded herself. *You're just friends.*

She gathered her belongings and grabbed the hat so she could return it to Jet. Then she stopped herself. She could hear her brother and Jet laughing in the kitchen. If she walked back there, this crush was going to get even more out of control than it already was.

Clara pulled in a deep breath and took one last look at the Stetson. Then she returned it to the hook and exited the building.

"IT'S LESS THAN two percent fat, because it's made with trimmed round steak. The trick is an aggressive marinade, then flash cooking at a high heat." Jet finished up his sales pitch as Hunter removed the Fit Burger from the grill.

Hunter cut off a bite, then chewed thoughtfully. The kitchen at Eighty Local was empty in the mid-afternoon. The only sounds were the ticking of a clock and the occasional car passing by on Main.

Jet forced himself to focus. He was here to sell a burger, not to speculate on whether or not Clara was still shuffling papers in a booth twenty feet away. There was nothing on earth as cute as Clara absorbed in her paperwork and sticky notes. Except for maybe Clara when she was smiling at him. *Should I have invited her over when she mentioned she wanted to meet the emus? Or was she just being polite?*

Jet thought about Clara's ability to choose who she was attracted to. He needed to learn that skill, quickly. He and Clara were friends now. That was perfect. He enjoyed her company, and being friends wouldn't interfere with his business relationship with Hunter. Anything more and he'd probably mess up again, and that was something he couldn't withstand a second time.

"How much did you run?"

Jet startled. *Right, they were talking about Fit Burgers.*

"I had the guys at Redmond Processing run two hundred pounds to start. It was a pretty simple operation for them, and I wanted to float it out to buyers before I get too involved. I figure restaurants won't want to invest too much in what is at present a novelty order."

Hunter took another bite.

"I like it. I could do this on a gluten-free bun, corn salsa, maybe some pickled onions?"

"Sounds like hipster food to me."

"Right on." Hunter nodded. "Every hipster on his way from Portland to Mount Bachelor will have no choice but to stop in for a Fit Burger and a kombucha."

Jet laughed.

"Seriously," Hunter continued, "my business is split between old ranching families and hipsters. It's a delicate balance, and this might come in handy. Want a bite?" Hunter offered the remainder of the patty to Jet.

"No, thanks. I prefer something less hip."

Hunter nodded. "I hear that." He studied Jet for a moment, then asked, "You run that whole place without pesticides?"

"Like my grandfather before me."

"I didn't know Hal was an environmentalist."

"He wasn't an environmentalist, he was cheap. Why spray when you have a grandson and a pickaxe?"

Hunter laughed, and in retrospect Jet could see the humor. "The summer before senior year I cut out three hundred and forty-seven thistles."

"You remember the exact number?"

"You ever chop out Scotch thistle? I remember every single one." Jet reflexively rubbed his left shoulder, remembering the persistent ache he'd had that summer. "But Hal left the place clean. I've got records going back thirty years, and I had no problem getting the organic certification."

"You're lucky."

"It didn't feel that way when I was seventeen, but I'm grateful now. I learned a lot working for my grandfather. In fact, I've got a few kids from the team coming out to help me tomorrow.

I'm starting renovations on an old cabin and thought some of the players might like something to do during the summer other than stare at their phones." Jet didn't mention the second reason he'd asked his players for help. He had an idea for a scholarship fund that was just taking shape, but he needed to run a few more numbers to make sure it would work.

"That's a great idea." Hunter nodded. "You gonna put my nephew to work?"

"If he wants to come."

"He'll show up. Kid still can't believe he's getting coached by the Exterminator."

Jet laughed, but he looked forward to the day people stopped using that nickname. He'd done a lot more with his life than catch a football. And while everyone else saw that night as a big victory, it had been a huge failure for him.

"Hey, you need any snacks for the guys? I could drop off sandwiches and lemonade."

"You sure?" Jet asked. He didn't want Hunter thinking he had to supply food for kids working on his project.

"Absolutely. I like the idea of the kids around here getting some real work experience, and I can write it off as a donation to the team."

"Then, yeah. Thank you. We'll get started at 9:00 a.m. Come out any time."

"Will do." Hunter turned back to his work, then seemed to remember something. "Since I'll be out at your place, do you have a rib roast you'd be willing to sell me? Just for myself, not for the restaurant. The rosemary at my parents' house is going nuts, and I need something to crust with it."

"Sure." Jet did a quick mental rundown of the contents of his freezer. He had at least two rib roasts and no immediate or future plans of cooking either, inasmuch as he had no idea how to cook them. "Let me give you one. I don't have much use for a roast around my place, with just me."

Hunter looked up from the remainder of the burger with the same introspective look Mr. Wallace used to get. Hunter was taller than his dad, his hair was longer, but the eyes were the same.

"I'll tell you what," Hunter said. "Why don't you have dinner with us on Sunday? I'm cooking up at the family place, for Ash and Jackson. You bring the roast, and I'll cook it."

The invitation was dropped so lightly. *Why don't you have dinner with us?*

Dinner at the Wallace house.

Jet had refused his first invitation to their house and hadn't ever expected to get another.

He'd still been baffled and hurt at the inexplicable rejection by Clara. It was senior year, the day before winter break, and most of the student population couldn't wait to stream out the doors of the school. Jet had been staring down the barrel of two weeks in a silent house, wondering if he and his grandfather would even celebrate Christmas that year.

After class, Mr. Wallace had set a file folder in his hands and basically demanded that Jet apply to the Rural Scholar Program by January 1. Jet had balked, not wanting to get his hopes up for a full ride with the prestigious scholarship. Mr. Wallace wasn't having any of it. When Jet had told him he couldn't get the application finished because they didn't have internet on the ranch, Mr. Wallace had a solution.

"You can submit it at our house," he had said. "Type it up on our computer, then stay for dinner. Lacy and I would love to help."

Had Jet imagined being invited to their house? To eat real meals at a table in the company of the two adults who made him feel like he mattered? To sit next to Clara and listen to her laugh? He thought about it all the time. But there was no way he was going to put himself anywhere near Clara now.

"Could we meet at school to submit it?" Jet had asked.

All these years later, Jet could still remember the choice he'd made at that moment. He was going to create a life for himself where he could be in Mr. and Mrs. Wallace's position someday. He would get the scholarship, complete the education, take a good job, make a ridiculous pile of money and come back to Outcrop on his terms. When he got married and had children, his kids would never wonder if there would be presents at Christmas.

Jet would put every piece together. He would have so much confidence that it would be easy to give confidence to others. He was on that road now. Coaching was rewarding, and if his scholarship idea panned out, he'd be able to help a lot of kids get the same kind of education he'd had.

"Will your folks be back?" Jet asked Hunter, trying to sound as casual as the invitation had been.

"Nope. They're still traveling. If my mom were in town, her rosemary never would have gotten so out of control in the first place."

Relief and disappointment spanned his chest. It would just be Ash, Jackson and Hunter. And Hunter, Jet realized, was becoming a friend.

This casual invitation wasn't offered to the desperately lonely Jet of the past but to the confident, successful man he had become. If he were to finally sit at the Wallace dinner table, it was under vastly different circumstances. He would go, enjoy the company of friends and spend no time scanning the house for signs of Clara.

"Deal," Jet said.

CHAPTER NINE

CLARA GRINNED AS she pushed open the door to Second Chance Cowgirl. She was here to do some reconnaissance. There were a few boxes that needed to be checked before she went ahead with Project Coach + Christy. And there was no place on earth she'd rather do research than this beautiful little shop.

The last few days had felt so out of control as she wrestled with her feelings for Jet. As she had gotten to know him better, she became more nervous that she would find a way to mess up their growing friendship. But that was ridiculous. She was an adult, and she'd learned to control the waves of panic she was prone to. If Jet made her feel like the world was spinning off its axis from time to time, she just had to manage it.

To that end, today she was going to do something she was good at: helping other people fall in love. It was much more satisfying than dealing with her own emotions.

"Hello, Clara," Christy Jones greeted her warmly. "What brings you in?"

Within the exposed brick walls were vintage dresses, designer finds, antique jewelry and rows of the most incredible boots lining the back wall.

"It's not so much that something brings me in, more that I couldn't stay out any longer."

Christy laughed. "I like to think of my shop as a gallery, and you are welcome to enjoy it any time."

"Plus, it always smells so good in here," Clara said. "The minute I walk in I just want to stay forever."

Christy glanced around the store at the other customers, then leaned across the counter gesturing for Clara to come close. "It's my own invention. Essence of rose with a dash of cinnamon oil. Calming, while inspiring positive thoughts. Perfect for shopping, yes?"

Clara tipped her head in acknowledgment. Christy was a good businesswoman, with an incredible eye. Like Coach, she knew what she wanted professionally and went for it. "Coach Kessler should try that with the football team."

Christy's brow knit. "Well, it would certainly confuse the opposing team."

Clara laughed. "Coach will try anything to get to the playoffs."

"I used to love going to football games." A ghost of regret passed across Christy's face, replaced quickly by a smile. "I guess it's time I found a new team to root for."

Box one: must like football. Check.

"I think I can help you out there."

Christy nodded, then exchanged a few words with her other customers, directing two teenage girls to a rack of vintage concert T-shirts.

"Can I look at those bracelets?" Clara indicated a tray of delicate, handmade jewelry. She didn't need a bracelet per se, but she wanted to look authentic and keep Christy's attention. If authenticity meant having to buy a cute new bracelet, well, in Coach's words, she'd take one for the team.

Christy pulled out the tray.

"Have you gotten to know many people in Outcrop yet?" Clara asked.

"Well, you. And your mom. Most of the women in town come in pretty regularly."

Box two: no men in her life. Yet.

"Have you been to Eighty Local?"

"No. I hear it's wonderful, though. I can't quite bring myself to go out to eat alone."

Score! That got their first date planned. This was all moving along as Clara hoped. What she couldn't quite understand was why Christy was single. Was it by choice or circumstance?

Clara picked up a delicate silver bracelet with a single charm reading *Embrace the Change*.

"That's made by the Sister's Guild," Christy said. "All proceeds go to helping women in financial need after divorce."

The little charm glimmered in the low lighting. Christy kept her eyes on the tray of bracelets. *Interesting.*

"That sounds like a great cause," Clara ventured.

"So many women of my generation were raised to think they don't have the financial savvy to make it on their own. The guild provides classes on personal finance and job training and offers low-interest loans to help women get on their feet after a divorce." A thoughtful look passed over Christy's face. "Some women stay in bad marriages because they don't think they have the resources to go it alone. The Sister's Guild…"

Clara was beginning to understand what might be holding this beautiful woman back from dating. It was abundantly clear what had helped her move forward in business.

"Does the Sister's Guild offer business classes?" Christy pressed her lips together and nodded. "They do. I took the small business class five years ago. Now I teach it."

That did it. Christy was pure awesome. Project Coach + Christy was officially on.

Clara held up the bracelet. "I'll take it. And if the Sister's Guild is interested, I could teach a class on relationships. It's hard to open up after a divorce, but I've helped a number of people do just that and finally find their happily ever after."

Clara handed Christy her credit card. The elegant woman focused on the task, asking, "How would a woman know she was ready for that? Opening up, I mean."

Clara accepted the little bag containing her new bracelet. "I think if someone asks for help, it means they're ready for it."

Christy met her gaze, a slow smile emerging.

The bells of the front door jangled as a new customer entered. Wait, no. Not a customer. Her brother, Hunter.

"Hey, Clara! I need your help." He gestured for her to leave the store. Clara stayed put.

"You need my help right now? I'm—"

"Shopping. Yeah, I see that." He seemed to remember his manners and gave Christy a salute. "Hi, Christy. Can I steal Clara? I promise to buy all her Christmas presents here for the rest of my life."

"You already buy all my Christmas presents here."

Hunter waved her toward the door, his hand slicing the calm, scented air of Second Chance Cowgirl with urgency. "I have eighteen unassembled sandwiches, three gallons of lemonade, seven hungry members of the Outcrop defense and apparently a flock of escaped emus. I can't deal with it because Caleb just called in sick."

Clara exchanged a look with Christy. "This may be the least appealing scenario I can think of."

"I need your help." Hunter looked so desperate she almost forgot how much she needed to stay here, doing the one thing she was actually good at. Being here, in this well-ordered, nice-smelling shop on the verge of helping a good person find love felt so right. But turning down her brother felt so very wrong.

She walked up to Hunter and spoke in a low voice. "Could I have just five more minutes? I'm exercising my superpowers here."

"Your superpower is bringing order to chaos," Hunter said, opening the door fully and gesturing to the street. "Would you please get in the truck?"

JET FOLDED HIS arms across his chest, staring at the old shack he'd shared with his grandfather. Jackson and six other members of the Outcrop Football defense stood with him, imitating his posture. Emus ran free all around them, but he and the boys had business to take care of. He'd deal with the birds once he got the guys started.

"You all ready for this?" he asked.

"Sure thing, Coach," Manuel said.

Jackson took a couple of steps toward the cabin. "We're happy to help."

"You're not helping, exactly. You're earning your future."

The boys exchanged glances. The inspirational language felt awkward, but Jet could grow into it. Coach Kessler and Mr. Wallace had left some big shoes. It was time for Jet to step up and step into them.

"This is where I grew up." Jet gestured to the building. "And that is where I live now." He indicated his custom home. The boys nodded, one let out a low whistle. A couple of the kids came from tough circumstances, like Jet had. They needed to be told they could reach well beyond their humble beginnings. "I got from here to there by listening to my teachers, taking a risk on going away for college and working my butt off once I got there. It was hard, but I knew I had adults back home who believed in me." Jet gestured for the boys to make a circle. "Huddle up."

The boys formed a ring around Jet. He channeled pure Kessler as he prepared to lay out the plan. He glanced around at the faces of his players, stopping short when a flat beak appeared in the ring.

"Just push that emu out of here," he told Manuel.

"He wants to be part of the group!" Manuel protested. The emu trilled in response.

"Fine." He addressed the bird. "Larry, you can stay for the huddle, but you are not going into the cabin."

Larry had a maniacal smile fixed on his face, the only expression emus were capable of. The bird shuffled his too-large feet with a *We'll see about that* attitude. Jet refocused on his players.

"We're going to start by cleaning this place out. Then repairs, then paint, then landscaping. It's gonna take a couple of months. When we're finished, I'm going to rent it out. The nicer we make it, the more I can charge."

"Money is good," Aaron said.

"It is. And all the money I make on this house will go to pay for your college educations." The boys shifted, eyeing each other to figure out if this was a joke. Jet pushed on. "It won't be enough to cover the entire expense for all of you, but it will be a start. And if you have to take out loans, this cash cow will still be producing money after you graduate and can help pay back those loans. Manuel, you're the only senior, so you get first dibs a year from now in the fall."

Manuel let out a whoop. Jet tempered his enthusiasm with a stern look.

"But you've got to maintain a 3.0 GPA."

"Not a problem. I got a 3.7 right now." Manuel did something that might have been a celebratory dance move. It wasn't going to get him many dates in college but indicated his time had been spent earning that 3.7, rather than learning to dance.

"Keep it up, then. As for the rest of you, work hard. The Outcrop Defense Scholarship will help, but there are a lot of other ways to fund your education. Good grades, keeping out of trouble and helping your community are all habits that will pay off during the application process."

Jackson glanced up at him. "You got the Rural Scholar award, didn't you?"

Jet nodded. "I've got your grandparents to thank for that. Now it's my turn to help out."

"Is this scholarship only open to guys playing defense for Outcrop?" Aaron asked.

"Nope. It's open to anyone willing to work on this project." He pointed to the old cabin. "You put in your time on the house, you get a slice of the pie. Who'd you have in mind?"

"I'll…I'll talk to you about it later." Aaron's gaze flickered between the shack and Jet's gorgeous home. The kid had an older sister, and Jet guessed in his family there was no money and even less encouragement to go to college. He dropped a hand on Aaron's shoulder.

"I know some of you have jobs and all of you have families who expect you to help around the house. Come work here when you can. Once you put in your share, you're in on the scholarship money."

The rent on the house wouldn't come close to covering seven college tuition bills. Which was why Jet had shifted a chunk of his investments into a special account to augment the scholarship. Jet had been hoarding the money he made in Seattle against disaster, acting as miserly as his grandfather had. There was plenty left in his personal account to weather any kind of setback.

If Hal Broughman knew what kind of yuppification was happening in his old cabin he would roll right out of his grave. But this project wasn't about honoring the past; it was about creating the future. His grandfather had done his best with the teenage grandson he'd never asked for. Hal had lived a good, honest life. Jet could honor him by digging out Scotch thistle by hand and keeping the land clean and productive. The old house itself was nothing but a symbol of where Jet had come from.

Jackson was already racing up the steps, pulling at the front door. "What do we start with?"

"For starters I want that sofa out. Then the rest of the furniture. Anything upholstered goes to the dump, but everything else gets piled in that pit I cleared out back. When we knock off work for the day we're going to burn it all."

"Yesss!"

"Let's gooo!"

The boys rushed the house. The excitement may have been more for the promise of burning a huge pile of furniture rather than college. But everything in its time. The screen door kicked open, and Aaron backed out holding one end of the sofa, Jackson following on the other. Tyler went long and caught the ugly cushions as Manuel hurled them out.

Jet smiled. This was going to be fun. Hunter was dropping off food for the guys. They could clear the house, then enjoy lunch while watching the bonfire. He'd texted Hunter to let him know that the emus were out, and when Hunter responded he said he might bring some extra help. Bowman would likely join them, and it would be cool to get to know him better.

It was shaping up to be a pretty good day. He felt good, finally moving forward in dealing with this old shack that reminded him of the lonely days of his youth. Remodeling it into something useful was another symbol of how far he'd come.

And should Clara ever step foot on his property, she'd only see his new house and maybe catch a glimpse of a renovated cabin in the distance. He might finally shake off the past that dogged him. The name Broughman would be associated with an innovative ranch, a nice house and the Outcrop Eagles defensive coach. And maybe, somewhere down the road, a girl like Clara Wallace wouldn't think twice about dating a Broughman.

CHAPTER TEN

"Wait, we're going to Jet's?" Clara asked, her heart lurching as they turned onto the highway. "I thought you needed help at the restaurant."

"No, some kids from Jackson's team are helping him out on the ranch and I told Jet I'd donate lunch." Hunter floored the gas, the coolers in the bed of his truck sliding to the back. Clara put a hand on his arm in a not-so-subtle gesture to slow down. Hunter sped up and kept talking. "I'm gonna drop you off, then you put the lunch together, okay?"

"Not okay. How am I supposed to get home? I have an appointment this afternoon."

"Jackson can bring you home."

"Jackson doesn't have his driver's license."

Hunter opened his mouth, but Clara spoke over him. "Your life may be crazy busy right now, but that doesn't mean I'm willing to take your crazy on for you."

He leaned back and let out a sigh, finally easing up on the gas pedal. "I know. I'm sorry,

Clara. If I can make it through the addition to Eighty Local, everything will be fine."

"Hunter, you need to drop something. You have too much going on right now. You can't keep helping out with the horse operation, run a restaurant and build an events center all by yourself. You've got to slow down."

"I'm fine." His jaw twitched, belying this statement. Then his face softened. "Look, I just want to support Jet in his efforts to get the kids in this town off the sofa and doing some real work this summer. He's doing something the rest of us should have done years ago. I didn't know Caleb was going to get sick when I agreed to help."

He was right. They should be supporting Jet in this endeavor. And she'd be fine setting up lunch for the guys. It was, in fact, the exact sort of thing a friend would do. This would be a satisfying challenge, testing her ability to be friends with Jet. She would be helpful and friendly and not stand around gazing into his warm brown eyes.

"I owe you, big-time," Hunter said.

"How big-time?"

Hunter nodded, knowing what was coming. "Fine. I'll go on your next group date."

"And convince Bowman to come, too?"

"And convince Bowman," he mumbled.

"Excellent. A day off will be just what you need to relax."

Hunter glared at her. Clara grinned right back at him.

"We'll take my clients to Smith Rock. You always make time for climbing."

And maybe Jet might want to come as well? As a friend...

Hunter grumbled as he turned off the highway. Clara scanned the property with interest. Jet's acreage rolled out to the west. Cattle dotted the landscape, and horses bent their heads to the sweet grass in a corral. A stand of trees obscured what looked to be a road or second driveway that ran along a creek.

The whole scene was idyllic, with the exception of the maelstrom Hunter was headed for. Teenage boys ran amok, piling old furniture into a pit behind a weathered shack. Young emus trotted through the mix, tripping up on their feet and getting in the way. At the center of it all stood Jet, calling out orders, picking up and redirecting emus and laughing with the kids as they worked.

Hunter pulled to a stop in the middle of the chaos. Jet glanced up at the truck with a big smile and waved. The smile, and his hand,

dropped the moment he saw her, horror crossing his face.

Not the most auspicious welcome.

Jet recovered and walked over to the truck. He
opened the door for her and helped her down.
"What are you doing here?"

"Sandwiches." She gestured to the coolers.
He looked skeptical. Clara glanced at Hunter
to get some support, but her brother was busy
pulling coolers out of the back of the truck. She
tried for a joke. "Right? I stand between the two
great sandwich makers of the west, and somehow this is my job?"

Jet gave a half-hearted chuckle, then glanced
nervously at the cabin.

"Sorry. You're stuck with Clara," Hunter said
as he stacked the final cooler next to the shack.
"I gotta get back to work. Clara, text me when
you finish, and I'll make sure someone gets out
here to pick you up before your appointment."

"I can take you home," Jet said.

"You sure?" she asked.

"Of course." He sent Hunter a look as he
hopped back into the driver's seat, then muttered to himself, "Now that you've seen the
house, my truck will look luxurious in com-
parison."

"Is this your house?" she asked. She understood he'd done pretty well in Seattle and re-membered something about him having built a new home. This didn't look particularly new. Or like a home.

"No." Jet was emphatic. "No, this is just an old shack on the property."

Her nephew emerged from the door of the building, barely visible behind the stack of old newspapers he was carrying.

"This is where Coach Broughman grew up, Aunt Clara," Jackson said.

Jet turned away sharply, like he hadn't wanted her to know this.

Manuel came out of the house holding a chair over his head. "Now he lives over there." He nodded to the west. Clara turned. From this van-tage point she could see a massive pine-and-slate home beyond the stand of trees.

Okay, so he did very *well in Seattle.*

Jet rolled his shoulders, like he sometimes did when he was uncomfortable. Then he took the situation head-on, as was also his habit.

"This was my grandfather's home. It's not much to look at now, but these boys and I are going to fix it up, and we'll use the rental money for their college funds."

"Wow." Clara wasn't entirely sure where that *wow* was aimed. Jet's generosity toward these kids or the realization that this shack had been his home. "That's so generous."

He shrugged. "A lot of people helped me out when I was young."

He took a few paces toward the shack, his jaw set in frustration. Clara stopped him with a hand on his arm. She was pretty sure she knew why he was upset. While she'd always known Jet hadn't come from a privileged background, she'd had no idea it had been this bleak.

She gestured toward the house and said quietly, "I didn't know."

He nodded, then studied the ground between the two of them. "Doesn't matter."

But it clearly did. This dilapidated shack was a key to understanding Jet. His drive to succeed, to give back to Outcrop, it must have started here.

"Careful on the steps," Jet admonished a young man. He trotted over to help the kid carry a musty recliner down the stairs and around the back to a pile of furniture.

Clara walked into the shack, trying to imagine what it would have been like for Jet, coming home here. Inside, the space was cramped and stale. A small table was pushed up against a wall in the kitchen area. Was that where Jet had done his homework and set himself on the road to a prestigious scholarship?

She stepped into a small back room. Old papers and receipts were stacked against the walls, blocking the windows and obscuring built-in bookshelves. Her parents spoke of Hal Broughman as a good man who wasn't able to negotiate the changing times and economic markets. Clara knew him to be stern and quiet. What had it been like for Jet to live here with Hal? And how had Jet made it so far?

Clara heard a quiet shuffling at the door to the room and felt eyes on her. She turned.

Only to find herself staring into a pair of unnaturally energized golden eyes. Blue skin was visible through molting feathers. The creature tilted its head and took two tentative steps toward her.

"Who let Moe in the house?" Jet's voice rang from the front room, his heavy boots scraping across the wood floor.

Moe turned at the sound of Jet's voice, weaving his head and shuffling his feet.

"You're headed straight for the recycling bin if you keep this up." Jet reached for the bird, then noticed Clara. "Oh. Hey." He shook his head. "Sorry about this."

She couldn't tell what he was sorry about. The bird, the papers, the whole house?

"Nothing to be sorry about," she said gently.

He flexed his brow, as though that statement was debatable. The emu wandered over to a stack of papers and pecked at it in curiosity. Clara took a step toward Jet.

"This is where you grew up?"

"This is where I lived for four years with my grandfather," he said.

"And before that?"

Jet shifted, clearly uncomfortable. Then he looked up, his gaze connecting with hers. "All over Oregon. In and out of the foster system. My mom…" He tried again. "She wasn't much of a mom."

Clara didn't want to push Jet to speak. She felt privileged to even have this information but desperately wanted to know the rest of the story. She struggled for the right words, then said simply, "I'm really glad you wound up here."

He nodded, then smiled. "Yeah. I was lucky."

That Jet could come from such difficult circumstances and still see himself as lucky was incredible. He really was an amazing man. There was something about his quiet strength and determination that made her feel stronger, too.

He shifted, then gestured to the back of the

house. "Hey, I promised the guys we'd burn all the wooden furniture and old paperwork in a bonfire once we got the place cleared out. That'd be a great time for lunch if it works for you."

"Oh, sure." Clara glanced around at the room. The temptation to organize this into a real office was strong. "Um…"

"Um?" he questioned.

"About lunch. It's pretty simple. So maybe—" Clara bit her lip and looked up at him hopefully "—maybe I can help here?"

"You want to help clear out the house?"

She waved her hands to indicate the room, her heart beating at the possibilities. "I would really, *really* like to work on this room."

Jet seemed confused. "You don't have to."

Clara gave in to the excitement and clapped her hands. "Please? The guys can make their own sandwiches. You have no idea how much I want to clear out this room right now. This would make an incredible office for someone."

Jet laughed. Encouraged, Clara admitted, "I really love getting rid of other people's clutter."

"Then, you've come to the right place. It's all gotta go." He wrapped an arm around the bird and spoke to it as he lifted it. "Including you, Moe."

"This is going to be so satisfying."

He shook his head. "If you say so."

"I say so. Thank you."

Jet looked bemused as he turned to leave.

Clara called after him. "And then I want to talk to you about paint colors."

"Paint colors?"

"I have so many ideas!"

She could hear Jet chuckling and Moe squawking as he exited the house. Clara gazed around the room. Helping Jet with this cabin was going to be so fun. And she would spend zero moments wishing this could be her office. It's what a friend would do.

WATCHING HIS OLD furniture go up in a blaze was much more fun than Jet would have expected. With the house completely cleared out and the doors and windows open to the summer breeze, he was beginning to see the potential.

Once they'd piled everything fit to burn in the pit out back and washed up, Jet gave the guys a sandwich-making lesson, creating a masterpiece for Clara as his example. Then he lit the fire, which scared the emus enough that everyone could eat their lunch in peace, without fear of a bird butting in.

The best part of the day turned out to be Clara. She had enjoyed the sandwich he'd made her, laughing at the antics of the boys and the emus. It was remarkably easy to have her there. Her natural sociability rubbed off on him, and he found himself making jokes and relaxing in her presence.

Over the last week, he'd come to recognize that Clara had two primary moods. Most of the time she was happy and laughing. Her face relaxed, her movements easy, the adorable dimples of her smile flexing. Other times he'd seen her tense up. In those moments she went on the defensive and seemed to struggle to regulate her breathing.

But she was obviously having a good time clearing out the old shack.

Once the boys had doused the last of the embers, he'd helped Clara up into his truck to take her back to town in time for her appointment. His high school self would have felt like this was a lifetime achievement, opening the door for her, taking her hand as she climbed up into the passenger seat. But then Manuel had come running over and asked if they could drop him off at his family's grocery store on their way into town.

So Jet had finally taken a drive with Clara riding shotgun in his truck. There just happened to be a large, talkative lineman sitting in between them.

With all the excitement of the morning, Clara was running late for her meeting. Fortunately, it was with Michael, who agreed to meet Clara at her house. He was waiting for them as Jet pulled up. Clara popped out of the truck, cheerfully greeting him, and explaining away her disheveled appearance.

As Clara and Michael chatted, Jet took in the color-coordinated flower bed, perfectly refurbished furniture on the little front porch and a cream-colored Schwinn leaning up against the railing. There was no mistaking who lived here.

"Jet, you want to see a picture of a woman I might fall in love with next weekend?" Michael asked.

"Sure."

"Come on in," Clara said, heading to the door.

"In your house?" Jet asked, before looking around for something to bang his head against. The depth of stupidity this woman could stir from him sometimes was impressive. *Get it together, man.*

"That's where I keep my stuff."

Michael patted him on the back as he moved into the house.

Jet followed them into a room that could only have been decorated by Clara. Pale pink, spring green and warm cream colors ran throughout. Polished hardwood floors anchored the room, and old-fashioned, double-hung windows filled it with light. Coved ceilings made everything seem snug. It was tidy in a way Jet wouldn't have thought possible, but still comfortable. It felt like a home. The furniture was pretty, the flooring was lovely, the woman standing in the middle of all of it was gorgeous.

"Nice house."

"Thank you." Clara tucked her hair behind an ear. "It's a mess right now. I wasn't expecting to be gone all morning."

Jet and Michael exchanged a glance.

"Yeah." Jet grinned. "This place is trashed."

"Your throw pillow's a good half inch off-center." Michael pointed to the sofa. "This is almost as bad as the cabin at your place, Jet."

Clara blushed. "I meant the table." She gestured to a small pile of papers at the center of a teak table. "And my desk is a disaster."

Jet glanced at the desk. It was home to hundreds of small, colorful pieces of paper. He moved closer.

Clara darted in front of him and snatched up

a piece of cardstock, catching a few sticky notes as they fluttered off it. She raised her chin. Jet was aware he'd tapped into a weakness.

"Do you have enough sticky notes?" he asked.

"No," she clipped back. "I may have to run out to OHTAF this afternoon and get some more."

"I didn't know Outcrop Hardware, Tack and Feed carried sticky notes."

"They do. There's an extraordinary selection."

Jet nodded, easily able to imagine who had talked Mr. Fareas into stocking small, pretty office supplies.

"What's this?" he asked. A corkboard hung over her desk. It was covered with pictures: horses, interiors of homes, a sun setting over a beautiful canyon, a wedding dress. Jet felt like he was looking at Clara's daydreams.

Michael came over to the board.

"That looks like your house, Jet," he said, pointing to a picture of a kitchen.

Clara came around to the other side of Jet and studied the board with him.

The kitchen was very similar to his. An image of her sitting on his counter, eyes shining as he made her a sandwich popped into his head. Jet forced his gaze up to the ceiling.

"That's for inspiration," she said. "When I see something I like, I put it there."

Jet glanced around her house. "That's how you did all this? How everything is so…" he wasn't sure what word to pick: *beautiful, adorable, perfect*? "…you?"

"Sometimes it's hard for me to make decisions," she admitted. "When I can look at something concrete, it helps me make a plan."

"And you wouldn't want to do anything without a plan?" Jet teased. Clara shuddered.

"Speaking of plans," Michael's voice pulled Jet's attention away from Clara. Michael held two eight-by-ten photographs, one on either side of his face. He stood grinning in the center.

"What do you think? Abby," Michael said and gestured with his head toward the right, "or Joanna?" He nodded to the other.

"They both look nice." Jet turned to Clara. "Are they right for Michael?"

"We're getting closer."

"Because we're following the Love Rules," Michael added.

"There are love rules?" Jet asked.

"Of course." Clara widened her eyes.

"You made up these rules?"

"My sister and I collaborated to give voice to

several truths regarding romance," Clara countered.

"Everybody has to memorize them," Michael said.

"And follow them." Clara pointed a finger at him. From her tone, he guessed Clara had heard about, and put an end to, Michael's communication with his needy ex-girlfriends.

Jet laughed, then found himself walking to the sofa. He'd had no intention of staying, much less sitting down. But Clara had patted the spot next to her, and here he was, planted in the middle of her sofa asking, "What are they?"

Clara looked at Michael, which was all he needed for a recitation and commentary.

"*Love Rule Number One: Never waste time on someone who isn't into you.*"

Jet nodded. "Reasonable."

"That effectively voids every romantic experience I have had until the last two weeks," Michael said. "*Love Rule Number Two: To find love, love yourself first.* Basically, you have to treat yourself the way you want others to treat you. This is an area of improvement for me, yes?"

"Yes," Clara confirmed. "You've made great strides."

Michael beamed at the compliment. "*Love

Rule Number Three: Know your core values, and seek someone who shares them."

"*Find*," Clara corrected. "Find someone who shares your core values."

"It's the same word," Jet said.

"It's not the same word." Clara's voice was firm. "*Seek* implies the act of looking. *Find* means you've found the person. In this business you have to keep your sights on the end goal. Lifetime happiness in a lasting partnership."

She was so serious Jet didn't feel it would be right to do anything other than nod gravely.

"*Love Rule Number Four*," Michael continued. "*Know your love chemicals, and choose when and with whom you release them.*" He paused and picked up one of the pictures. "I would really like to release some chemicals with this woman."

Clara snatched the photo away. "No chemicals." Michael gave her a pleading look. "No chemicals until you're fairly certain she's the one."

"Chemicals?" Jet asked.

"Michael has had fun studying the chemicals," Clara said dryly, dropping on the sofa next to Jet. Jet didn't have the first idea about love chemicals but knew something was going on as his body adjusted to Clara's sitting next to him. Whatever chemicals were involved, they all seemed to be taking shots and doing an impromptu conga line.

"There are so many!" Michael enthused. "They are part of what we feel as we go through the process of falling in love. But right now, Clara is talking about oxytocin, which is released by human touch. So, when you hold a newborn baby, you release oxytocin, and it helps you bond with the baby. Every time you hug someone, you release oxytocin. It even happens when you hold hands."

Jet knew his eyes had jumped to Clara, because he was staring at her. Could you blame involuntary eye movements on chemicals?

Michael kept talking. "Oxytocin and vasopressin are responsible for attachment. So you know how I'd go out with a woman, realize intellectually that she was horrible but still think I wanted to marry her?"

"I remember a few of those," Jet said.

"I was releasing chemicals with the wrong women."

Jet took a cautious glance at Clara. She leaned forward, beaming as Michael spoke.

"I'm impressed," Jet said. "You know your stuff."

"Love chemicals are super important," Clara said, tucking her hair behind her ears again. "You need to be cautious about them during the dating process. But once you commit, the more oxytocin, the better."

"Right."

"I always tell my clients you need to make touch a priority, particularly after you get married. Couples need to do what it takes to connect as often as possible."

Clara looked straight at him. Jet's brain wrapped itself around all the ways he and Clara could release oxytocin, then locked. Clara kept talking while Jet worked incredibly hard to keep his thoughts to himself.

"Because then you feel attached, and in love, and that becomes a great cycle of feeling love and expressing love."

Jet struggled to dredge up thoughts of anything to stop his body's reaction to Clara. *Drought, financial instability, emus.*

"Have I mentioned I'm looking forward to this?" Michael asked.

"You have. Okay, Dr. Williams. What's the final Love Rule?"

"*Look good, feel good.*"

Here Michael shrugged. Scrubs, nerd shoes and thick-framed glasses: he was not a poster boy for style. But he was so dang happy.

"I should probably change out of the scrubs when I leave the hospital," Michael said.

"No." Clara's smile flexed. "For you, scrubs are fine."

"Blue is a good color for you," Jet said.

"And scrubs say, *I have a steady income in a growing industry*," Clara added. "And in your case, the rule could be reversed. *Feel good, look good*."

Jet glanced at Clara. She understood and appreciated his friend. Michael held up the two pictures again.

"I did buy a new outfit for the Smith Rock trip. That's where I meet this one, right?" He held out a picture of a dark-haired woman with deep blue eyes.

"Yep," Clara said. "Joanna. And my money's on her."

Michael studied the picture more seriously. A funny look passed over his face, then he carefully set the photograph down. "How's the old house looking?"

"It's amazing!" Clara said. "I'm in love with that back office."

"You were right, Michael," Jet admitted. "When we finish, it'll be a viable rental property."

"Maybe a retreat for a writer," Michael said.

Jet nodded as Clara and Michael threw out ideas. The building that had been an eyesore and a reminder of his difficult upbringing now seemed to have unlimited potential. It could serve any one of the purposes Michael and Clara were brainstorming. Personally, he couldn't help thinking it might make a nice office for a beautiful matchmaker.

CHAPTER ELEVEN

CLARA HOPPED OFF her bicycle the second she hit the gravel drive of her family home. She walked quickly, clutching the handlebars and pushing her bike along the drive. Then she dropped her bike on the front lawn and broke into a run, as she did every other Sunday afternoon.

Piper appeared at the door and headed straight for her, the two colliding in a hug and rush of conversation.

"I'm so glad you're home!"

"I'm so glad you're here!"

"I have to tell you about a guy I dismissed this week. Is your dress from Gallo?"

"Yeah, I just got it."

"I totally ordered the same dress!"

"In the vintage pink?"

"Obviously."

"I totally thought of you when I saw the pink. I brought a nice cheese."

"Perfect, I have bread." Clara waved the baguette, then held out a pastry box to Piper. "And

I made a batch of ginger crisps for you to take back to Portland. No sharing with the brothers. They're all for you."

Piper opened the box and inhaled the scent of her favorite cookie. She slipped her arm through Clara's.

"You are the best."

"No, you're the best. That's why I made you cookies. To celebrate your bestness."

Arm in arm, the twins made their way onto the front porch of the family home. While Clara would never begrudge her sophisticated sister a life in the city of Portland, there was nothing on earth like being back in one another's company.

They paused at the front door. Warm, sage-scented air settled around them, cocooning them. Once they were inside there would be no brother-free chatter for the next several hours. While Clara loved her brothers, there were some things only her twin would understand or even know to ask about.

"Seen anything of Jet?" Piper asked.

Clara bit her lip and grinned. Piper was the one person she could talk to about the confusion Jet sparked in her. She'd called her sister six times in the last three days, and that was before she helped clear out the little house on his property.

Piper laughed. "I have got to see this guy again."

"He is so—" Clara searched for the word. She couldn't come up with anything that described the complex, intelligent, funny, kind man she was getting to know. Instead she went with, "We burned a pile of furniture together. It was awesome."

"Of course. Smoldering furniture. Sounds serious." Piper held Clara's gaze. "Are you interested?"

Clara let the words swim around in her head. "I don't know. Kind of. Obviously, yes. But I shouldn't. And is he…?" Clara hesitated, then pulled a piece of cardstock covered with sticky notes out of her leather binder and handed it to her sister.

Piper shook her head slowly. "You're using office supplies to determine Jet's intentions?"

Over the past few days Clara had spent an embarrassing amount of time sorting out various signals she'd received from Jet. Pink sticky notes for signs he could be interested in being more than friends, green for signs he wasn't, and purple for points of confusion.

"What else would I use?"

"I don't know," Piper said, mugging a confused expression, "a straightforward question to the man himself?"

Clara shuddered, then reached up to make sure the clasp of her necklace was still at the back of her neck. "I love sticky notes."

"But sticky notes will never love you back."

Clara gazed down at the paper. She might never be able to open up to a relationship with a guy, but her devotion to sticky notes was well established.

"Maybe not, but I'm pretty sure the people who manufacture them can't live without me."

Piper chuckled as she took the paper from Clara and set it back in the binder. "We were talking about Jet," she said simply.

Clara pressed her lips together. Jet was complicated. All the sticky notes in the world couldn't pin down the emotions he stirred in her.

Piper took her hand. "Clara, when was the last time you dated someone?"

Clara shrugged. "There was that guy, in January."

"Yeah. That lasted, what, four dates?"

"Three." She tried to keep her expression disinterested, even when her heart slammed up against her rib cage and started rattling. She knew where Piper was going with this.

Piper looked down at their hands. "Which

makes it the longest relationship you've had in the last five years."

Clara blew out a puff of breath. "He wasn't right for me."

"And can I assume you still haven't—"

Clara cut her sister off. "Actually kissed anyone? No. And it's not a big deal."

"You're twenty-eight."

"I'm not going to run around exchanging chemicals with men I don't want to commit to just because I'm…almost thirty." Clara hung her head. Piper pulled her into a hug. "It's weird. I know. I'm a freak."

"There's nothing wrong with waiting for the right guy."

Piper was only halfway correct. There was nothing wrong with waiting for the right guy. But hitting twenty-eight years old without a real kiss? That was just sad. She'd come close a few times, but whenever the opportunity arose she'd start questioning whether this was a guy she wanted to bond with. Nothing killed the mood quicker than someone practicing deep breathing techniques, or explaining she needed to go for a quick run to work a few things out.

And while she did a great job of pretending it had everything to do with good decision-mak-

ing and nothing to do with anxiety, it got harder
and harder to believe herself the older she got.

*Particularly when there's a guy I'm really
interested in kissing.*

"I wish a lot more people would wait for the
right guy. I'm only asking because you have a
hard time making big decisions." Piper pulled
back and looked Clara in the eye. "It's okay to
make a mistake."

"Do you think Jet's a mistake?"

Piper shook her head. "I think you like him.
And I want to make sure you like him because
he's a great guy, not because he isn't interested
and that makes him safe."

An uncomfortable buzzing rattled in Clara's
head. She pushed back from her sister's embrace. "I'm not afraid of dating. In fact, I'd love
to. But now that I've waited this long, I may as
well wait for my forever guy."

"I didn't say you're afraid of dating."

"Good. Because I'm not. That would be ridiculous."

Piper just smiled. "No, sweetie. You're afraid
of falling in love."

Clara squared her shoulders, then crossed
her arms for good measure. Piper squinted her
right eye.

Ugh. It was so unfair when Piper was right about her personal failings.

"Okay, fine. Love is messy."

"And beautiful. Clara, you've done an extraordinary job managing your anxiety. It's incredible, really, and I couldn't be more proud of how far you've come. But our life mission is to make the world a better place by helping others open up to love. Shouldn't we include you in this equation?"

Piper was right, but Clara had no intention of admitting it. She rolled her eyes. "You date enough for both of us."

"I'll stop dating when I find the right man."

"Then I'll start dating when I'm ready." She pushed open the front door, ready to be done with this conversation. "But Jet's a great guy. We may only ever be friends, and therefore he's totally safe, but he's definitely a great guy."

The hundred-year-old, Craftsman-style farmhouse had been updated under their oldest brother's ownership, but still had the same warm and inviting feel it had when they were young. Ash had fewer piles of paper lying about than their parents had, and Jackson was better about doing his chores than any of them had ever been, but it was still home.

"Hi, Aunt Clara," Jackson said, bending slightly to give her a hug.

"You've grown," Clara accused. "You were not this tall yesterday."

"That's exactly what I said," Piper chimed in.

"I turn around, and you're a foot taller. This has got to stop."

Jackson rolled his eyes and picked up his phone. Even the Best Nephew Ever had limits on the amount of auntie-nonsense he could tolerate.

"Hi, Bowman." Clara greeted Hunter's twin with a hug. "How was Yosemite?"

"So beautiful," Bowman said. "We climbed Pre-Muir."

"Is that some horrible, scary, far-from-the-ground death trap?" Piper asked.

Bowman laughed. "I'm safer rock climbing than you are in Portland traffic."

Piper shook her head. "That's not true."

"Statistically, it is," Clara said. Piper, for some reason, had never been comfortable with rock climbing. "I ran the numbers. So long as Bowman takes the correct precautions and checks his equipment." She turned to her brother and made eye contact. "Every. Single. Time. He's fine."

Bowman chuckled. "I do."

"No, his work at the fire department is way

more dangerous. In fact, if you want to worry about Bowman, rock climbing is among the safest things he does." Clara flipped open her notebook. "I have a list of worry rankings if you want to see it."

Piper set her hand over the list. "Aaand this discussion is officially over." She pointed to Clara's baguette. "We've got bread."

"And cheese," Clara said.

"Everybody's in the kitchen." Bowman grinned at his sisters. "Careful on the way in. More people died from accidents in their own homes last year than in all climbing accidents combined."

"That's not funny." Piper's eyes flashed dangerously.

Bowman laughed anyway. "But it *is* true."

Clara took confident steps toward the kitchen. "Bowman, stop teasing her," she commanded as she pushed through the swinging door.

"Oomph!" She smacked into something big and solid on the other side. Piper crashed into her from behind.

Clara weaved unsteadily as a strong hand gripped her shoulder. She looked up into warm brown eyes and felt the world compress into nothing more than the man before her. Kissing, again, seemed like a really good idea.

"Well, hello, Jet Broughman," Piper said.

"What are you doing here?" Clara asked, as Jet said, "I didn't know you were coming."

"I invited him," Hunter said from where he stood fussing over roast vegetables, "so stop staring, and offer the man a beer."

"I'm not staring." Clara shot her brother a look. "Here, slice this." She dropped her baguette on the counter and turned to Jet. "May I offer you a beer?"

"Yes, thank you." Jet looked as uncertain as she felt.

"I'll grab it," Piper said, tossing her cheese to Jet. "Slice this." Piper headed out on the back porch where Ash kept a fridge for drinks. Clara followed her. As the screen door slammed behind them Clara heard Jet say, "One of them is like a whirlwind, but man, together they make a hurricane."

JET HUNG BACK as the Wallace family filled in around the table. Arguing, teasing, shuffling back and forth into the kitchen, everybody was busy and perfectly at ease.

Except for Jet.

Since issuing his invitation, Hunter had told Jet about the food he would cook, plans for the roast and what to expect from Ash but nothing about Clara coming. *Who does that to a guy?*

It had taken a good deal of his mental focus to think about anything other than Clara for the last week. And that had become significantly more difficult after spending the day with her cleaning out the old cabin than learning about the love chemicals.

His gaze jumped to Clara again, as ideas for releasing oxytocin took over all other thoughts.

"Here." Piper tapped the back of an empty chair.

Grateful for the direct instruction, Jet pulled it out and sat.

Roast veggies, Yorkshire pudding and jars of Hunter's pickled onions and relishes were scattered across the table. Applesauce, rolls, horseradish sauce and mustards, all homemade, it was like some kind of feast for the Greek gods—if the gods had relocated to the central Cascade Mountains.

Finally, Hunter came in bearing the platter with the rib roast, and the family broke into applause.

"Thank you for the roast, Jet," Ash said from the head of the table.

"Thank *you*," Jet replied. "I wasn't expecting to be included with the whole family."

"Hunter loves strays," Piper said, serving herself a slice of roast.

Jet's heart sank. Right, he'd been invited because he was a stray. Hunter probably invited some lonely person every week.

"Which is why you're here, with nothing in your hand but a stinky cheese," Hunter said, throwing his napkin in his sister's face.

"It's not stinky, it's artisan."

"That's what they said about your last boyfriend," Bowman quipped.

"I can't believe you're making fun of me in front of a guest," Piper cried.

"You called my guest a stray," Hunter shot back.

Bolting for the door seemed like the best option. Jet was on the verge of excusing himself when a soft hand came to rest on his. His gaze met Clara's.

"Nobody thinks you're a stray."

Jet looked down at Clara's hand on his, then back into her eyes. Just in time to see Bowman's napkin hit her face.

"I'm not even in this argument!" she cried, snapping the napkin back at Bowman.

Jet started to laugh. Ash cleared his throat and immediately the squabble stopped.

Helping himself to roast vegetables, Ash asked Jet, "How's the team looking?"

"Great," Jet said, then nodded at Jackson.

"Coach asked Jackson to swing up on defense, and with a little more work I think he can take offence, too."

"You played wide receiver and safety, right?" Ash asked Jet.

"Yeah."

"What's the safety do?" Piper asked Clara.

"They play football?" Clara guessed.

"Don't you two remember anything I've taught you?" Jackson asked.

"Sorry, sweetie," Piper answered. "Your aunties are remedial sports fans."

"But you were cheerleaders. You have to know something about football to cheer, don't you?"

"Absolutely not," Piper said to her nephew. Jet couldn't help but laugh.

"But we intend to make up for our misspent youth by watching your team," Clara said. "And I have a plan to match Coach Kessler with the most elegant woman."

Jackson made a face implying his aunt couldn't have said anything more ridiculous, which set the whole table laughing.

"You gonna go for quarterback?" Bowman asked Jackson. "That was your dad's position."

Jackson shook his head, looked at his dad, then back at Jet. He smiled. "I'm going for safety."

Jet nodded in appreciation. Jackson turned

his attention to the food in front of him but kept smiling.

"What's this football player cabin restoration project?" Piper asked. "I heard something about scholarships and burning furniture?"

"It's the Outcrop Defense Scholarship," Jackson said. "Everyone who works on fixing up the house Jet grew up in gets a share of the rent money to go toward college."

Jet confirmed this but didn't say much as the family filled Piper in on it. The siblings talked fast, interrupting one another to explain the project that Jackson had already summed up perfectly. Then Clara's gaze fixed on him and the room quieted as she asked the one question he wasn't prepared to answer.

"What's the rent going to be?"

Jet had a number in mind, but if a certain matchmaker inquired about renting, he had every intention of lowering the price substantially and augmenting the scholarship fund with his own earnings. It was important that the kids see real money toward their educations out of their investment of work on the cabin. But if he wanted to fund some of that out of his own pocket while supporting his local matchmaker, that was his affair.

"Still trying to work that out," he said.

Jet tucked into his dinner, trying to eat slowly. His best meals were always at Eighty Local, but this was food on a whole different level. Focusing on his plate, he felt himself relax. The conversation ricocheting through the room was rapid, funny and competitive all at the same time. He could enjoy it but was at a loss to engage.

With the social blizzard raging around the table, he studied Clara and Piper. They were identical twins, but Jet had never had any trouble telling them apart. Clara's hair was highlighted blond, worn in shining waves, whereas Piper's was darker and straightened. Clara was vivacious, Piper cooler and more sophisticated.

"Why didn't we hang out in high school?" Piper asked him abruptly.

Jet started to make an excuse, then stopped. Piper probably hadn't given him a second thought since graduation, if then. He told the truth. "You all were pretty intimidating, back in high school."

"We were?" Clara asked.

"Yes."

The family looked confused.

"We were intimidating?" Bowman asked.

"Yes," Jet said again. "Perfect family, perfect parents."

Silence settled around the table. Jet cleared his throat. *They have to know how lucky they are, don't they?*

"I hadn't realized our parents were perfect," Piper said.

"Right." Clara glanced at the head of the table. "You'd think perfect parents wouldn't have named their firstborn son after a tree."

"Or their second and thirdborn sons after animal-killers," Piper finished.

"You'd think perfect parents wouldn't have raised their daughter to call my guest a stray," Hunter said.

Jackson met Jet's eyes, then he addressed his aunts and uncles. "You guys have two nice parents."

The table quieted. Ash shifted uncomfortably. Clara leaned over and squeezed her nephew's shoulder.

"You're right, Jackson. We have great parents."

"What do they do now that they're retired?" Jet asked.

"Travel," Clara said, as Piper said, "They're always traveling."

"When Ash came home to take over the horse operation," Hunter told him, "the two of them took off on vacation, and they've barely been home since."

"What's this trip?" Jet asked.

"Kenya," Ash answered. "Mom is looking at relics from the twelfth century Indian Ocean trade, and Dad wants to see some bird."

"Dad wants to see a Taita apalis," Bowman said.

"Oooh! Fancy bird name," Piper teased.

"That's great. I'm glad they get the chance to travel." Jet paused, unsure of how much to say. "Your parents had a big influence on me. Your dad… He's the reason I got my scholarship to University of Washington. He encouraged me to apply to the Rural Scholar Program and wrote me a letter of recommendation."

"I didn't know that," Clara said.

"Yeah. There's no way I could have paid for college, and I wouldn't have known about Rural Scholar. I owe him a lot. And your mom…" Jet stopped. He couldn't say she was like a second mom to him, because he didn't really have a first. He knew Mrs. Wallace had taught thousands of people and treated each of them with the same care and respect she showed him, but she still managed to make him feel special.

"Right, everyone loves Mom," Piper said. "Just like everyone loves Clara."

That was the reminder Jet needed. Like her mom, Clara managed to make everyone feel special and cared for. It was a good quality, and so long as he could remember that and remain friends with her, everything would be okay.

"ANYONE UP FOR a walk?" Clara asked. Hunter and Bowman jumped up, as did Piper. Ash would doubtless prefer to take a break from the family for the thirty minutes they were out ranging the property. "Jet?"

"Sure," he answered.

Clara felt the bizarre urge to issue a little clap of excitement.

This was getting ridiculous. Jet was walking with the family, not a big deal. Obviously, he would choose to stick with Hunter, rather than spending his time in the house with her oldest brother. Ash was not only named after a tree, he was almost as talkative.

Still, Clara felt a hum of rightness as she skipped down the back steps. Jackson and Jet were deep in conversation about football. Piper walked between Bowman and Hunter, making them laugh with stories about Portland. They turned onto the running path and began to head up along the west pasture, like they did every other Sunday after dinner. Clara followed. She would catch up and join a conversation soon enough, but the pasture and trees and her family and Jet were so beautiful, she wanted time to soak it all in.

A twinge of worry about her parents sparked. Clara combated the concern with three deep breaths. *They're fine. They're happy. Kenya is a lovely place.*

Her stomach churned.

Kenya was a lovely place, and it was on the other side of the world, and her parents had a bad habit of changing plans mid-vacation.

A familiar rhythm of hoofbeats caught her attention. Clara looked up to see Shelby galloping toward them. His mane caught the wind, and the evening light gleamed against his glossy brown coat. She heard Bowman laughing as they watched the horse gallop over to Clara.

"Hello, best horse," she said as Shelby skidded to a stop. She stood on the bottom rail of the fence so she was face-to-nose with her friend. She scratched under his mane and kissed the crescent on his forehead. Shelby leaned his head into her shoulder. The horse had always been able to sense her moods, and on her most difficult days he had been known to escape from the pasture and walk up to the house to check in on her.

"Hey, there," Jet said, joining her at the fence.

Shelby gave Jet a stomp and a nudge, then returned his attention to Clara.

"I'm good," she whispered. "You can say hi to Jet."

"We met last week," he reminded the horse.

Shelby gave Jet a glance and swished his tail. Then he shook off Clara's attention and started walking along the fence as though he were another member of the family.

Which, of course, he was.

"Does he always join you on walks?" Jet asked.

"He'll walk along Clara's path as long as he can," Hunter said. "But when it veers from the pasture he gets mad."

"Dad did *not* think about Shelby when he made this trail for Clara," Piper said.

Clara watched Jet take in the trail, a wide swath of wood chips her father had built the fall of her first year in high school and maintained meticulously since then. It ran along the border of their property, skirting the west pasture, through the woods, along the ridge of the hill, then down past the east pasture, looping the big pond and back to the house.

"Your dad built you a running trail?" Jet asked.

"We all use it," Clara replied, shooting her family members a warning look.

"When you make us take a walk every other Sunday after dinner. But you were the only one out running laps at ten o'clock at night on a regular basis," Bowman said.

Clara could feel Jet looking at her.

"I'm not making anyone walk." Clara crossed her arms. She glanced up at Jet and met his eyes. His body radiated warmth and strength as he walked next to her. She could get used to having Jet on these family walks. A sense of ease snuggled in.

"Clara has two channels," Hunter said, knocking any sense of ease right out of her.

"Hunter," she warned.

"Humming and buzzing."

"Please stop."

"Humming is good," Bowman explained.

"And buzzing is bad," Hunter finished.

"When everything is perfect, the world is humming." Bowman gave her a wicked grin.

"And by perfect, we mean Clara-perfect," Hunter clarified. "Which means your hair looks good, the stars are aligned, and you have a fully functioning set of sparkly pens lined up, ready for work."

"There are zero things wrong with liking good hair, aligned stars and sparkly pens," Clara said.

"But if one strand of hair or one star is out of alignment," Bowman said in a warning voice.

"Buzzing," Hunter finished.

"I like order," Clara defended herself.

"Liking order, totally reasonable," Hunter said.

"Worshiping order," Bowman frowned, "leads to problems."

Family tales of her perfectionism could roll on all evening. Clara's eyes darted to Piper for help. Piper held her gaze, clearly saying that if things were going to go anywhere with Jet he needed to know about this. Clara took in a deep breath. *Will things with Jet go anywhere, anyway? Did he really need to hear all this?* She glanced up to see a sheepish smile light his face.

"So when you match up the right clients, it's humming?" Jet asked.

"Yes." Clara shot her brothers a satisfied glare. "That's my mission, to create more beauty and joy on earth by helping people find the right relationship."

Bowman gave a fake cough. "Because you've had so much experience being in relationships."

"Has she ever even had a real boyfriend?" Hunter asked rhetorically.

Jet didn't seem to register the brothers' patter. He looked thoughtful. "And when one of your clients shows up with a friend in tow who questions everything you say—" Jet was grinning now "—that would be buzzing?"

Clara laughed. "It wasn't my favorite first-meet."

Jet stopped walking and looked down at her. Clara's heart kicked up. There was definitely humming involved.

Which was completely derailed by Hunter. "You should have seen her pouting. She barely ate a bite of my soup."

"That's not even true. I had two bowls of it."

"And then she came back here and went for a run," Bowman tattled. "How many laps did you do? Six?"

"I have no idea." Clara glared at her brothers. "And it's too bad you have so little going on in your life you have time to count how many laps someone runs."

Bowman's expression shifted. "Someone always counts." His voice was quieter as he said, "We worry."

Clara's gaze dropped to the path.

"Do you run laps when you're angry?" Jet asked.

"No. I run...I run when I need to." Clara sighed. If she didn't tell this story, someone else was going to. "My first year I was having trouble transitioning to high school. Sometimes I couldn't…sometimes I couldn't make simple decisions, or I would get really wound up about things that didn't matter. Running always helped, so Dad built this path." She turned and gave her siblings and nephew a regal nod. "You're welcome."

Jackson, ever the peacemaker, came to her defense. "I run on this path all the time, Aunt Clara."

"I'm glad. Running is good for the soul." She shot her brothers a look.

Hunter reached out and ruffled her hair. Bowman dropped an arm around her shoulder. Clara tried to smooth down her hair and shrug off Bowman's arm but just wound up hugging both her brothers instead.

Family.

"Are we walking, or are we hugging?" Piper asked. "Because I thought Clara was making us go for a walk."

The group continued, stopping only when Clara had to say goodbye to Shelby as the path veered from the pasture. Predictably, Shelby stomped and snorted and expressed the indignity of being left out of the walk.

"Poor guy." Jet ran back to scratch his ears.

Shelby, sensing an ally, inclined his head to Jet. "It's no fun being left out."

"You're just encouraging him," Bowman called over.

"I'm looking out for him," Jet said to the horse. Shelby gave him the high compliment of nosing his pocket to see if he had any treats.

"He's a little overdramatic," Clara admitted.

"Wonder who he gets that from," Hunter muttered.

Clara rounded on her brother. "Okay, enough! You wipe that mirthful glint out of your eye right now, and stop teasing me in front of our guest." Hunter backed up a few steps, but Clara was quick and launched herself at her brother.

"I have no mirth!" he protested, laughing.

"You're not gonna have any by the time I get done with you."

Hunter turned to Jet and said dryly, "Yeah, Clara's not dramatic at all."

Jet laughed, and Clara felt the heat ride up her neck. She gave Hunter a good slap on the arm, then marched over to join Jet at the fence line. Shelby ignored her in favor of his new best friend. Clara ran a hand along Shelby's nose. "He's going to go straight back to his buddies the minute we leave."

"I still feel bad."

"I know, but in Shelby's world he would walk this trail with us, then join us back at the house for dessert."

Jet grinned at her. "And all humans would keep horse snacks in their pockets?"

"Exactly, and I would spend all day, every day, following him around with a currycomb."

Jet gave Shelby one last scratch on his ears. "We're taking off, buddy."

Clara tugged at Jet's hand, and his fingers curled around hers for a brief moment as they walked away. The magic she'd felt when she'd kissed his cheek pulsed around them.

Does he feel this, too?

She glanced at him; he met and held her gaze. The champagne and disco heartbeat came back full force.

The air cooled as the sun began its descent. An owl, perched in the branches of an Oregon white oak, hooted as they passed by. The path wound deeper into their property, and Clara found herself getting wound further into Jet. He was here, on her path, in the woods she'd played in as a child. She liked the way he laughed with her brothers and talked with Piper about the differences between living in the city and being back in Outcrop. She liked him, and it would take a lot of bravery on her part to see it through.

What was she so afraid of?

Failing. Starting to succeed, then self-sabotaging the relationship.

Hurting him again. Hurting myself.

And even if it all worked out and they fell in love, she'd have a million new things to worry about. It was exhausting enough calming her anxious fears about her daredevil brothers and city-girl sister. Throw in her parents traveling to remote corners of the earth, Ash refusing to talk about his failed marriage, and Jackson having his driver's permit, and she was fully booked for worry.

"What's that look for?" Jet had dropped back from the pack to walk next to her.

"What look?"

He gestured to her face. "The furrowed brow, distracted expression, biting your lip."

Clara took a deep breath, relaxed her face and gave him the brightest smile she could muster. "Hunter made two kinds of pie for dessert, and I'm going to have to pick one. It's a tough choice."

He grinned at her, clearly not buying her excuse but willing to play along. "Want to jog it out? Might help make the decision?"

"Or it might make me hungry enough for two slices of pie."

He laughed. "I had that thought. Let's go."

Clara gave a little skip as she ran next to Jet. *He is a good guy.*

But even if she did manage to open up and risk her heart, there was no guarantee this was going to wind up any differently than the last time she had a crush on him.

"THANK YOU," Jet said, holding out a hand to Ash. He'd been at the front door, almost leaving, for several minutes. Clara was snuggled up with Piper in a window seat, deep in conversation. It was incredibly hard not to look at her and not to want her to look at him.

He had to back off. He could not fall for Clara again. She charmed everyone. He understood now that her kindness wasn't manipulative. She was a genuinely sweet human being, with a big heart. But one bright smile and thoughtful comment didn't mean that she liked him more than any other human, horse, kitten or living creature on earth.

"Come back anytime," Ash said.

Jackson looked up from his phone. "What are we doing in drills tomorrow?"

"Speed and agility," Jet said, loud enough that Clara should be able to hear him. "Then a Kessler-style inspirational speech, followed by a severe chewing out to anyone who doesn't perform."

Jackson laughed, but Clara didn't pause in her conversation. It was fine. She was with her sister. He should just head home. The evening had turned out to be great, and that was a good place to leave it.

But he'd been fascinated to learn more about Clara. He'd often noticed her stopping to gather herself or taking deliberate breaths. The plans she came up with and executed with such precision made sense in light of her struggles.

Was it possible that her hesitation to date was linked to the anxiety she felt? How such an incredible woman could be single was a mystery, but that would explain things. And if her chemistry did keep her from dating, what kind of man would it take to help her open up?

Definitely not him. The role models he'd grown up with weren't a great setup for success in a relationship. He'd reacted so poorly the last time she'd turned him down he didn't want to think about it. Now they were friends. He didn't need to mess this up by pushing Clara into a relationship she wasn't interested in.

The memory of her fingers, curled inside his as she pulled him away from Shelby along the path came unbidden. The briefest touch had sent what Clara called *love chemicals* flooding through his system. He had to shut this down before it got any worse.

"See you, man," Hunter said, then glanced at Clara and asked, "Did you rope Jet into coming Saturday?"

Clara trained her gaze on him, a hopeful spark forming there. Jet's heart leaped and strained against his rib cage. He placed a hand on his chest.

Because that would keep his heart in place?

"Wait. What? You're leaving?" Piper asked, seeing the coat in his hand.

"Can you come Saturday?" Clara grinned, then bit her lip.

Say no.

"Where?" Jet asked.

"Smith Rock, remember? I've got a group date, we're climbing. Hunter and Bowman are coming."

"If you try to set me up, I will disown you," Bowman said.

"If you try to set me up, I will sneak into your house and rearrange everything in your closet," Hunter told her.

Clara shuddered.

"Shirts next to pants. Summer dresses against winter coats."

"Stop it!" She was laughing now.

"Total disregard for color," Hunter said.

"Okay, I'll be super clear. The brothers are off-limits."

"*Clear* means you need to tell everyone we are only there to climb and help others climb, and we will not be calling anyone, no matter how good a fit their matchmaker thinks we would be," Bowman said.

"I'll put it on the waiver." Clara turned to Jet and widened her eyes. His puppy dog of a heart rolled over on its back and sighed.

Come up with a good excuse, because you are not spending next Saturday falling in love with Clara Wallace.

"You're taking your clients rock climbing?" he heard himself asking.

"I honestly don't know why you do that," Piper snapped.

"It's a great group date," Clara defended herself. "Everyone has a lot of fun. Do you climb, Jet?"

"Sure." In Outcrop, the little town in the shadow of world-famous Smith Rock, everyone grew up climbing. Everyone except for Jet, who'd had no one to teach him. He took rock climbing his first trimester at University of Washington and had made sure he got good at it. When he had kids, he'd be Crag Dad along with the best of them.

"This will be a sport-climbing trip," Hunter said.

"This will be a Gumby-fest," Bowman inserted. "We're the rope guns, setting up for all Clara's clients."

"They're not all inexperienced," Clara protested. "There are several good climbers joining us."

"You're not including Michael on your list of good climbers, are you?" Jet asked.

"Of course not." Clara's eyes met his and shone with a conspiratorial smile. "But if you came, you could help him out. Then he could catch the eye of Joanna or Abby, and fall in love and be happy for the rest of his life."

"You're gonna get Michael on a rope?"

"Yep. You in?"

The room silenced at this conversation. Jet found himself at the center of attention, a place he was rarely comfortable. His eyes came to rest on Clara, who was all smiling and sparkly and beautiful.

Would one day really make this any worse than it already was?

"To see Michael rock climb? I'm in."

CHAPTER TWELVE

"AND MR. FAREAS, again, I'm sorry to be such a bother," Clara said, picking up her paint samples.

The older gentleman waved away her apology, but Clara could see by the set of his shoulders that he was looking forward to her exiting his establishment.

"The colors really are almost perfect, and I love the sage."

He raised a bushy eyebrow.

"And thank you for letting me test so many swatches."

The indulgent smile he'd been holding back finally broke. "This matters to you," he said, shaking his head.

"It does matter." She held the paint samples closer. Clara had tried twelve different colors before settling on three options for the loft in Jet's cabin, using up several hours of Mr. Fareas's time in what was currently a six-dollar purchase. "Thank you."

The keeper of Outcrop Hardware, Tack and

Feed nodded, rang up the paint, then uttered a sigh of relief as he moved on to a new and more lucrative customer.

Bells jangled as someone opened the door. Clara glanced over from her perfect cans of paint.

"Oh, hey!" she said, looking up at the man who was fast becoming her favorite person to look up at.

"Hey." A smile lit his face as he held the door for her. Jet wore work boots, jeans, one of the clearly expensive but in-no-way showy T-shirts he favored and a worn cowboy hat. No, it wasn't just a hat. Jet had on a vintage Stetson that looked like it had belonged to his grandfather's father.

Clara hoped the clunking sound she heard wasn't her jaw hitting the wooden porch of OHTAF.

Nope. She'd dropped a can of the paint it had taken her way too much time to get right.

Jet chased down the rolling can onto the front porch. Clara followed him out. Jet examined the can.

"What are you working on?"

"Just gathering some ideas for the loft in the cabin," she said as casually as she could.

He looked surprised but happy about it. "Thank you. This is a nice color. Would it work for the rest of the cabin, too?"

She wrinkled her nose. "No. Don't you remember? We talked about using a wide array of colors that reflect the landscape."

A bemused smile crossed his face. "Right. The array of colors. Sounds great."

Clara shook her head. "You're not even trying to have an opinion on color choices, are you?"

"Not one."

Clara laughed at his response. "Well, if you're not here for paint, what are you in for?"

"I need to order some more fencing. After the last emu break, I think I have to replace all the old stuff at this point. Mr. Fareas is going to get sick of me if he isn't already."

"I imagine he can tolerate you all right."

Jet shrugged.

"You order your fencing here? Doesn't HomeStore in Bend have all kinds of fencing in stock?"

"Are you kidding me?" Jet gestured to the hundred-year-old building. "I love OHTAF."

"Me, too."

"Michael and I plan on being old men on the front porch."

"You might have some competition," she said, nodding to a group of elderly gentlemen sitting around a chess game.

Jet crossed his arms and studied the octo-genarians.

"You're right. I wouldn't want to tangle with those guys. Fortunately, there's the bench." Jet sat down. Clara took a step, then another, and found herself sitting next to him. She gazed at him, taking in the old porch, the show window behind them and the perfection that resonated from Jet.

"What?" he asked.

"Nothing."

He pulled off his hat and examined it. "This hat is really old. I probably shouldn't wear it in public."

"No!" The word shot out of her mouth. "No," she tried again, with more control. "It's a great hat. In fact—" with one hand she indicated him, the store and Outcrop in general "—it's all very satisfying."

Okay. That was the weirdest thing I could possibly say.

Jet peered at her closely. "Satisfying?"

"Not like, *satisfying* satisfying, but like…right. Like everything is how it should be. It hums."

Jet grinned. "Glad to know I hum."

A soft breeze fluttered through the porch, but it wasn't quite enough to cool the hot blush flooding her face.

"So should I stay here at OHTAF?" he teased.

"No, by no means. You also work well at Eighty Local," she said, then clamped her mouth shut before she continued with *and on a horse, and in my family home, and basically anywhere I can lay eyes on you*. She cleared her throat. "You and Michael have plans for this porch?"

Jet rested the hat on his head, then leaned back crossing one leg over the other. "Yup. When I decided to move back here, Michael was finishing up residency. He'd heard lots of stories about Outcrop and wanted to check it out. When he saw OHTAF, that was it. He contacted the hospital in Redmond, then gave me the task of spending enough to keep the store open. I'm doing my part."

Clara held up her can of paint. "Here's my contribution."

Jet nodded his thanks, then got the most adorable grin on his face. It was like all those years ago when he'd made the unexpected touchdown. Like he didn't expect good things, but something good happened anyway.

"It was fun having you at dinner on Sunday," Clara said.

"Yeah. The food, and your family… Jackson's a great kid."

"He is the best kid," Clara confirmed.

"It's cool how you all look after each other."

Clara could sense his unspoken questions. She glanced around the porch. This was a good man, and this was as good a moment as any to tell him.

"They take care of me."

"Is it anxiety?" Jet asked.

"It's complicated. No, not complicated, just…" She looked up at Jet. "Do you mind if I psychobabble at you to explain this?"

"Babble away."

"Okay, so I get anxious, but I've learned to manage my chemistry so it doesn't develop into a full-blown anxiety disorder."

Jet nodded. Clara let out a breath before continuing. She'd never discussed this with anyone outside of her family. Except the therapist, and even that had been a bit of a struggle. She glanced up at Jet and allowed herself to soak in his calm strength. He smiled encouragingly. *She could do this.*

"We all have our quirks, but for something to be considered a psychological disorder, it has to be maladaptive, unusual, disturbing and atypical. I'm wound more tightly than most people, but my behavior doesn't generally fall into all four categories. Unless someone finds the excessive use of sticky notes disturbing."

Jet laughed. Clara steeled her courage and

continued. "If my feelings of anxiety kept me from thriving, then it would be a disorder."

His gaze traveled over her face, took in her clothes and rested on the can of paint. It occurred to Clara that her outfit coordinated with the paint *and* her manicure.

"And you're clearly thriving."

Clara blushed, which probably didn't go with the outfit.

"I've learned to handle my chemistry pretty well. And honestly, I like it. I like that I have something inside me that doesn't quit until things are done well, be it a match or the organization of my books. I like knowing when I take something on, I will do it to the best of my ability."

"But?"

"But the problems occur when there is a major change, or I'm in a situation where I don't have much control." Clara glanced at Jet to check his reaction, then got a little lost in his gorgeous brown eyes.

"On Sunday, you said your dad built the running path because you were having trouble transitioning to high school."

"Right." She bit her lip. "Do you really want to hear this?"

"Yes." Jet's response was swift and solid.

He *did* want to hear, and strangely enough, she wanted to tell him.

"The first few months of high school were the worst downward spiral of my life. Everyone was busy with the start of the school year, so no one in the family realized what was happening. I worked pretty hard to hide it, but I was routinely staying up until three in the morning doing homework assignments four or five times over and still feeling inadequate. School days were a blur of panic." She drew in a breath as she remembered how poorly she'd treated her family. "I fought with Piper over nothing. I withdrew from everyone."

"That must have been horrible."

"Yeah. It was. Bowman found me sobbing out behind the bleachers during lunch one day. My parents put the pieces together, and I got help." Clara smiled, remembering the way everyone had rallied around her. "Piper took charge."

"I'd expect that," Jet said.

"She kept me by her side, coming up with projects like running for student government together, and trying to convince the school to get a cat. Hunter packed my lunch every morning, serving me linemen's portions of my favorite foods. Mom took me to a therapist in Bend once a week.

I learned to be smart about what I ate, how much time I spent on my phone and how much sleep I got. Everyone in the family learned to employ Three Deep Breaths." Clara paused and looked up at Jet. "And Dad built me the running path. I spent hours on the path, burning off the persistent buzzing. I still use it when I've had a bad day."

Jet exhaled. "I'm impressed."

"I don't want to make it sound like anxiety is easy to overcome. Mine is pretty mild compared to a lot of people, and I have every advantage that makes it possible to cope with my chemistry," Clara said. "I have an amazing family and work that allows me flexibility and control. This has been hard for me, but I can't even imagine what it's like for people who don't have my resources."

Jet leaned forward, elbows resting on his knees, looking out at the street before them.

"I imagine there are a lot of people with all your resources who don't handle this as well as you do."

"I do like handling things well," she admitted.

"But change is hard?"

"Change is difficult. Like when we graduated. Or when Piper moved to Portland. But I make a plan and follow it. And if things start going sideways, I know the signs and can get help."

"I guess I always assumed you didn't have any problems. From the outside, it looks like you have a perfect life."

Clara gazed into Jet's eyes. She felt relaxed, and somehow more free in sharing this information with him. She'd always assumed people would think less of her if they knew about how she'd struggled with anxiety and panic attacks when she was younger. But Jet had been through some difficulty of his own and came out the other side stronger. He understood.

"My life is perfect," she joked, holding up the paint can. "It takes considerable energy to keep it that way."

Jet laughed, leaning back to study her. A spark raced between them.

"And what about you, Jet Broughman? Was it weird, going to Seattle all on your own at eighteen?"

Jet's expression shifted. "I'd been alone throughout high school. My grandfather was an excellent man, but no one could call him a hands-on parent. College was a tailspin, but I'd been a fish out of water for so long I knew how to do it by then."

A creeping feeling tugged at Clara's heart. "Were you a fish out of water in high school?"

"You could say that."

"And I was like…"

"A big fish in a tiny pond."

Clara buried her face in her hands.

Jet continued. "With all the other fish swimming with you wherever you went." Clara groaned. Jet laughed as he kept teasing her. "Telling their fish parents they had to get fixed-gear bicycles because Clara Wallace had one."

She shook her head. "I'm sorry if my high school self failed your high school self aquatically."

Jet's laughter eased. "It was a long time ago." He shifted his gaze to Main Street. "I probably wasn't the easiest person to get to know."

"You weren't! But I did try."

Jet nodded. "I know." A smile played on his lips. "So say a guy really liked you in high school."

Clara felt a blush heating her cheeks. "I'll try to imagine that."

His smile broke into a full-on grin. He studied his hands.

"If that guy caught you off guard by buying you tickets to go zip-lining, would that have made you feel anxious?"

She laughed, bumping his shoulder with hers. "If it was a guy that I really liked, and I'd been out on a limb, trying to flirt with him for weeks, I would have been pretty wound up by the time he asked me out." Clara shook her head. "And zip-lining—"

"Is the coolest date an eighteen-year-old can come up with!" Jet laughed as he defended his former self.

"Be that as it may, I would not have had the skills to handle it well."

Jet nodded, his smile warming her to her toes. For the first time she didn't feel completely rotten about her response to him all those years ago. She felt understood.

JET GAZED DOWN at Clara.Her big brown eyes were sincere, tangling up his insides. She had tried to talk with him after her rejection of the date. It must have been incredibly difficult for her to step outside of her comfort zone to vie for his attention in the first place, much less speak to him after her panic attack.

As he remembered her floating down the hall toward him with her bright smile, the old feelings of frustration or anger weren't there anymore. His heart began to pulse, waves of blood swirling fast, like a river in late spring. He pulled in air, hoping it might help connect the synapses in his brain. No luck. Every neuron was firing at once with no connections being made.

A loud piano sonata snapped him back to earth.

Clara pulled a phone out of her bag. "I'm sorry, it's my parents. They're calling from Kenya."

Jet stood, despite every nerve in his body demanding he sit right back down beside her. "I should get going."

"You should say hi." She motioned for him to sit. His body responded before his brain was able to weigh in on the issue.

She tapped her phone, and Mr. and Mrs. Wallace appeared on the screen. "Clara!" he heard her mom say. The voice hit right in his gut. How much had he missed Mrs. Wallace's kind, cheerful voice?

"Hi, parents!" Clara beamed back at her phone. "How are you? How's Kenya?"

"Incredible," Mr. Wallace said, as Mrs. Wallace said, "Beautiful!"

With Clara focused on her phone, Jet took the opportunity to study her. Her dimples danced across her cheeks as she engaged in an animated conversation with her parents. She quizzed them on their health. Were they drinking enough water? Were they keeping out of the direct sun?

Jet listened as they dodged her questions with commentary on all they'd seen and were doing.

"We thought of you and Piper the other day," Mr. Wallace said.

"We met a matchmaker!" Mrs. Wallace chimed in, both of them pointedly not answering Clara's question about sticking to their original itinerary.

"No way!" Clara said. "What was she like?"

"It was a man," her father said.

"That's cool." Clara grinned at Jet. He shook his head, mouthing the words *I already have a job.*

"Who's with you?" Mrs. Wallace asked.

"Take a guess!" Clara said, handing the phone to Jet.

The move was so unexpected he didn't respond right away. He stared at the images of two of the most important adults in his life, unable to get a word out.

"Jet!" Mr. Wallace cried. "What are you doing back in Outcrop?"

"He lives here." Clara leaned over Jet's arm to address her parents on the screen.

"I thought you were working for that computer company in Seattle," Mrs. Wallace said, as her husband added, "Glad you made it back home. Are you working the ranch?"

Jet held up the phone, trying to focus on both the Wallaces at once. Nervousness constricted his chest. Then Mrs. Wallace smiled and said, "Jet, it is so nice to see you," as she had so many times when he wandered into her classroom with nowhere else to go.

"It's great to see you, too, Mrs. Wallace. Ash told me you two were checking out rare birds and the Indian Ocean trade cities."

"We've seen the Taita apalis," Mr. Wallace said. "Along with a fulvous whistling duck and a vulturine guinea fowl."

"Fulvous whistling duck?" Clara started to giggle.

"That's fantastic, Mr. Wallace."

"You wouldn't believe it," he said. "We're planning on hopping over to Madagascar to try to find a sickle-billed vanga while we're here."

"Wait, what?" Clara grabbed at the phone.

Jet held tight to the device as her father excitedly described the birding in Madagascar.

"Can I have the phone, please?" Clara asked.

"Just a minute," he responded. "Mrs. Wallace, did you get to see the ruins at Kilwa?"

"Kilwa is in Tanzania, and we might go check them out. But we went to the Gedi ruins here in Kenya, which were amazing."

Clara lunged for the phone, yelling, "You

can't go hopping over to Madagascar. Jet, give me the phone."

"I want to hear about Gedi," Jet said, exchanging a look with Mrs. Wallace on the screen and holding the phone farther from Clara's reach.

"Stop hogging the parents," she said, making Jet laugh out loud.

"I'll only be a minute," he said, resting his hand on her arm. He didn't want to interfere with her phone call, but it felt so good to talk with the Wallaces.

"But I planned this time to talk to my parents."

"Not everything always goes according to plan," her dad said.

"People have to follow the plan for things to go according to plan," Clara said. "And not go hopping off to Madagascar."

"Clara…" Mrs. Wallace's tone immediately had Clara sitting back on the bench. "Do you see how your father and I are sharing the phone? You and Jet try it."

Jet turned to Clara who was still scowling. He gingerly held out the phone in his left hand. Clara moved closer. Jet lifted his right arm so it rested on the back of the bench and Clara leaned in to him to look at the screen.

And there he was, with Clara under his arm and Mr. and Mrs. Wallace on the phone in front of him. Jet had to summon all his strength to act casual, as though this weren't the single most amazing thing that could happen in a person's life.

"There," Mr. Wallace said. "That's better. Now, Jet, how did you wind up back in Outcrop?"

Time simultaneously stretched and constricted as Jet sat on the bench in front of OHTAF, Clara snuggled up against him. He managed to keep from wrapping his arm around her and pressing his lips into her soft hair. It was harder to keep his heart in check. He felt so connected to her and her family at this moment. But he knew it could all be swept away. Learning about her anxiety, and how hard she worked to manage it, made him determined not to upset her or disrupt their budding friendship. He was a coach and mentor to her nephew, friends with her brothers and parents. Even Piper seemed to have warmed to him. If he hurt Clara, all these connections would be at risk.

He didn't think he could handle being abandoned by the Wallace family.

Jet forced himself to focus on the screen. This was just a friendly conversation.

"What brings you both to the front porch at OHTAF?" Mr. Wallace asked.

"Jet's practicing to be an old man," Clara said.

"Clara's been throwing paint cans around," Jet answered. "I'm just here to grab them before Mr. Fareas finds out what she's up to."

The Wallaces laughed, sending a wave of pleasure through Jet. He tore his gaze from the screen to see Clara laughing with her parents. *This was what a family felt like.*

Even though he knew he should be happy as their friend, he couldn't quite convince his heart that he didn't want more.

CHAPTER THIRTEEN

JET STOOD AT the open door. He felt alive and restless as the evening air drifted over his skin. Daylight dimmed as the sun dipped behind the pines. His kitchen was bright behind him, a computer in his work nook reminding him of work he didn't feel like doing.

The sun sunk a notch lower, sending warm rays through the tree trunks. His climbing harness and a couple of ropes were laid out on the counter. He'd practiced tying knots, then practiced teaching other people to tie knots. If he was heading out to Smith Rock tomorrow, he needed to get his work done now. But there was no use running figures when every fiber in him was focused on the next day.

He turned back to examine his kitchen. It was ridiculous. A huge expanse of state-of-the-art appliances, windows, custom cabinetry and enough counter space for every member of the French Revolutionary Army to make themselves an omelet. All for a man who lived on cold-cut sandwiches and takeout from Eighty Local.

Michael was far too nice to laugh at his house, but his comment about filling it up with a family rang true. Michael was being proactive about finding his family. But Michael was enthusiastic, resilient and completely willing to put his heart in someone else's hands.

Jet had to admit that while he'd come so far putting together the life he wanted, there was one area in which he was holding back. He'd made friends, business connections and was now coaching and mentoring kids in Outcrop. But somehow, he'd been assuming a wife and family would just show up in his life.

The right woman had shown up all right. He had to keep himself from making the wrong move.

He was falling for Clara Wallace. That made him nervous. He'd been in a number of relationships but could admit that he'd never been attached to any of the women he dated. If he were completely honest with himself, he'd known at the time he wouldn't really commit to anyone until he came back to Outcrop.

And if he were totally, soul-searchingly honest, there was only one woman in Outcrop he'd ever been interested in. Sitting with her in front of

OHTAF, talking to her parents, had felt so right. If he and Clara were dating, that type of easy, casual conversation would take place all the time.

But if we broke up, it would never happen again.

An uncomfortable chill ran through him at the thought of failing in a relationship with Clara. She was the expert in love. If they couldn't make it together, it would be his fault. And he knew in his soul that if Clara left him, he would never get over it.

Could he learn the skills of being in a successful relationship? Michael had sure turned around in the last few weeks. Then again, Michael had an excellent teacher.

Jet hadn't checked out the Love, Oregon website yet. It was probably chock-full of Love Rules and relationship surveys.

He glanced at his computer.

Nah.

Instead he opened his fridge, thinking about cooking himself dinner.

Clara and Piper's business was about more than just matching people up. They helped people figure out what they wanted and then pointed them in the right direction. The transformation of Michael over the last few weeks was impressive. It was like they had some find yourself formula.

Which he could probably find on their website.

Jet slammed the fridge door. It did not matter how hard he looked, all he had were sandwich fixings.

He turned around and grabbed his laptop, then headed into the living room. Flopping back on the sofa, he engaged his web browser. He could do this.

He hesitated before typing in his search bar. Then he hopped back up, ran into the laundry room and scooped up the baby chick. He didn't have a ton of time to spend with Taffy, but she liked to hang out while he worked on his computer, and he could use some support.

The Love, Oregon site popped up on the first page of his search, with a beautiful picture of Clara and Piper laughing, the family ranch spread out behind them and the Cascade Mountains in the background.

Jet clicked on the Testimonials tab.

Hundreds of entries flooded the screen, along with pictures of one happy couple after the next. Old, young, urban, rural, tattooed, pierced, people of every creed, interest and ethnicity were all snuggled up to someone else, grinning.

This is the best money I have ever spent...

Everyone can find true love...

We thank God for Love, Oregon and Clara Wallace...

Jet felt an uncomfortable pressure behind his eyes. Someday Michael would post here.

He read through the mission statement, a typically Clara declaration about creating beauty and joy by helping people fall in love.

Get started, a link at the bottom said. Jet let the cursor hover over it for a moment, then clicked. Along with information about policies, pricing and confidentiality, there was a questionnaire entitled *Who Are You, and Who Are You Looking For?*

"What do you think?" he asked the chick. Taffy fluffed her feathers. "You're right," he said. "It couldn't hurt."

He hadn't registered on the site so Clara would never know he'd been there. The very last thing he wanted her to think was that he was hoping she'd set him up with someone. *Unless she took someone to mean her.*

Jet leaned back in his seat. *What do matchmakers do when they wanted to find a date? Is there some sort of quid pro quo among them? Or would Clara be more likely to try it DIY?*

He shook his head. If Clara wanted to find a date, all she'd have to do is look up from her sticky notes and beckon the first man who happened to be walking by. *Am I good enough to be that guy?*

Jet scrolled down to the first question.

What are your best qualities?

His fingers hesitated over the keyboard, then he typed.

Hardworking, loyal, smart.

He reread his words, then erased them after realizing he'd described the ideal dog.

Jet picked up his phone and texted Michael.

Jet: What are my best qualities?

His phone buzzed back an answer before he was able to set it down.

Michael: Are you doing the Love, Oregon survey?

Jet: No.

Michael: Right.

Jet: Just sitting around, wondering what my best qualities are.

Michael: You are smart, hardworking and loyal.

Jet grimaced.

Jet: Thanks. I think.

Michael: And you're a brilliant sandwich maker.

Jet: I am.

Michael: Dude, your sandwiches are incredible. You're also the best friend a guy could ask for. And you're good at math.

Jet: Thanks, man.

Jet set down his phone and looked back at the survey. His phone buzzed again.

Michael: Let me know if you need help with question number six.

Jet glanced down at number six.
What does love look like? Describe a relationship you admire.
I'm good, he texted back.
That was easy: Mr. and Mrs. Wallace. But what was it about their relationship he admired? Jet started a list.
Mr. Wallace would walk Mrs. Wallace to her classroom every morning.

Mrs. Wallace would grab an extra cup of coffee during her prep period and take it to her husband during class.

They supported each other's passions, like looking at old, ruined port cities and strange birds.

They used to walk down the halls of the school holding hands.

They'd smiled at each other during the phone call, like they still shared secrets.

Jet had never allowed himself to want a relationship like that. Up until now his greatest relationship wishes were to meet someone, get married, avoid screaming at each other and not get divorced. It was an incredibly low bar. But he didn't want to get his hopes up only to be disappointed. If everyone could have a relationship like the Wallaces, wouldn't they?

An hour later Jet was leaning back in his chair, still working on the questionnaire.

What does your life look like five years from now?

Jet surveyed the room. For years he'd imagined a wife who would help him connect with his community, bringing if not love, then color and laughter into his world. He had done absolutely nothing to bring color and laughter into his own life. Unless he counted the emus. He had imagined a house full of parties, watching a wife host those parties. Taffy peeped at him, revealing an uncomfortable truth. He had thirty-five hundred square feet of house, and so far he'd hosted more birds in it than people.

It was time for that to change. Jet inhaled a deep breath and picked up his phone.

CLARA'S PHONE BUZZED on the table. She set down the files she was cleaning out and saw an unfamiliar number on the Love, Oregon line, so likely a new client.

"Hello. Love, Oregon."

"Hi, Clara," the voice said, then paused a moment when Clara didn't respond immediately. "This is Jet…Broughman."

"Jet!" she said, so much more enthusiastically than she wished. "Hi, this is Clara. Which you know. Because you called me." Clara began to beat her head against the wall as quietly as possible. "Hi."

"Hi." Jet laughed, making her a little more comfortable.

"What's up?"

"Well, I was calling to ask for your help."

"Absolutely." Clara nodded vigorously. *Because he can hear me nod?*

"I thought you could help me host a party.

For the guys who are helping out with the cabin. And their families. Maybe even the whole team, and anyone who is an Eagle football fan. We could have it here, in my home."

Was he kidding? Had Hunter put him up to this?

"I…I have a big home." He was speaking uncertainly now, and Clara knew no one had put him up to this. "And a really great driveway."

"A great driveway?"

She thought she could hear a faint thump, as though Jet was hitting his own head against the wall.

"Every party needs a great driveway," she said.

"What I meant to say—" Jet's laughter warmed her "—is that I have a big house and plenty of space to park, and I never have anyone over. I should do something for the guys, but I've never hosted a party before. Could you help me?"

Clara dropped into a chair. He was serious. "This is the sweetest thing ever."

"I-I was thinking…" Jet began.

She spoke quickly to remove any awkwardness. "It's a great idea. I love it." She thought for a moment. Jet had done so much for young people in Outcrop in the short time he'd been back. What was driving him? Tentatively, she said, "You take good care of your players."

"It's the least I can do." Jet was quiet on the other end of the line for a moment, then he said, "Clara, do you realize how much your parents did for kids like me?"

"I know they helped a lot of people. But, no," she admitted. "I was pretty unaware at the time."

Jet cleared his throat. "Most kids who grow up like I did wind up exactly where they started. But your parents saw greater possibilities in me. They made me feel like someone who could succeed. Like somebody who mattered."

Clara felt tears building behind her eyes. She'd known her parents were good teachers, but she had no idea of the effect they'd had on their students.

"Coach Kessler taught me the meaning of giving to a cause larger than myself. Being on that team was more than playing football, it was about giving your best for others, even when the odds felt impossible. I took that lesson with me to college and into the business world, and now it's time to pay it back."

Clara pulled in a breath against the emotion rising in her.

"I owe this community a lot, way more than a party. But it's a good place to start." Jet's tone changed, humor came creeping back into his voice. "And of all my friends, you seem like the most likely to know how to throw a shindig."

Clara smiled against the lump in her throat. "I'm honored with the accolade. Thank you for asking. I love parties. I would love to help."

"That's what I was hoping." She heard relief flood Jet's voice. "I have a grill."

"And a driveway," Clara teased. "What more does a party need?"

"Just people."

With those words everything clicked. Jet had returned from the big city and needed to give back to a community he loved. Why hadn't she seen it before?

"Jet, this is awesome. It's going to be super fun. I'm so glad you asked so I can finally pay you back. I'm in your debt for helping with the trail ride and agreeing to go to Smith Rock. Right now, you are better than my brothers when it comes to helping out with my business."

Jet's low voice set off a steady hum that resonated through her body. "There's no need to pay me back. It feels good to watch people fall in love and see them move forward in their lives. It feels good…"

"What?"

He paused, then said, "You have a cool business. I like helping out."

Clara's heart beat strong in her chest. Jet understood and appreciated her work. "I'll like helping you out, too. Plus, I've never seen your real house, and I hear you have a great driveway."

He laughed. "Yeah. We'll get most of it catered. And I can grill," Jet offered.

Men and their passion for meat over an open flame.

"That would be great. But I don't want you to get stuck cooking for the whole party. You'll want to talk to people."

"Oh, heck no," he said. Clara burst out laughing at his response. "I want to have people over. I don't want to *talk* to anybody."

She giggled harder; tears were starting to roll. "Jet, you are a complicated man."

"I'm not complicated." He sounded more serious. "I'm just not like Michael or you." He paused, then finished his thought. "I'm shy. Until you get to know me. And then I can't shut up, which you've probably figured out by now."

Clara laughed again.

"I'm trying to put together the life I always wanted, but I'm probably going to have to host five or six parties before I actually start talking to anyone."

Clara bit her lip. "What kind of life do you want?"

Jet didn't speak for a moment. Clara was afraid she'd misread his signals and gone too far. But she let the silence hang.

"What everyone wants," he said. "A family, financial security, emus who stay in their appointed pasture."

"The American dream."

After setting a date and agreeing that Eighty Local was the only caterer either of them were ever likely to call, Clara forced herself to end the conversation. She bid Jet goodbye with what she hoped was an appropriate expression of enthusiasm due when a gorgeous man asks you to host a party with him.

Then she started dancing. Not a demure skip of joy but deeply funky moves of bliss. She cranked up the music. Every dance class routine she'd ever learned came popping out of her cerebellum, and when those ran out, she switched to kickboxing.

Her canon of choreography exhausted, Clara walked to the west window and stared out at the sun as it set. Her heart was definitely fluttering, and it wasn't just the cardio.

But she couldn't rush in with Jet. She suspected she was right when she told him he would fall in love once and hard. There was absolutely no guarantee she was that woman. While he'd asked her to help host a party, he hadn't actually asked her out. She still didn't know how *she'd* react if he did.

What would she say if this happened to one of her clients? She'd probably call the request to cohost a party *a strong indicator of interest.*

Okay, one more shimmy!

Clara glanced at her computer, then at the pile of folders she should be going through. She looked back at the computer.

One quick scan of their compatibility wouldn't hurt.

Clara dropped into the chair at her desk and opened up her compatibility program and set to work. Ninety-four percent.

Then she ran their astrological signs, despite the fact that she'd never believed in astrology. Ninety-seven percent match.

Maybe there was something to star signs?

A pinging sound intruded on Clara's thoughts. She was humming so deeply, the sound confused her. Eyes blurry, she turned from her computer to see her phone flashing. She pounced.

Six texts from Piper, the last one demanding, You gonna let me in on this?

Clara switched over to the Zoom application on her laptop.

"Hey!" she said as Piper answered her call.

"What is going on?" Her sister had her hair wrapped up in a towel and was wearing a robe.

Clara folded her arms on the desk and sighed as she dropped her chin on her forearms. She could feel the goofy grin spilling across her face.

"Someone's smitten," Piper said.

Clara propped her head up with one hand, feeling, and no doubt looking, a little drunk. "Jet Broughman is the sweetest, funnest—"

"Hottest," Piper interrupted.

"Most adorable…" Clara filled her lungs with air as her addled brain searched for more adjectives. "Am I too old to use the word *dreamy*?"

"The word was used to describe a seventy-year-old client of mine last week. I think you're good."

"Oh, Piper. He's so—"

"Sweet, fun, hot, adorable and dreamy?"

"Yeah." Clara sighed.

"You do remember the last time you felt this way about Jet?"

Clara straightened. "This is different."

"Well, what happened that's made you so loopy?"

She launched into a long story about OHTAF, an old worn cowboy hat, sharing a phone call to Kenya and a nice but empty driveway. Piper's reaction was all interested noises and probing questions. It wasn't until Clara admitted that she'd run their astrological signs for compatibility that Piper interrupted her.

"This is serious."

Clara sat up, shaking a bit of her Jet-induced delirium off. *Serious.*

"You ready for this?" Piper asked.

Clara switched her focus from Piper's image on the computer screen to her little cottage. Crickets chirped outside in the evening air. Her home was tidy and perfectly organized for one person. Was she ready? She'd come so far in creating a life where she wasn't hampered by her anxiety. Falling in love could be messy.

And then, what if they got married? Clara's heart danced at the thought, then tripped on its ventricles and fell flat. She intended to marry someday, but there were absolutely no guarantees. Then children? Kids had always been a far-off proposition. She wanted them, for sure. But she need only look at her four siblings to know that kids were unpredictable, and parenting was pretty much the messiest job out there.

Clara shook her head and refocused on the screen.

"Nope!" she said cheerfully. "But help me figure out what to wear while I get ready."

CHAPTER FOURTEEN

Pink rays hit the golden rock formation, illuminating Smith Rock at dawn. Geese honked in the cool morning air. Jet shrugged out of the new Outcrop Football sweatshirt. It couldn't be more than fifty degrees yet, but he was already warm.

"I'm probably going to die today," Michael said cheerfully, joining him at the canyon's rim. He was dressed in brand-new adventurer's clothing. Everything was sweat-wicking, off-the-charts SPF and covered with more pockets than a man could possibly use.

"Clara won't let you die," Jet told him. "It would be bad for business."

"Good point. Still—"

"You'll be fine." Jet glanced around. He checked his phone. They were early. "Besides, I told Clara I'd come specifically because I want to see you up on a rope. I'll make sure you don't fall."

"You'd better." Michael began, then stopped and studied Jet.

His friend had always been smarter than he was.

"You've been hanging out with Clara?"

Jet tried to shrug casually, but he wasn't very good at it. "She… Well…"

"Hello!" He heard Clara's voice. He and Michael turned to see Clara exit a rented van, followed by a number of her clients.

"You've got some explaining to do," Michael told him. Jet nodded, repressing a smile.

"Gather up, everybody!" Clara called.

"Gather up," Jet muttered to Michael, gesturing.

"You gather up," Michael shot back with a grin.

Clara was somehow even more beautiful than she'd been two days ago. It took considerable effort, but Jet forced himself to examine the clients she'd brought. The group was smaller than the trail-riding party. Mostly fifty and younger, they appeared to range from incredibly fit to moderately active. Clara was chirping out instructions. They would hike down into the canyon, then around Smith Rock to Waterfall Slab, where there were climbs ranging from 5.4, very easy, to 5.11, significantly more difficult.

"Welcome to Smith, everybody," she said. "My friend Jet will help us out, setting ropes and belaying."

Jet nodded in response.

"Belaying? That's when someone holds onto the rope attached to my harness and keeps me from falling, right?" Michael asked.

"Yep." Jet clapped Michael on the shoulder, reminding him, "No one's going to get hurt today."

Michael rolled his eyes as though that were debatable. A woman in the group giggled at his antics. Michael smiled back at her.

"My brothers are already down at the slab, getting ready for you. Lorna and Ryan are amazing climbers, so please don't hesitate to ask them for help. Wendi, you've done some climbing, too, right?" Clara asked a woman in her early thirties.

"Some," Wendi answered.

"Great. Michael, Joanna, Helen, Greg, Maddy and Howell, we won't let you fall. I promise." The group laughed at her perception of their fear. "Ryan, Wendi, why don't you two lead the way?"

Jet shouldered his pack and fell in next to Clara at the back of the group. She looked great. Form-fitting climbing pants, athletic tank top, light sweatshirt and a ball cap were practical for the situation. Pearl earrings and her gold necklace were a reminder that she was still Clara, the girl who made a living out of romance.

"So what's the plan? How will all your clients help out on this trip?"

Clara looked up at him with a gleam in her eye. "Obviously Lorna and Ryan will be showing off their skills, but their age difference is enough that I hope it's clear they're not a pair. Wendi is so athletic, all she needs to do is be herself. As Joanna and Howell are both teachers, I'm assuming they will be encouraging as everyone tries their best. Greg will be able to tell us about any wildlife we see and hopefully will finish falling in love with Helen. And Michael will be on hand in case anyone gets a scratch. Speaking of which, if no one is injured, would you be willing to ask him about that cut on your knuckle, loudly, in front of either Joanna or Maddy?"

Jet glanced down at his hands. They were covered with nicks and cuts from struggling with the fencing.

"You've got it all planned out, don't you?"

"I do." She grinned up at him. "And you haven't even asked me about the adrenaline, yet."

"Adrenaline?"

"Right. It's a powerful love chemical."

Jet instinctively reached out to take Clara's arm as she slowed down around a steep, tight turn in the trail.

"More love chemicals?"

"Totally. Chemicals are not the be-all and end-all of love, but they seriously help. Adrenaline is one of my favorites. It's like a litmus test for love."

"How so?"

"Adrenaline is what makes you feel like anything is possible when you fall in love. Like you can fly. You know the feeling?"

"No," Jet lied. In truth, he could probably launch off the canyon's side at any moment and join the eagles circling overhead.

"Well, it happens. And natural adrenaline will heighten any emotion you are already feeling. Think of it this way. You and I like each other, right?"

Jet sputtered. "Y-yeah."

"So by exerting energy, hiking together, we are releasing adrenaline. Studies show that by the end of this hike, we will like each other more because of the power of adrenaline. You know how sports teams are always really bonded with each other, or how after dancing with someone you feel more strongly about them? That's because of adrenaline."

"Cool."

"But if you don't like someone, you will like them even less after exerting yourself."

Jet stopped walking. A breeze rose up from the Crooked River, cooling the canyon hike for a moment.

"Seriously?"

"Yep."

"I think that's happened to me."

"It happens to everyone, all the time."

"I'd been on a couple of dates with a woman, then I asked her to go on a bike ride."

"And?"

"A mile into it I knew I would never call her again."

"Exactly! So on this date, people will have a greater sense of who in this party they want to get serious about and who they don't. Isn't it fun?"

Jet allowed himself to appreciate just how good she looked in a ball cap. Could he blame that on chemicals? "It's brilliant."

The trail to the back of Smith Rock ran along the river, rising and falling just enough to elevate everyone's heart rate. It was also narrow: no more than two people could walk abreast. As the group hiked, Jet watched people settle in next to those they were drawn to. By the time they reached Waterfall Slab, a few people had paired up already. Including Michael.

As Jet helped people check their climbing harnesses and taught them to tie knots, he kept an eye out for his friend. He was still chatting with the same woman.

"Who is Michael talking to?" Jet asked Clara as he pulled his harness out of his pack.

"That's Joanna," she said, eyes bright. "You saw a picture of her at my house the other day."

Michael grew confident as Joanna kept her focus on him. He relaxed.

"She's a third-grade teacher." Clara's fingers crossed tightly as she watched them.

"Can you help me with this knot?" an athletic woman asked Jet.

"Sure," he replied, checking to see if Clara noticed his skills in teaching people how to tie into their harnesses. "You've got it," he said encouragingly to the woman.

"Thanks." Her smile was bright and sincere. Jet wondered who Clara was hoping to set her up with.

"I'm going up!" Michael proclaimed.

"I've got your belay," Jet said.

Joanna came to stand next to them, her deep blue eyes wide. "Good luck."

Clara spoke to the teacher. "Joanna, do you

have a phone on you? Someone needs to take a picture of Michael so he can show his patients."

"Great idea!" Joanna said.

Jet shot Clara a look. Michael looked ridiculous in his outdoor ensemble and climbing helmet perched on his head. Why would he want a picture?

Clara raised a brow, and Jet knew she had her reasons.

"Okay, buddy, go get it," Jet said.

Michael slowly and carefully started climbing. Joanna breathed in sharply as he got ten feet off the ground.

"This is horrifying!" Michael cried in his cheerful voice. "I am never, ever doing this again."

"You're doing great, man!"

And he was. Jet had always been impressed by Michael's ability to jump into any activity and make the best of it. He hacked his way through the route with no grace but obvious determination and courage.

"Jet?" A woman's voice intruded on his attention. Jet noticed the athletic woman standing beside him again. "Can you give me a belay?"

"Sure. Just gotta get my old friend through this."

"Wendi, can you help Ryan find this route?

I think it's up the trail," Clara said, handing Wendi a guidebook and pointing out the route.

"Okay," Wendi replied, then she said to Jet, "I'll be right back."

Jet nodded, but his attention was on Michael. "You got it, man!"

"I'm going to pass out!" Michael said, which set Joanna giggling.

Jet turned to her. "You're next."

Michael slapped the anchor at the top of the route, fifty feet off the ground. "Woo-hoo! I did it."

"Nice!" Clara called out.

"Now, get me out of here."

Jet lowered his friend. Michael's trembling fingers and the rush of blood to his face had nothing to do with the exertion of the climb.

"You did it," Joanna cried.

Michael, still tangled in his rope, reached out for Joanna. Without a pause she hugged him, and the two of them were exclaiming over the climb. Jet took a step back, then another and stood next to Clara.

"Is that—?" Jet gestured to Michael. He could feel the power of the connection his friend had with this woman.

Clara nodded, a smile spreading across her face. "I think this is it."

Jet's throat constricted. He felt Clara's hand come to rest on his back.

"She is absolutely wonderful," Clara said. "I've been working with her since January. I thought she might be good for Michael, but I had no idea it would happen so quickly."

"This is powerful and—" Jet searched for the word Clara had used at OHTAF "—satisfying, right?"

Clara laughed. "Yes, Smith Rock, the Crooked River, people falling in love—" she glanced up at him "—super satisfying. Tell me you can't feel the hum right now."

Jet felt a lot of things, and *hum* was as good a word as any.

"Michael has wanted this for so long. You made what had been so hard for him easy." He gazed at Clara. Lots of chemicals involved. "Thank you."

"High five for love!" Clara said, holding up her hands.

Jet slapped his palms against hers, then let his fingers curl around her soft hands for a brief moment. Her pupils darkened. She bit the edge of her lip, then smiled up at him.

"High five for love."

SHE HAD KNOCKED this one out of the park.

Try as she might to stuff her smile back down, Clara couldn't help but grin. Michael was paired up with a wonderful woman. Jet got to watch it happen with her. And not that she had a ton of experience with such things, but that had to be the most romantic high five ever performed.

Predictably, Joanna had taken pictures of Michael on her phone, and once she shared them with Michael, he would have her number. Clara caught snippets of their conversation: children they worked with, favorite films, area restaurants. When Joanna saw a chipmunk, the two of them could barely contain themselves. Clara hoped they'd wait at least a week before either one proposed.

Now Jet belayed Joanna. She was not as brave a climber as Michael and took a fair bit of encouragement. Jet and Michael were more than willing to give it. Clara knew that in Joanna's mind she was achieving something monumental.

"Off to your right, can you see the pocket in the rock?" Jet called out to her. He had been giving her steady instructions for some time. Clara grinned at him. This climb was literally easier than a stepladder, but there were always a few people who needed talking up. He winked at

Clara. Her body lit up like Main Street during the local business fair.

"Hey." Wendi appeared at Jet's side. "I'm back."

"Okay." He smiled at her. "Your turn next."

Clara felt her grin snap off. Beautiful and confident, Wendi was understandably picky. She was a lawyer from Bend and disinclined to settle. And she kept circling back to Jet.

Jet, Clara had realized, was largely oblivious to his hotness. That, combined with his sweet streak, made him an easy target. Wendi had her sights on him.

Clara turned from the group and looked out over the Crooked River. Had it only been two days ago they'd snuggled up together at OHTAF, talking to her parents? She closed her eyes and went back to that moment, feeling Jet's warmth, his masculine scent wrapped around her.

"Clara?" Wendi called.

Clara turned around to see that Jet had lowered Joanna to the ground and was fist-bumping her. Wendi coiled up a rope and grabbed Jet's climbing shoes.

"Jet and I are going to head around the corner to give Kunza a try," Wendi said.

"Great." Clara forced a smile.

"Let me know if you need me to get this

scrape checked out," Jet said, pointing to the cut on his knuckle. Clara warmed.

"I think we're good." She nodded to where Michael and Joanna sat together talking.

"You're amazing," Jet said.

"Isn't she?" Wendi said, heading off toward the next climb. Jet followed.

Clara watched the two of them go. As they rounded a corner, Wendi looked back and gave Clara a huge grin and a thumbs-up. Clara's heart slumped against her rib cage, and she pouted.

But there was work to do—keeping people moving, encouraging them to climb, getting everyone fed. None of that stopped the buzzing irritation she felt. Clara had invited Wendi to meet Ryan, a handsome, fun-loving entrepreneur with whom she was a strong match. Instead, Ryan was busy helping Howell, a fifty-six-year-old English teacher and emerging novelist. The two men were having a great time, but she wasn't here to help people make friends. Wendi hadn't understood, or was deliberately ignoring, Clara's remarks about Jet being a friend who was here to help. Meanwhile, Hunter and Bowman, who were supposed to be helping, were attempting some ridiculous climb neither of them could even get started on.

Clara took three deep breaths, then scampered over rocks scanning the group for good news. Michael and Joanna sat together, overlooking the Crooked River, deep in conversation. Her brothers had set up the ropes for everyone, and watching Jet joke with them definitely set her humming. Clara tried to focus on these good things.

"What route is this?"

Clara looked up at the sound of Jet's voice.

"Sabotage," Hunter said. "Aptly named."

"You get it yet?" Jet asked.

"Nah," said Bowman. "The start is the crux. My elbow is still jacked from Yosemite."

"Can I try?" Wendi asked.

Clara didn't like that idea at all. Wendi would have to climb for at least sixteen feet before she could attach her rope to a bolt for protection, and the start moves looked impossible.

"Ryan?" Clara called. "Can you give Wendi a spot? I don't want any twisted ankles."

"I can spot her," Hunter said.

Clara gave her brother a look, attempting to remind him that they were here to help these people fall in love. Unless he was willing to marry Wendi, he needed to get out of the way and make room for Ryan.

The speed with which Hunter hopped back suggested he got the message.

"I think it's the matchmaker's turn to get on the wall, don't you?" Jet asked, leveling a heart-stopping grin at Clara.

Clara felt herself go all warm and fuzzy as she met Jet's eyes. Then his words hit her. *Get on the wall.*

Clara didn't climb outdoors. In a gym, with nicely padded floors and employees who checked every piece of equipment daily, sure, Clara loved climbing. Her aversion to outdoor climbing was irrational, but she didn't have to face that particular fear right now. Or ever.

"I'm working today." She gestured to the couples all around her.

"One climb. I've got a rope up on a 5.9 here." In a normal setting his smile and attention would have made her giddy. Why couldn't they be at Eighty Local right now and the challenge something more like the consumption of a Burma Mile burger? Jet looked around at the party. "Don't you all want to see Clara climb?"

The blood was pounding so heavily in her head she couldn't really hear the cheer that rose up from her clients. Something twisted in her gut. Smith Rock, the vegetation surrounding it and even Jet began to blur.

Suddenly, Jet was much closer. His head bent down toward her ear. "I'm sorry," he said. "I didn't think—"

"I'll be okay."

"Buzzing?"

"Yes." She gave him a small smile. "Loudly."

"I'm such an idiot."

Clara laid a hand on his arm, and Jet stopped speaking. She allowed herself to lean in toward him. His scent wrapped around her like a hug.

"I can get you out of this," Jet said, taking her hand in his, making her hand very, very happy. "I'll say your harness is too big, or we can make up an old football injury."

Clara laughed. Jet was smiling at her with deep concern in his eyes. Somehow both of her hands were in his, and she'd managed to move even closer to him. Then she glanced at the rock. She felt, for the first time in a long time, that she could do anything.

She felt like she could fly.

"You're right," she said. "I've asked everyone else to do this. I can get up there myself."

"I shouldn't have brought it up. I just thought it would be fun to give you a belay."

Clara met his gaze. "It's okay. I'm here, my brothers are here, you're here. This is a good time to try. But realize I'm going to have a massive adrenaline release up there. I'm going to really like you when I get finished."

"Or hate me," Jet said.

"I am never going to hate you, Jet."

He picked up the end of the rope and held it out to her. Clara tied into her harness.

"I sure hope not." He gave her knot a tug, examined his belay device, then stepped back. "Ready?"

Clara looked up at the route. She laid her hands on the rock and felt strong. She smiled over her shoulder at Jet. He grinned right back at her.

Wow.

"Climbing," Clara said.

"Climb on."

She curled her right hand around a pocket in the rock. Tightening her abdominal muscles she swung her foot up, then balanced as she reached for the next hold. The flow of the climb felt easy, what with all the adrenaline moving through her. Clara placed her toes on a nubbin of rock and pushed up.

"Whoa! Clara, Clar, hold back there," Bowman shouted. Clara glanced down at him, confused.

"What?"

Her brother gestured for her to climb back down a few feet. "Did you check your knot?"

Clara glanced down at the knot she'd tied into her harness. She'd felt so good in Jet's protective gaze that she hadn't even thought about it.

"I checked it," Jet said.

Bowman shook his head, mock disappointed. "You're supposed to check your own equipment. Every. Single. Time." He reached up and turned her knot so she could examine it from both sides, then tugged at it. "Knot looks good, harness fits correctly. You're good. Climb on."

Clara scanned the route, then glanced back at Jet. The feeling of freedom and security washed over her again. Anything felt possible when he looked at her like that.

"AND THEN SHE says she always wanted a Newfoundland puppy. Can you believe it?" Michael leaned back against the passenger seat in the truck. "She is so awesome."

Jet nodded, again. He hadn't done much but nod and agree as Michael talked nonstop about Joanna on their drive back to Outcrop.

After a three-second break in his Joanna monologue to point out a field of llamas, Michael said, "And she sounds like such a good teacher, the way she talked about her students. I can't believe how perfect she is."

"I'm happy for you," Jet said, again.

"Clara Wallace is a genius."

Jet looked out the window at the earth and rock racing by. "She is."

That snapped Michael out of his Joanna-induced haze.

"You like her."

Jet shrugged, unable to press his lips together hard enough to keep from grinning.

"Dude! You have a crush on my matchmaker."

Jet tried to glare at Michael, but when his eyes met his friend's he burst out laughing.

"She is…" Jet let out a breath and shook his head. "She is so sweet."

"And cute," Michael egged him on.

"So cute. Have you ever seen anybody so cute?" Jet shook his head. "I don't know how this happened. But yes, like the rest of the world, I am smitten with Clara Wallace."

"You've been hanging out?"

"I guess. Mostly I've been helping her with things." Jet rubbed his right shoulder. "I haven't actually asked her out."

"Do it."

"I don't know."

"What do you have to lose?" Michael asked, in his typical, the-glass-is-always-full, grass-is-green-everywhere type of manner.

Jet let the question sit. What did he have to lose? *Her company. My pride. Friendship with her family. My deal to supply Eighty Local with beef.* So much was at stake. But what if he didn't ask her out? Jet swallowed, trying to clamp down on the mix of fear and exhilaration rising through him.

"She says everyone falls a little bit in love with her," Jet said. "You can see it happen. Even you were all starry-eyed when you met her."

"Sure, but I used to fall in love with everyone. Now that I've learned about commonalities, expectations and attraction, the three pillars of relationships, I have nothing but respect for her."

"Well, I don't know what you're talking about, so maybe I should learn it and I'll stop feeling this way."

"Jet, I've known you for a long time. You light up around Clara. You're more relaxed and fun when she's around. She sparkles at you."

"She sparkles all the time."

"She likes you. It's obvious. Go for it."

Jet placed a hand over his chest, hoping to steady his heartbeat. Clara did brighten when she saw him, but then she was happy to see everyone. She'd always been that way.

"I did…I did ask her to help me host a party."

"You?" Michael nearly choked on the word. "You're throwing a party?"

"Yes, I am throwing a party. How's that for having it bad? And you'd better show up."

Something in the console buzzed. Both men reached for their phones. Michael's lit up with a text, and Jet found himself unreasonably disappointed. Which was stupid. Any text he might receive would just be from his old boss Ken, trying to get him to move back to Seattle.

"It's from Joanna!" Michael said, happily punching away at the screen. "She sent the picture and said today was really fun." Michael studied the text as though it was an abnormal artery in a two-year-old's heart. "What should I write back?"

Jet did his best to help his friend formulate a response, but he needed to come up with a response of his own. Clara had been so brave that afternoon and risen to his challenge despite her fear. Now it was his turn to be brave and risk falling himself.

CHAPTER FIFTEEN

CLARA WAS LATE for her second first-meet that month, and just like last time, it was because she was too wrapped up in Jet. She parked her bicycle in front of Eighty Local and pushed her kickstand into place, pulling her leather notebook out of the basket. She'd just spent half an hour on the phone with Wendi, trying to explain that Jet was only on the climbing trip to help, not to meet anyone.

Then Wendi, an excellent lawyer, had pleaded her case by explaining what a great guy Jet was, specifically contrasting Jet's reaction to Clara's failure to check her knot to that of Hunter and Bowman.

Clara swallowed hard, and another wave of fear flowed through her.

What if her knot hadn't been tied correctly yesterday?

She steadied herself on the wall of Eighty Local. She'd been stupid not to check her own knot, but it wasn't that big a deal. Jet had checked it. Instinctively she must have known that Jet checked it.

But she should have checked it herself. She forgot. She forgot because she was humming in a fog of love chemicals that apparently no one else, least of all Wendi, had noticed.

At the time she was so wound up in Jet it didn't even faze her. She kept climbing and reached the top, and all of her clients had gathered around, cheering. Climbing outside was a pretty big achievement for her, and under Jet's gaze it wasn't hard to face her fear. But the minute her feet touched solid ground again, Hunter and Bowman would not stop teasing her about forgetting to check her knot. At one point Jet butted in, reminding her brothers that he'd checked it.

Bowman had slapped him on the back, saying, "We know you did. You weren't going to let her fall." Then he and Hunter cracked up again.

Clara glared at her brother's restaurant. What if the knot hadn't been secure? What if she'd forgotten to tie in entirely?

She closed her eyes as she imagined the rope slipping loose. She'd have scrambled to hold onto the rock, slipped, fallen. Piper would be devastated if Clara hurt herself climbing. It could happen. Really good, responsible climbers got distracted and didn't tie in correctly. Clara's stomach churned, she felt dizzy, like the world kept spinning as she came to a stop, frozen in her fear.

Was this what falling in love was going to do to her? Make her reckless and irresponsible?

"Clara?"

She looked up to see her brother poking his head out the front door.

"You okay?" He didn't wait for her response, just came out and wrapped her in a hug. "Want me to send your client home?"

"No." Clara straightened her shoulders and pulled in a breath. "I'm fine."

"Are you still upset about yesterday?" he asked.

"I'm fine," she snapped.

There was no sense in being angry at Hunter. He and Bowman seemed to think failing to check her knot was some kind of breakthrough for her. There was less sense in being angry at Wendi. She'd come climbing with the belief that Clara would have a few potential men for her, and she'd picked the one she liked the best.

The tough, sweet, good-looking rancher guy.

No, the only person she had to be angry with was herself.

Wendi had been so excited when they talked on the phone, making Clara promise to tell Jet she was interested and give him her number. She had half a mind to bury the request. Would Wendi even know?

But that would be lying. On the long list of rules Clara followed to keep her anxiety in check, a prohibition against lying was near the top.

Had Jet said something to Wendi to make her think he was interested? They'd been off by themselves, working on a climb that Clara couldn't imagine completing in her dreams.

She didn't like this feeling, out of control and unsure. She'd never felt like this: stressed out that a guy liked her, or didn't like her, or did and would inspire her to completely lose control of herself. The buzzing in her mind increased, drowning out the sounds of the small town. She should have gone for a run. *But no, I'm on a streak of bad decision-making. May as well ignore the signals and push through with work.*

"Sis, I'm sorry we were teasing you yesterday. It was honestly cool to see you so relaxed while you were climbing," Hunter said gently. "Did something else happen?"

"No, the group date was fantastic, a total home run."

Unless you count picky, pushy clients taking a liking to Jet.

Clara squared her shoulders and headed to the door.

Hunter's brow furrowed. "Why don't you take the day off? Go for a run."

"I'm good," she said. "There's nothing I like better than matching people up. Nothing."

"Not even sweet potato fries?" he asked.

Clara hesitated. She *was* still annoyed at Hunter from the day before, but sweet potato fries would go a long way in helping her find the grace to forgive him.

"I guess I'm willing to help you out by doing quality control on your fries."

Hunter grinned and held the door for her.

She popped open her notebook and looked over the information on her new client. A man in his late thirties, athletic, part-time rancher, gourmet cook, never married. He'd forgotten to fill in some of the information, like his birth date, and name, but that wasn't unusual. People got nervous taking this first step. Clara pulled up her best attitude. She loved helping people find love, and she was heading in to do just that.

The bells on the front door rang cheerfully, and Clara felt better being in her brother's establishment.

"He's in the booth," Hunter said, gesturing

to Clara's regular spot. Clara headed over with purpose.

There she came face-to-face with a man who was fifty if he was a day, with a ratty Outcrop Football sweatshirt covering an athletic-ish frame and a wide grin.

"Coach Kessler?"

"I'm ready," he said.

"Late thirties?" Clara accused.

"I feel like I'm in my twenties!"

"Coach, we celebrated your fiftieth birthday several years ago."

"So I split the difference."

"Gourmet cook?"

"Gourmet cook, gourmet eater, same thing."

Clara dropped her leather notebook on the table and sank into the booth.

Hunter butted in from across the counter. "I told you it wouldn't work, Coach."

"But I want to find love," he said.

Clara started to close her notebook. Then her favorite history teacher leaned back in the booth and sighed. She reopened her notebook.

"Of course you do," Clara said. "And I've actually been constructing a plan to—"

"That's how this works, right? I hire you, and you help me fall in love?"

"It's a little more complicated than that."

"Bring it on!" Coach said. "I'm ready."

Clara pulled in a deep breath as the train wreck that was this day lost several more cars in a screeching fury. She hadn't felt this close to a panic attack in years, not even when she was fifty feet up a cliff at Smith Rock the day before.

Now she had to embark on an incredibly awkward conversation with a former teacher she respected and adored. She'd spent considerable time helping Christy get ready to meet a nice, honest man, and that nice, honest man was now reinventing himself to get a date?

Not on her watch.

Clara refocused on Coach. "For starters, you don't pay me anything."

"Now, wait a minute—"

"No," Clara sat up and pointed a finger at Coach Kessler. "Teachers don't pay. Love, Oregon policy. Second, you have to be completely honest about who you are."

"Can't you spice me up a bit?"

"You are a kind, sincere man, a fun and supportive teacher and coach. That's plenty spicy."

Coach snorted and looked out the window.

"How's your plan going?" Hunter leaned across the counter, polishing a glass with a flour-sack towel. "The one to set him up with Christy Jones."

Coach sat up with enough speed to upset his water glass. "Can you do it?"

Clara closed her eyes. "You want to date Christy Jones?"

"Clara, you've gotta help me," Coach begged. "I walked into her store three times last week."

"Okay." Clara tucked her hair behind her ears. "That's good. What did you talk about?"

Coach slumped back in the booth. "I couldn't think of anything to say."

"You walked into her store three times and said nothing?"

He nodded.

"Did you buy anything?"

He nodded again.

"What did you buy?"

"I don't know. I wasn't paying attention. She's very beautiful."

Clara rested her forehead against her fingers. "It's a women's clothing store. You walked in and silently bought women's clothes?"

"I know. It's hopeless. Do you want some clothes? They're still in my truck."

Clara must have let out the breath she'd been holding, because Coach asked, "That bad, huh?"

"You're not starting off on a strong foot," she admitted.

"But you can do it? People say you're a miracle worker."

Clara studied her former history teacher. "Don't think of me as a miracle worker. Think of me as a coach. In order to get the best out of my clients, they have to start by being honest with themselves."

"I am honest. I honestly have no chance with her. Unless we make me look better than I am."

"Play that scenario out to the end. I tell Christy she's meeting a thirty-eight-year-old gourmet cook. Then you show up and try to pretend to be something you're not for two hours? There are zero chances of that working."

He nodded, looking more defeated than she'd ever seen him, and that included a horrible night at the district semifinals in 2016. She had to help him, no matter what was going on in her personal life. Clara felt calmer as she pulled her focus from Jet to an area in which she knew what she was doing.

"Tell you what. Give me a couple of days to come up with a plan. I'll give you some coaching on how to ask her out and what to do once you're on a date. I know from a little research of my own that she wants to meet more people in the community, and she's ready to date. I can't think of a better person to connect her with than you."

"Even after the clothes?"

"I refuse to shy away from the challenge."

"Deal." Coach Kessler shook her hand. Clara stood as he kept speaking. "You're going to have to work some of your magic, though."

"I don't have any magic. I do, however, have a series of forms I want you to fill out." Clara plucked a dating plan out of her folder and slid it across the table.

"Worksheets?"

"Serves you right. You're lucky I'm not making you give a class presentation. Please have this finished by Wednesday." Clara stood and picked up her leather binder. "I'll do my best to help you with Christy."

"Your fries are up," Hunter said, reappearing at the table with a loaded basket.

Clara glanced at her phone, then back at the fries. She needed to call Jet and tell him about Wendi. Get it over with. The fries would taste a lot better once this task was finished.

"Coach, you start in on the fries. I need to make a quick phone call. Hunter, do you mind if I head out back?"

"Sure. I'll take care of your client here."

Clara rolled her eyes.

She walked slowly through the kitchen. Wait-staff and a second cook would come on for the dinner rush, but this afternoon Hunter held down the fort on his own. After she called Jet, she'd ask Hunter if she could pull espresso, if only to have something familiar to focus on.

Clara kept walking, past the storeroom and into the back parking lot. She had no idea how Jet would react to Wendi's request for his number. Her brothers were the ones warning her not to set them up with her clients, not Jet. On the other hand, that was before OHTAF and before he had called and asked her to host a party with him. An uncomfortable tension formed in her chest.

Why didn't I sort this out with sticky notes before I left the house?

She liked Jet, a lot. She knew enough about the business of love to understand that she was falling for him. What she didn't know was if she could handle it. She'd hurt him the last time. Would she do the same thing again? Was it better to let him explore the possibility of Wendi, rather than take a chance on her?

She loved their growing friendship and couldn't stand the thought of losing that. But in her heart, she knew she really wanted more. Everything more.

And that was way more frightening than forgetting to double-check her knot.

Clara pushed open the back door and stepped into the bright afternoon sunshine. She was a professional. She would let Jet know about Wendi and let him decide what to do about it. Jet had done extraordinary things with his life and was certainly capable of pursuing the woman of his choice. She had no control over his feelings. All she could control were her actions in this situation. Clara pulled out her phone and started to scroll for Jet's number.

A crunch of gravel drew her attention. Jet's restored dirty truck came bumping into the back lot. Clara dropped her phone in her bag, her heart speeding up at the sound of the aging transmission system.

The truck came to a quick stop, and Jet jumped out. His grin met hers and he jogged toward her. Clara's heart pulsed against her rib cage.

"Hey." His eyes were bright, and his smile hit her so hard she nearly lost her balance.

"Hi. I was going to call you."

"Oh." He stopped, right in front of her. "I was hoping to see you." Clara felt her body respond to his, drawing her closer to him. "Thanks for having me along on Saturday. It was fun."

"Yeah, all the clients had a great time." Clara paused, waiting to see if Jet was going to mention Wendi.

"Especially Michael. The guy is hooked."

Clara nodded, her breath coming in short. "Michael and Joanna did great, and…then there was this other thing."

Jet smiled down at her, his gaze connecting with hers. Clara had seen that look before. He felt this, too. A soft breeze blew her hair across her cheek, bringing the smell of juniper with it. Warm sunshine fell around them.

Clara felt a twinge of trepidation. This was such a huge move. Was she really ready?

"What thing?" he asked.

She gazed at Jet, then bit her lip.

"Wendi was really into you," she said, testing the waters. "She asked me to give you her number."

Jet froze, his eyes searching her face. "Wendi?"

THE PARKING LOT started to spin. Jet took a step back to steady himself and get out of the reach of Clara's perfume.

"Wh-who is Wendi?"

"Wendi. From Smith Rock."

"Wendi." Jet focused on the gravel, trying to dampen down the roar of emotions kicking up inside of him. He glanced at Clara. She was so pretty. He tried to speak, stopped himself, then tried again. "You want to set me up with *Wendi*?"

"Well, no, but—"

"No?"

"Not exactly. Okay, here's the deal." Clara smiled cautiously. How many times had he told himself to be wary of that smile? "Wendi is really picky and looking for an exceptional man."

Clara dropped her hands and looked at Jet expectantly. This wasn't happening. This couldn't be happening.

"So I'd be doing you a favor if I called her?"

Clara's smile fell. She reached out like she was going to take his hand, then held back.

"No." Uncertainty flickered across her face. "No, Jet. You don't have to call anyone. She just asked me to give you her number. She assumed you were a client of mine, and she's so picky. I invited her there to meet Ryan, but…" Clara smiled again, dimples flashing. "She liked the sweet, tough, good-looking rancher guy."

Jet fought against the anger rising within him, but when he was able to move past it he was hardly able to stand the sadness that came rushing through. If Clara thought he was so sweet and good-looking, why didn't she want to date him?

The baffled feeling of rejection shot through him. All the times his mom promised she could take care of him, then waved as he drove away with another social worker a few months later. All the families who pledged forever, then sent him away saying it just wasn't the right time for them. Every time he got into a social worker's car, holding back the tears, the hurt, the anger. He'd always kept the emotions to himself. He never railed against those who rejected him, keeping the *Why?* deep, deep within him.

In his heart, he'd always known why. He didn't deserve to experience love and family like other people. He would never experience love and family.

Jet glanced down at Clara. He needed to walk away, right now. He needed to master his disappointment and save this friendship.

"I thought I should tell you," she said. Her fingers pressed against the pendants on her necklace, her other hand checking the clasp. She was nervous.

Nothing could have been more hurtful.

"Why?" The word came out much harsher than he intended. Clara stepped back. "Clara,

I don't want to call Wendi. I'm…I want to be with *you*."

Stress flickered across her face. He could almost hear the buzzing feeling she'd described. That's what he was to her, a source of stress and anxiety. He had to stop, just walk away. But the hurt he'd spent years damming up had broken free.

"I thought…" He could hear the pain in his own voice. "I thought we were falling for each other."

Color drained from her face, just like it had so many years ago when he'd asked her out. His heart went into free fall, taking any chance of joy with it.

"I don't know if I can do this," she said quietly. "I'm sorry."

"Sorry?"

"This is a big step for me…" She seemed to be grasping at any excuse. "I'm not ready—"

His control slipped. "I've never been ready for you. You just come into my life like this gorgeous wrecking ball and I stand around and watch while you demolish everything."

She laid a hand on his arm, unleashing hope even in the face of all the evidence that this was a hopeless situation. Her steady gaze begged him to settle down, to listen to her. Then she shuddered and pulled away, shattering any hope he had of handling this rejection well.

"What even was this?" He gestured between them. "We've been hanging out. You're helping with the cabin renovation."

"It's a great project. I want to help out."

He exhaled. This was happening. Clara was rejecting him, again. He worked his jaw to hold back the tears building behind his eyes. "Right. You're right. You were just helping out, supporting the local kids."

"Jet, I didn't mean—"

"Meanwhile I'm thinking the cabin would make a great office for a beautiful, talented matchmaker in town."

Tears welled up in the corners of her eyes. "You said we were friends."

"Friends," he echoed. Just friends. Nothing more than friends. How could he have been so stupid?

Everyone falls a little bit in love with me, she'd said.

And she was right. Beautiful, sweet, golden Clara. Of course everyone fell in love with her. He was no different.

As a friend, she was offering Jet what she considered to be the greatest gift she could give him. She wanted the same happiness for him that she wanted for Michael, for all her clients, for the whole world. She wanted him to fall in love, just not with her.

Jet tightened his jaw. He would not be at Clara's family dinners on Sunday afternoons. He would not exchange a smile with her across the room of a party they were hosting together. They would never laugh together as a newborn baby kept them awake all night long.

He'd done it again. Despite every warning sign, he'd let himself think he deserved the kind of happiness reserved for people with stable up-bringings. Clara had been clear from the start; he'd just been too stupid to listen.

She was speaking, something about needing time and talking again later, something about wanting to be ready. Jet didn't need to hear it. She'd rejected him. That's all he needed to know.

He took a few steps toward his truck. Clara was still talking, but nothing made it into his head. She would never understand this pain. Right now, he just needed to get away from her. But the hurt, lonely child within him couldn't resist a show of indifference in the face of rejection.

He pulled out his phone. "It doesn't matter," he said, speaking over her apology. "What's Wendi's number?"

CHAPTER SIXTEEN

"DUDE, WHAT HAPPENED?"

Jet looked up at the sound of Michael's voice. He glanced around, bleary-eyed. Chunks of firewood were strewn in every direction. It looked like he'd dumped a stack of juniper logs into a giant blender and flipped it on High without putting the lid on.

The axe fell at his feet, and Jet swayed. How long had he been out here?

"I've called you five times," Michael said, using his doctor voice.

"Aren't we meeting for lunch?"

"It's three o'clock."

Jet dropped onto the chopping block, sweat running down his face and back. Four days later, he was still angry, but it was hard to say who with. He'd seen nothing of Clara since he'd left her stammering some kind of apology in the parking lot of Eighty Local.

Since then, he'd received three short, businesslike texts about the upcoming party. Clara hadn't been near OHTAF or her brother's restaurant or any other place they might meet up.

Yeah. He'd ruined that friendship, and that meant he'd lose Hunter's business and any chance of connection with her family.

Michael sat on the other side of the block. "What's going on?"

Jet rubbed his face. The hollow feeling in his chest expanded.

Michael was smart enough to figure it out. "I'm sorry."

"She…" Jet could only manage one word before all the air washed out of his lungs. He reeled in his anger and the pain that surfaced beneath it. "She just wants to be friends. She tried to set me up with someone else. Someone named Wendi."

"She was trying to set you up?"

Holding back tears became physically painful, fast. The yard blurred again. Jet battled to get a breath.

"But she spent the whole day at Smith with you," Michael said. "She laughs at all your jokes, even the bad ones."

"It's called drawing focus. She had me do it on the trail ride. If she seems interested in me, it's a signal to other women that I'm interesting. It works."

Michael wore a kind, serious expression. The one he used with the parents of his patients, as every dream they had fell apart.

"You're going to get through this."

Jet stared at the back of his massive house.

"You've never opened up to anyone before. And I get why you would let your guard down with Clara. She's great."

Jet let out a hollow laugh. "I knew better."

"You cannot fault yourself for falling for Clara Wallace. Everyone—"

"Everyone falls in love with Clara." Jet ran his hand over his chest. "You know what she said about me? She said I would fall in love once, hard and fast. She was right."

"Jet," Michael warned.

"No, she was right. I'm not going to get over this." He tightened his jaw against the pain.

"I'm going to call you out here. You've been pushing away women since your first year in college. You condemned yourself to being alone because no one was ever right enough. Now, you are recondemning yourself by saying you'll only love once, and it was Clara. That's unhealthy."

"Unhealthy, but true."

"I'm sorry, but from what I've observed, things could still work out with Clara."

"They're not going to work out. A girl like Clara Wallace doesn't go out with a Broughman."

"Jet, in all the time I've known you, you have never let a woman in." Michael looked thoughtful. "You aren't going to like this next question."

"Get it over with."

"Did you do anything to shut Clara out? You don't handle rejection well. Sometimes I think you end relationships before they get serious so you don't get hurt."

Jet stared out at the grove of pine trees beyond his yard. That was the question. What had he done to mess this up?

Michael was right on one count. Jet had ended relationships with a number of smart, beautiful women. The pattern was always the same. Jet's logical brain would examine a woman's attributes and assess that she was worth dating, and he would try. But the women always tried much harder. Eventually, Jet would conclude that, although whoever he was dating was nice, he wasn't excited about her, and he would walk. Every time.

But it wasn't because he was afraid of being rejected. It was because nothing had ever come close to the magic of Clara.

He shook his head. "No. I was heading into

Eighty Local, and she came running up to me. I had it all planned. I was going to ask her if she wanted to bring her horse out here and ride around my place. I guess I thought six thousand acres, two hundred and twenty head of cattle and a handful of emus might impress her." Jet remembered her nervous smile as she came toward him, her eyes concerned. He felt the conversation again like a kick in the chest.

Then he remembered what he *hadn't* done: listen to her. Just like the last time, he took her rejection and wallowed in it. She still wanted to be friends, and he'd made sure that couldn't happen. And now they had to host this party together. It was ridiculous, thinking he could ever be anything to this community, or any community. His players might show up, but no one else would. He'd have this ridiculous house, more food than anyone could need and six defensive players wandering around bored.

He bent forward, rubbing his face with his hands.

Michael's hand came to rest on his back. "Ever since I've known you, you've been Jet Broughman, the phoenix rising from the ashes. You've put together an incredible life. Any one of your accomplishments flies in the face of statistics, and yet here you are. You made it. You don't have to work again if you don't want to. You have this ranch and this incredible home."

"What's your point?"

"Maybe it's time to stop seeing yourself as the kid defying the odds. Maybe it's time to just be Jet. This isn't going to vanish." Michael gestured at his home. "You put the pieces together to get exactly where you wanted to be. Put some more pieces together. Be patient. Fall in love and create the family you always said you wanted."

Be patient. That's where he'd messed up.

Michael stood. "You're hosting a party with Clara in two days."

Jet raked a hand through his hair. "If anybody shows up."

"I'm showing up. And I'm bringing my amazing new girlfriend." Michael picked up a log and threw it on the stack. "You may be a great friend and the best sandwich maker I know, but this place is a mess. Let's get it cleaned up."

Jet let out a hollow laugh. How many times had he invented some task to get Michael over a broken heart? Now the tables were turned.

Michael grinned, as though he could read Jet's thoughts. "You're gonna be okay. We'll get you through this."

He might get to *okay* someday, but he wasn't going to get over Clara. He could, however, apologize for his reaction this time. Michael was right: he'd come a long way in his life. But he still felt like he had so far to go.

CLARA KEPT WALKING down Main Street. She'd given herself five days to be upset, and it was time to start putting the pieces back together. Supporting Three Sisters Chocolatier was probably the best way to start.

No. Apologizing to Jet would have been the best start. But she still couldn't figure out how she could possibly make up for her behavior.

She couldn't have hurt Jet more if she'd spent months planning it. The one man who inspired her to change and grow past her fears probably never wanted to see her again. And why would he? She knew how hard it was for him to open up, after a childhood of abandonment. But all she could think about in the moment was herself, *her* fears, whether *she* was ready. Not only had she destroyed her possibility of happiness, but she'd hurt Jet so deeply. That was something she could never forgive herself for.

The lights from Outcrop Outside still crisscrossed the street. A wave of sadness rippled through her. Clara swallowed hard and kept walking. For a long time now, she'd convinced herself she was okay. Told herself and anyone who would listen that the predisposition for anxiety didn't hamper her in any tangible way.

That was a lie. As big a lie as she'd ever had a client try to pass off on her. Her whole life was dedicated to helping people open up to love. She'd barely cracked open the door before slamming it in her own face.

And that just made her furious.

Clara marched on down Main Street. First chocolate, then radical self-assessment and change. The little bracelet she'd bought from Christy Jones sparkled on her wrist. She was going to *embrace the change* like nobody's business.

She glanced over at OHTAF, allowing sadness to settle as she remembered the phone call with Jet and her parents. Just like that afternoon, old-timers sat in the rocking chairs, and a couple of men had their heads bent over a chess game.

More specifically, Coach Kessler had his head bent over a chess game.

Clara peered into the window of Second Chance Cowgirl. Christy Jones was alone in her perfect, beautiful shop.

Clara stopped. She took two steps backward, then turned and jogged into the flower shop. One massive bouquet later, she headed up the steps at OHTAF.

"You. Out of the chair," she demanded.

"Just a minute." Coach jumped one of Mr. Jungert's pieces and picked it up.

"No minutes. Up." Clara gestured with her thumb. "You're coming with me."

"But I'm winning."

"Win later." Clara tugged at Coach's arm. He moved one last piece, then allowed Clara to marshal him down the stairs.

"Did we have a meeting?" he asked. "I'm sorry if I missed it. I filled out some more of those forms you gave me."

Clara thrust the flowers into his arms and dragged him across the street. Coach looked up at the Second Chance Cowgirl sign, then at the flowers and finally back at Clara.

"I'm not ready."

Like she was gonna buy that excuse.

"Actually, you are. You may be scared, but you're ready."

"But—"

"I am not in the mood, Coach. You are a classic late bloomer in love. You weren't ready to settle down in your twenties or thirties. And yes, I've heard the stories so please don't try to pretend I don't know. By the time you got to your forties, all the good ones were taken."

"That's true," he said, like this was the first time he'd ever considered it. "That's exactly what happened."

"I see it all the time. And it can be limiting. But *you* have a window of opportunity. You're ready to commit. There is a fantastic woman on the other side of this door. Go get it done."

Coach hesitated. Clara didn't want to bring up the obvious, but there was no other option.

"Did Jet hesitate in the state playoff game? Did he pause before jumping up to catch that ball? Did he think to himself *What if I try but fail?* No. He seized the opportunity."

Coach raised his eyes to meet Clara's gaze and gave a determined nod.

"This is bigger than the playoffs. This is life."

Coach Kessler squared his shoulders and reached for the door handle. A bell rang as he opened the door. Christy looked up from a rack of vintage dresses and smiled. Clara gave her favorite history teacher a light shove, then closed the door firmly behind him.

She pulled in a deep breath, then two more.

She'd see Jet at his party the next day. That gave her twenty-four hours to get it together and come up with an apology worthy of the man she owed it to.

CHAPTER SEVENTEEN

"LET'S MOVE, GUYS," Jet called. "Guests will be here in a few hours. If anyone decides to show up at this party, we need this shack looking good."

Manuel and Aaron set the young aspen tree they were carrying into the hole Jackson had dug for it. Aaron's sister, Carley, turned the tree in its place until she was satisfied with the orientation of the branches, then Jackson started filling in the hole.

"The whole town's going to be here," Carley said.

"The whole town's invited," Jet clarified. He'd be happy if the families of these kids showed up. His chest constricted as he remembered that Clara would be here, too. She hadn't backed out of helping him with this party, even though she had every reason to. It had hurt when she gave him Wendi's number, but his reaction had been inexcusable. They'd been friends, and she acted on that friendship.

"Everyone is coming, Coach," Manuel said. "My dad can't get anyone to work at the store because everybody's like, 'Jet's house! Party!'" Manuel did his own approximation of a dance move, setting his teammates laughing.

Jet nodded. He hoped the kids were right but suspected they were wrong. He just had to put his head down and get through this awkward party with Clara and his players. He'd done plenty of hard things before. He could apologize to Clara and make it through the party.

"Would you quit messing around?" Carley snapped at her brother. "I need to go home and get dressed. And I'm hoping you all have the decency to shower and dress nice."

"Collar and tie, right, Coach?" Jackson asked.

"Collar and tie, game day attire," Jet responded. Then he shook his head. "Wait, I don't have a tie."

The guys laughed. Jet's spirits lifted, if only for a moment.

"I can bring you one of my grandpa's ties," Jackson said.

The memory of Mr. Wallace's science-themed ties washed over him. Jet shook his head. There was no sense in wishing he could be a part of that family now. All he could do was hope to salvage the working relationship with Hunter.

As though on cue, Hunter's truck appeared at the gate. It was too early for him to start setting up the catering. What was he doing here?

Hunter jumped out of the truck to open the gate. He didn't look happy. Jet's chest constricted.

"I'll be right back, guys." Jet jogged toward the gate. Hunter saw him coming and slammed his truck door. He leaned up against it, arms folded. *Not a great sign.*

"I just came from Clara's house."

Jet closed his eyes against the memory of the tidy little bungalow that smelled like Clara.

"Is she okay?"

"No," Hunter said, without hesitation. "No, she seems pretty bad." He leveled a glare at Jet. "Is this about you?"

Jet fought the sickness rising in his stomach. He shrugged his shoulders, waiting for the hollowness to recede before trying to speak.

Hunter's gaze intensified. "You say something to her after Smith Rock?"

Jet swallowed hard. He'd lost Clara, he would lose Hunter's friendship, too. He would lose Hunter's business and any standing in this community he'd scrambled to get.

He met Hunter's stare, frustration overriding the pain. "Yeah, I said something. After she tried to set me up with one of her clients."

Hunter's arms dropped, and he glanced back in the direction of town, then at Jet. "She tried to set you up?"

Jet clenched his jaw, turning away from Hunter's disbelief.

Hunter let out a low whistle. "I didn't see that coming."

The pain in Jet's chest threatened. He swallowed, then turned back to Hunter. He could barely get any words out. "I didn't see it coming either."

Hunter shook his head. "Man, I'm so sorry. We all thought—"

"Yeah. So did I." Pain washed through him, fresh and unrelenting. "I didn't react well."

"Of course not." Hunter ran his fingers through his hair. "What was she thinking?"

"She was thinking she wants me to date someone else."

"No," Hunter said. "I know my sister. She may have said one thing, but she didn't mean it."

Jet appreciated the sentiment, but Hunter hadn't been there; he hadn't seen her smile as she offered him Wendi's number. "I don't know if I can deal with this," Jet admitted. "Being in town, seeing her."

"Well, you're gonna have to deal with it,"

Hunter said, dropping a hand on his shoulder. "Outcrop's not letting you go."

Hunter's blunt words snapped Jet out of his self-pity. "What?"

"I know your old boss keeps calling, trying to get you back in Seattle, but forget it. I'm not interested in finding another supplier and the Eagles won't find a better defensive coach. Jackson and his friends look up to you," Hunter gestured to where the kids were working. "Every other sentence out of that kid's mouth these days starts with *Jet says*. I'm sorry you have a broken heart, and I'm really frustrated with my sister right now, but you're stuck here. You matter in this town."

Jet managed a dry laugh at Hunter's assessment. "Thanks."

"I mean it." Hunter shook his head, concerned. "And I am sorry. She doesn't always act in her own best interest. Change is hard for Clara."

"She told me that once."

"Think about it. She's a matchmaker who has never been in a real relationship. This has probably been pretty confusing for her."

Jet let that sink in. If she had been falling in love, that would have been unnerving. Possibly more frightening than zip-lining.

"Look, I've been watching this go down all

summer," Hunter said. "It's hard not to be frustrated with my sister right now, but I can tell you this, she really likes you. Her anxiety gets out of hand, but it happens so infrequently now she's not good at recognizing it anymore. I know her. She has a pattern to put herself back together, and if you can give her some time, I think there's still a chance for you two."

Hunter's words opened up a sluiceway of mixed emotions. Pain and love and loss conflagrated in his gut, but overriding all of it was tremendous respect for Clara, a beautiful, complex woman. Could there be another chance?

Hunter was distracted by something happening over at the cabin.

"Are your emus supposed to be out?"

Jet groaned. *Some things never change.*

"I gotta go," Jet said. He looked at Hunter. "Thank you for this insight."

"Good luck." Hunter nodded to where Larry was pecking curiously at the new landscaping. "With everything."

Jet trotted back to the cabin. He was determined to let the laughter and camaraderie of the kids muscle through some of his sadness. They were working together, turning the old eyesore of a shack into a great place that would help fund their college educations. He'd created this opportunity for the kids and could do even more to help his community.

While he was proud of how far he'd traveled, Michael was right. Holding on to the pain from his childhood was keeping him from the happiness he wanted for his future. He needed to move forward, past Jet rising from the ashes. He could just be Jet: rancher, friend, defensive coach, emu-wrangler.

He was still heartbroken over Clara—that wasn't going to change. She was still in town, still the sweetest, most beautiful woman he'd ever met.

And she was still single.

Hunter was right when he'd said this had to be confusing for Clara. Jet had been too wrapped up in his own heartbreak to consider how hard change was for her. She grappled with anxiety, and he needed to be there for her, rather than worry about his own wounded ego. They could still be friends, after all. And as a friend, he could be the one to help her open up to something more when she was ready.

"I'm open. I'm open!" Jackson's voice distracted Jet from his thoughts. Clara's nephew ran past Manuel, then juked around Aaron. Carley launched a small pot of lavender into the air. Jackson caught it, pulled the plant out of the plastic container and dropped it in the hole that had been prepared for it. "Touchdown!" Jackson cried.

Jet laughed at their antics, really laughed for the first time in a week. It reminded him of another time there were still a few seconds left in the game and he needed to keep playing.

He grinned. This wasn't over yet.

CHAPTER EIGHTEEN

CLARA PARKED, THEN CLUTCHED the steering wheel with one hand and the door with the other. She took three deep breaths. This was going to be uncomfortable. That was fine. She shook off the buzz rattling around in her head and took one last glance in the rearview mirror. *At least she looked good.*

Her feet touched down on the paver stones of the extraordinary driveway, and she glanced up at Jet's home.

A massive front door framed with pine pillars stood open to welcome the guests. The whole scene was so Jet: a smart use of local materials to create something you couldn't stop staring at. Clara felt her insides sink.

She closed her eyes and pulled in another breath. There would be other opportunities, other men. She could make different choices in the future. When her eyes opened she was staring directly at the gorgeous house. Clara whimpered. She really wanted *this* man.

Jet appeared at the front door, then came trotting out to greet her. He looked nervous but determined, like when he'd walked across OHTAF to join her at the stock tank of chicks all those years ago.

"Hey." He waved, then returned his hands to his pockets.

"Hey." She waved back. She had to say something friendly, something normal. "This is a great place."

He glanced back at the house and shrugged. "It's too big." His gaze reconnected with hers, then softened. "Clara, I—"

A rush of nerves swept over her, and she cut him off. "Do Hunter and his crew have everything set up?"

Jet paused, then continued walking toward her. "Yeah. It's all good."

Clara nodded. She opened her mouth to apologize, but Jet spoke first.

"All I have to do is grill burgers." He gave her a determined smile. Clara guessed this was as hard for him as it was for her. But one thing was clear: they both wanted the other to feel okay about the situation. That was a start.

"And have fun." She smiled up at him. "It's a party, remember?"

At that Jet looked down at the ground, but

after a few moments, his gaze came to rest on her face. He placed his hand on her arm.

"Jet—"

A vehicle turned into the drive, and Jet's hand dropped. Clara looked up to see an old International Harvester Scout bumping down the road.

"Looks like Coach made it," Jet said, the relief on his face transforming to curiosity. "And he seems to have a date."

"Yes!" Clara clapped her hands together, then pressed her fingertips to her lips. She might have royally messed up with Jet, but she'd nailed that match.

"What is it?" Jet asked.

Clara bounced on her toes as the Scout pulled to a stop. "This is my masterpiece."

Coach Kessler, in his trademark Hawaiian shirt, hopped out of the driver's seat and trotted around to the passenger side. He opened the door, offering his hand to Christy Jones. She was so elegant in a long skirt, vintage boots and turquoise jewelry that it was hard to believe she and Coach came from the same planet. But there was nothing mismatched about the look they gave each other.

"You did this?" Jet asked.

Clara bit her lip and grinned at him. "I'm pretty pleased with myself. It took a stern talking-to with Coach and a long pep talk for Christy, but I managed to get them both to take a chance. From there they fell in love in about fifteen seconds."

"You are a genius." He shook his head, the brilliant smile flashing.

"I did try to tell you that, at the first meeting with Michael. But no, you didn't believe me." Clara waved her hands in mock dismay.

A flush crept up Jet's neck as he groaned. "I'm still sorry about that. Is there any match you can't pull off?"

Clara glanced up into his eyes. "Just one."

Jet shifted, holding her gaze. A steady hum vibrated through her mind.

"Can I, um…" Jet gestured toward the old cabin. "I was gonna ask…"

Clara took in a deep breath. She was ready for whatever he was going to say. If she was so lucky as to get another chance, she would not mess it up.

Jet glanced down at his feet. Then he said, "Do you still have time to discuss paint colors?"

"Paint colors?"

He blew out a breath, like that wasn't what he'd meant to ask but kept on with it, anyway. "Yeah. See, we're still gonna have to paint the interior of that…thing, and—"

"I'd love to help."

"You would?"

He looked so surprised, like he hadn't expected her to say yes.

"Absolutely."

"Clara." He glanced back down at the ground between them. He was clearly having trouble speaking. "Clara, I'm sorry—"

"You're sorry?" she interrupted him. "I'm the one who—" She met his gaze, and any words she might have been able to come up with vanished. Not for the first time, she felt like he understood her. His smile bathed her in its warmth and pulled her toward him. The memory of brushing her lips against his cheek warmed her. She put a hand on his arm, raised herself onto her tiptoes.

A horn startled them both. Clara glanced up to see a Sprinter van parking next to Coach's vehicle. Manuel and his family climbed out, hollering greetings and exclaiming over the house. She dropped back onto her heels.

Another car arrived. She looked back to see a whole line of vehicles coming down the highway.

"It looks like everyone's coming," Jet said. "People are actually coming to my party."

"Well, yeah. Of course everyone's here. And

early." She checked her watch. "There's no such thing as fashionably late in Outcrop."

Jet nodded. "Okay, then. We should—" He indicated the house.

"We should," Clara agreed. "I'll stay up front and greet the guests," she said, reiterating the plan they'd made.

"And I'll grill out back."

"But don't get stuck there."

"That's the whole point of grilling. To get stuck."

Clara laughed. His gaze connected with hers, and he shook his head. "You'd think a match-maker would know me well enough by now. I have an excuse for not mingling at my own party, and I intend to use it."

"Understood." She nodded, then pulled in a breath. "I hope once these people get here and settle, you don't mind if I…come and mingle… with you?"

His smile flashed, like it had all those years ago when he'd caught that pass. He nodded. "I'd like that."

It seemed everyone in town turned out to support the team and welcome Jet back to Out-crop. Clara had followed the guests into the house. They were all happy to see her, but what they wanted was Jet.

And this, she realized, was what she wanted too—the sweet, messy unpredictability of being with Jet. And it didn't matter if she had to run a hundred laps on the path to get herself settled enough to move forward with a relationship, she was going to do it. Yes, there were things she was going to have to give up in order to have Jet, and that scared her. She would have less control over her day-to-day life if she had to factor another person into her plans.

Less control but considerably more snuggling.

The whole room seemed to tilt as Clara came to this realization. She was surprised that no one else lost their footing as the earth shifted and rearranged itself.

She found herself one step closer to the kitchen, and then one more. It felt like each atom in her body was moving toward Jet of its own volition. But the house was packed. She pushed and bobbed past people. Did Outcrop Football seriously have so many supporters? Time seemed to bend and twist as she battled her way toward the opening into the kitchen. She could smell the burgers Jet was grilling on the back patio. She would find him at the grill and—

And what? What would she say?

I never meant to hurt you, but in doing so I realized how much I love you?

I'm sorry I asked you to call someone else, when I really meant to ask if we could take a long, slow drive in your truck and decide to love each other forever?

Do you mind if I spend the rest of the party staring at your biceps? Because it's kind of exhausting not to.

Clara stopped, and party chatter filled the room as she waited for the buzz of anxious thoughts to fill her. Her stomach should be dropping about now, her throat dry and panic commandeering her brain.

But nothing came. Her heart continued its strong, steady push, and every other physical reaction said nothing more than *Jet, please!*

She was ready.

The opening to the kitchen was a few feet away and completely blocked with people. Ordinarily, the sight would have filled her with satisfaction, but right now she could only wonder why there were so many people in between her and Jet. Clara glanced left. A hall led past a second staircase. She knew enough about interior design to sense a well-placed laundry room leading to an exterior door. She made a break for it.

THERE WERE NEARLY fifty people on his back patio. Jet doubted this many human souls had ever been on the entire Broughman property in any given year, much less packed into such a small place. The whole community had turned up, and the party had taken on a life of its own.

"These are up," Jet called out to Michael.

Michael managed to peel his attention away from Joanna, but not his arms or most of his body. Steeped in Clara's encyclopedic relationship knowledge and, Jet suspected, several love chemicals, Michael and Joanna were doing great. They'd practically manifested a flock of bluebirds carrying ribbons and hearts to circle them at all times.

"I'll grab them," Joanna said, landing a peck on Michael's cheek before she came to grab the platter. Jet shook his head at his old friend. Michael widened his eyes as if to say *Can you believe I'm here with this woman?*

Yeah, he could believe it. Michael had put himself out there, taken risks and allowed himself to hope. Jet had further to travel along that road than Michael did, but he could still get there.

The party swirled warm and happy around him. What if this were his life? As Clara's husband, he would get to stand at the grill for a hundred such parties, watching his beautiful wife entertain their friends.

Jet laid more burgers on the grill, nodding as people called appreciative comments over to him. This could be his life. He had to stay in the game. *I need your help with paint colors* wasn't the smoothest line, but he could try again.

I am your friend. I will wait until you are ready.

These were the lines he needed to try out next. He'd overcome poverty, survived in Seattle and finally begun to create the community in Outcrop he'd always sought. He could do this.

"Hunter!" Jet heard a female voice call. Jet turned to see Piper come barreling out onto the back patio. She did not look happy.

"What's up?" Hunter was replenishing condiments along the trestle tables.

Jet kept his eyes on those tables, trying to look casual as he strained to hear what had Piper so upset.

"This." Piper gestured to the back patio.

Was something wrong with his patio?

"I know," Hunter said.

"Like, I was baffled before, but now I'm downright furious. Did you see the living room? That picture of the mustangs?"

"Right." Hunter shook his head and laughed.

What was so funny about his living room? Sure, Jet had handed the decor over to someone else, but he thought that room was cool.

"That bowl? And the windows?" Piper held her hands up in air quotes and mimicked Clara saying, "It hums."

Piper glanced in his direction. Jet refocused on the grill, hoping she hadn't noticed he was listening in.

"It does hum." Hunter spoke just loudly enough that Jet could hear him. "You know, I never really got what she meant before, but yeah. This place hums."

Okay, humming was good. That had been established. So why was Piper mad?

"I'm not mercenary by any means, but that driveway? You could justify marrying someone for that driveway."

Hunter laughed. "In addition to the driveway, he's also a good guy."

"Exactly. Intelligent, funny, kind. His steadiness helps ground Clara. Her charm balances his shyness."

"I know," Hunter said. "You do realize our sister could qualify for the Olympics of self-sabotage."

"I'm so done with her self-sabotage. There

is nothing worse than watching someone place the dynamite and strike a match themselves just when everything is looking up."

Jet kept his gaze straight ahead, despite an intense longing to throw himself into the middle of their conversation. This must be how the emus felt right about now, forced to watch a party they weren't allowed to attend.

"I've seen the way he looks at her. The man melts anytime Clara so much as glances at him."

Okay, so it was that obvious. Not like he was the first guy to have that problem.

Piper was still speaking. "And why shouldn't he? Clara is literally the best person on earth. Plus, she's super cute. No, if I was confused about the turn of events after talking with Clara, now I'm downright furious. She's crazy about him."

A frisson of both fear and hope ran through Jet's body.

Hunter spoke. "And you're just plain crazy."

Jet closed his eyes and tried to remind himself that their sibling banter was endearing.

Heat wafted up from the grill. Jet looked down to see flames where he expected burgers. *Oops.*

"You need help?" Michael asked.

"I'm good." Jet fished around for an excuse that would get Michael to be quiet so he could keep listening in on the conversation. "Fit Burgers are supposed to flash-cooked at a high heat."

"Are they supposed to be blackened and crispy?"

"I'm still getting the hang of it. Look," he pointed, "Joanna's watching the emus. You should go tell her about the time they escaped."

Michael took a step back as Jet doused the flames, but he kept his eye on the grill.

Hunter said something Jet couldn't make out. Piper responded, also in a low voice. Jet risked a glance in their direction, but Hunter looking straight at him. Jet turned sharply back to the grill.

Whoa, return of the flames. Time to flip the burgers.

"Clara was falling in love with him." Piper spoke slowly and clearly, as though trying to get Hunter to understand her point. "And she got scared and messed things up. She did it her junior year in high school, and she did it again last week. I've had enough of this."

Jet's mind raced through the possibilities.

Clara had been falling in love. With me. And that would be frightening to anyone battling with anxiety. If that were the case, he needed to get in the house as quickly as possible and let her know they could take it slowly, step-by-step, until she felt comfortable.

Distracted, he began lifting the burgers off the grill. Charred on one side, pink on the other. It was fortunate he'd be handing the plate over to a doctor who would manage the food accordingly.

Blood converged from every part of his body to flood his face. He could do this. He could walk in and find Clara and tell her he would wait.

But what if she rejects you?

Jet let the question sit. His eyes landed on the now-neat stack of juniper logs out back. He was a successful adult, and the chaotic patterns of his childhood didn't have to apply anymore. He'd survived two rejections. It was possible he could live through another. Either way, he had to let Clara know that he was there for her.

"This is not entirely her fault," Hunter said. "The guy took Wendi's number when she offered it."

Okay. That's it.

No one was going to accuse Jet Broughman of being interested in anyone other than Clara. Jet set the spatula aside and pulled off the Eighty Local apron Hunter had loaned him.

"Michael, can you get this?" Jet gestured to the grill.

"I thought you'd never ask."

Jet turned toward the house, taking long strides for the kitchen.

"Jet!" Hunter called as he sped past. "This smells fantastic. Are these Fit Burgers?"

"No, I, um, not sure." Jet tried to look past Hunter to see if Clara was in the kitchen.

"I lined up one set of condiments for the pulled pork and another for the beef. I figure people can mix and match." Hunter kept speaking, but none of it made it into Jet's head. Jet tried to shift past him, but Hunter laid a hand on his shoulder. He was still talking about condiments.

"I need to…" Jet searched for the appropriate word. Most of what came to mind were not things he could say to Clara's older brother. "Go," he finally finished.

"Go?" Hunter asked, exchanging a smile with Piper. "Go where?"

"I need to go. Into my house."

His focus left Hunter completely, but not before picking up on his broad grin. Clara was in the house, upset, and Hunter was out here grinning? Jet pushed through the tangle of people on his patio toward the doors. He glanced back just in time to see Piper and Hunter exchange a high five. He loved the Wallace family, but there was no doubt they could get a little weird.

Jet's kitchen was as crowded as the patio. People were draped across the island, hugged the countertop, and full on blocked the opening into the living room. A man was actually standing in the open door, gripping the frame. Jet would have to knock him off his hinges to get through. Clara probably wouldn't like that.

He turned right to walk through his work nook, passing his computer and paper-strewn desk. Light fell from high windows in the hall, eliciting a golden sheen from the tile work that made his laundry room feel like a shrine.

And there was Clara, racing toward some new hosting emergency. She stopped when she saw him, staring up at him like she had something to say but couldn't quite remember what it was.

She was so beautiful in the early evening light washing through the windows. Big brown eyes met his, and Jet was a little worried he might fall in.

"Jet," she said, her dimpled smile flashing.

That did it. Jet was conscious of his hands coming to rest on Clara's waist. He lifted her and set her on top of the washer, leaving his hands on either side of her. Her eyes got impossibly wider. She was clearly shocked but not complaining.

"I really like you," his words fell out. "And I don't know how to say it to you, but you're…" Jet tried to compose something debonair, but it came out "…so pretty. Smart. Fun." His hands edged closer to Clara until he felt the softness of her sweater against his knuckles. It took considerable strength to keep talking.

"I like you, and I like the way we are when we're together. You have a lot going on, and it's a lot for me to ask. Please, let me be the guy you didn't plan on. Because I know this is what I want." Jet gestured in the direction of the cheerful voices. "I want to watch you shine in a house full of people. I want to be part of your plans. And if that's just as your friend, I'm in. If it's going to take time for you to adjust to the idea of being more than friends, I'm a patient man."

Clara's face turned up toward his, her lips parted. She placed her fingers on his bicep. The touch shot through him, making him sway on his feet. Her hand curled around his arm, drawing him closer. Her breath was warm against his cheek.

"So," he said as he felt heat rise in his face, "if you want to spin one of your webs on me—" he swallowed deeply "—or release some chemicals…" she was smiling now, her dimples flashing "…I am ready."

CLARA GRIPPED JET'S bicep and the back of his head, pulling him closer. She was simultaneously conscious of floating and being irrevocably tethered by Jet's touch. But rather than riding on a flying carpet, she was cruising through the stratosphere on a washing machine.

"Clara," Jet exhaled her name, pressing his forehead to hers. She gulped in air as she tried to remember whatever chemical it was they were secreting at the moment. Paraffin? No, that wasn't right.

"I didn't think I was ready." She bit her lip. "Apparently, I was wrong."

Jet laughed. His lips were so close.

"I…" He looked up, gulped in more air, then repeated, "I like you. A lot. Everything about you." Clara ran her hand down his cheek, relishing the trace of stubble at his jawline. She breathed in deeply, feeling heady at the scent of… *What were those chemicals?*

"You are so pretty." His eyes traveled her face. Something seemed to occur to him, and with effort he said, "But if I'm not what you want…" He pulled back. Every inch of Clara's body joined in angry protest at his departure.

"Jet, you are what I want." Her fingers moved slowly up his arms, curling around his muscles. "You're worth the risk."

Wonder filled his gaze. "So you don't need more time? Or space or...?"

She shook her head. "I don't need anything. Just you."

Jet lifted his hands to either side of her face. "All there has ever been is just you."

He lowered his lips toward hers. Clara couldn't believe this was finally about to happen.

"I'm scared," she whispered. "I want this, but I'm really scared. I'm really happy we're here, in your laundry room, but, um..."

Jet shifted, gently moving so he could look into her eyes. "But you want to take it slow?" he guessed.

"No." Clara was a little embarrassed at just how loudly that word came out. She lowered her voice. "It's just that I've never..." She stopped, swallowed, then took in a deep breath. "I haven't gone very far with men, at all." She looked into his eyes. "I mean...I haven't *really* kissed anyone before. And I'm super excited about, you know, kissing. And everything else. With you."

Jet's expression shifted slowly, comprehension, a flash of confusion, then something she couldn't quite read.

"Y-you've never…"

She shook her head. "Nope."

The sweetest baffled expression crossed his face. "How is that possible?"

Clara slid a little closer. "You know, the chemicals, and the bonding."

Jet shifted again, distancing himself once more. That was going to have to stop. "Right. *Love Rule Number Four: Know your love chemicals and choose when and with whom you release them.*"

"You remembered!"

"Oh, yeah."

His smile warmed her completely, wiping out any concerns. Clara leaned toward him, his hands ran down her arms.

"Wait." Jet's eyes shone with a mixture of panic and hope. "You've never kissed *anyone* before."

Clara shook her head. "Not like, *kissing.* Not romantically."

"And you want to."

She bit her lip and nodded.

"Kiss me?" he clarified.

"Yes, Jet Broughman. You."

"You don't want to wait until a special occasion? Like a first date?"

Clara laughed. "I like this occasion."

"I mean, we could wait until we get married if you wanted to."

"Oh, are we getting married?" she teased.

There was such sincere pleading in Jet's gaze. *He wanted to marry her.*

And this was not a good moment for teasing.

Clara leaned in and kissed his temple, then his eyelids.

"I don't want to wait until we go out or get married for my first kiss," she whispered. "I don't want to wait at all."

He looked into her eyes, and in his expression she could see the depth of his vulnerability. Hurt and abandonment had been the companions of his childhood. He'd spent years building up protective layers but now offered to shed them for her. The gift was so precious it took her breath away.

Jet swallowed. His hands repositioned along the side of her face. "I'm in love with you, Clara. I always have been."

She smiled, all her gratitude and hope bubbling over. His thumb drifted to her dimple. He smiled back.

"I love you, Jet."

His scent enveloped her as he leaned in. His lips brushed hers softly. Clara drew his face closer and fell into his kiss. *Magic.*

It was some time before a familiar noise intruded on Clara's senses. What was that clinking and humming? It was like a bunch of people were talking all at the same time.

Clara pulled back. "Oh, wait. The party?"

Jet leaned in to kiss her again.

"What?" he mumbled. His lips brushed hers softly. Her eyes closed, and she drew his face closer. Warm and easy and endless kisses were all that mattered, right?

"The party." Clara breathed out after another kiss. "The one we're supposed to be hosting right now."

Jet pulled back, puzzled.

"The party?" His expression shifted as he remembered. "We have a crowd of people here."

Clara decided that zero of those people mattered as Jet leaned down and placed a delicate kiss on her cheek, then another on her nose.

"Whoa. There's a party. And I'm grilling. And we're hosting." Jet shook his head. "We should probably—"

"Yeah," Clara agreed.

Disco and champagne bubbles were the only thing she felt responsible for at the moment.

"Or maybe they'll leave?"

"Uh-huh." Jet's eyes lingered on her lips.

Clara dug around in her Love Rules to come up with any reason not to make out in a laundry room during a party. Nothing was jumping out at her.

"Clara?" a deep voice called out from the kitchen. "Is she back here?"

Jet turned away, running a hand over the back of his neck. Clara slipped off the washing machine and wobbled on her feet.

"Hey, Clara." Hunter whipped around the corner from the kitchen. "Have you seen..." Hunter trailed off as he noticed Jet. Then he looked at Clara, then back at Jet again. "Jet?" he finished his sentence.

"Um, yeah," Clara said, pointing. "He's... um, right here."

Her brother turned back to her and said dryly, "Thanks."

"Did I, uh, leave the grill unattended for the last ten minutes?" Jet asked.

"Try thirty," Hunter said. "Michael's been stuck there, and somehow doing a worse job than you were." He glanced around the room, then did a double take at the utility sink. "Dude, is that a chicken in your sink?"

"Uh, yup."

Clara leaned over to see the little chick she'd thrust into Jet's hands at OHTAF nested cozily in a cardboard box. Jet wrapped an arm around her waist. She felt warm and safe, with endless possibilities unfolding before them.

Hunter groaned. "Come on. You two can come back here and discuss detergent options after the party. You go host," Hunter said, pointing to her. Then he looked at Jet. "And you go relieve Michael at the grill."

"Bossy," Clara muttered. She looked up and around the laundry room, noticing the clever design, high windows and framed prints advertising various national parks. "This is a nice room."

Jet paused before heading back to the kitchen. "Is it…satisfying?"

"Not yet," she said and grinned at him.

JET HAD SPENT his summer dreaming about being with Clara: watching her smile, enjoying her sense of humor and intelligence, getting to know her family. But there was another element to being with her that hadn't occurred to him until it happened.

The miracle took place on the patio. A long, painful twenty minutes had passed since he and Clara had walked out of the laundry room in opposite directions. Jet had spent the time cooking what would go down in Outcrop history as the worst burgers ever to be served at a party. He stood over the grill, completely disinterested in the meat. It felt like his body had been taken apart cell by cell, infused with sunshine and put back together again. Then he glanced up from the patties he didn't realize were burning to see Clara step out onto the patio. She smiled and headed straight toward him.

"Hi, sweetheart," she said. Placing her hand on his arm, she stood on her tiptoes to kiss his cheek.

And just like that, in front of the entire community, he was claimed by Clara Wallace. Of all the men in the house, in central Oregon, in the world, she chose him. After a lifetime of being passed along, overlooked and ignored, the world's most incredible woman had walked into a sea of people and let them all know he was hers.

His arm slipped around her waist.

"Hi, beautiful," he said. "You hungry?"

"Starving." She broke eye contact and glanced around the patio and waved. "Hey, Michael, Joanna. How's it going?"

If Michael was shocked, he didn't show it. As a pediatric surgeon, he had practice at not reacting to outrageous impossibilities. Joanna, on the other hand, let her eyes shuffle from Jet to Clara and back again.

Jet cleared his throat. This was the time to take the lead and clarify the situation. "You guys have plans for tomorrow?" he asked. "Because I was thinking maybe we could go get brunch together?"

Michael looked at Joanna for approval, which was quickly and enthusiastically forthcoming. "That sounds great."

"So like a date?" Clara grinned up at him.

"Yeah. I thought we could go after our morning date."

"Which is?"

"We're going to take a trail ride around my property, then discuss color options for the cabin."

Clara's laugh rang out. Jet felt so good he kept going. "We'll go for a trail ride, meet Michael and Joanna for brunch, then head off to our afternoon date."

"And that would be…?"

"You wanted to check out my laundry room."

"Oh." Clara paused and did that trick where she made the rest of the world disappear. "I thought we were going to check out the laundry room later tonight, after the guests left?"

"There's a lot to do in there."

Clara wrapped her arm around his waist and ran her hand along his side. She turned back to Michael and Joanna and said the words that would keep him up for nights to come. "He is literally the best boyfriend."

The party rolled on. Guests rotated through the patio. Hunter eventually muscled Jet away from the grill, muttering something about having a reputation to uphold. And throughout it all, Clara never left Jet's side. It was like she wanted to be with him more than anyone else.

Now they stood together in the entryway of his house, saying goodbye to guests. Folks were clearing out, and Clara wasn't going anywhere.

"Sis, I'm off!" Piper swept toward the door. "This was awesome. Thank you."

Clara wrapped her arms around her sister.

Piper glanced at Jet, then back at Clara. "You still coming to Portland next week to shop?"

"Of course. It's on the calendar."

"I didn't know..." Piper gestured to Jet.

"It's on the calendar," Clara said again. "And obviously we need a sleepover to talk."

"And you probably need a whole new wardrobe."

"This relationship can clearly be celebrated with new clothes."

"Everything can be celebrated with new clothes." Piper gazed at Jet. "Thank you for hosting us. And for listening to me complain."

He started to comment. Piper hadn't spoken a word to him the whole evening. Sure, he'd been listening in on her private conversation with Hunter but—

Through the fog something clicked in his brain. Jet looked at Piper, then glanced over at where Hunter leaned against the wall, smirking. They hadn't intended that conversation to be private at all.

Piper leaned over and gave him a hug, whispering, "You're welcome."

EPILOGUE

THE SCREEN DOOR clapped shut behind them, and Jet found himself reaching for Clara. He stood behind her on the front porch of her family home, wrapping his arms around her. Wallace Ranch was glorious. The sun shone warm against the bright blue sky, and the smell of pine and sage persisted.

Jet felt sweat prick his brow, despite the cool late-morning air. Michael's latest text still burned in his mind: Let's do this!

They'd made their plans carefully over the last week, and today was the day. It just all seemed so much easier when they were sitting on his back patio discussing strategy.

"You okay?" Clara asked, turning to look up at him. She was beautiful, wearing a pale green sundress, her gold pendant necklace sparkling against her throat. He had another piece of jewelry tucked in his pocket he hoped she might like as much as that necklace.

He tightened his arms around her waist. "I'm great."

Ash's truck came crunching up the gravel drive, Jackson and his driver's permit at the wheel with Ash beside him. In the backseat sat two of Jet's favorite people.

From behind Jet, Hunter let out a whoop. Bowman and Piper started waving. Jet felt a wave of nervousness pass over him. Clara squeezed his arm and gave him a smile that wiped the worry right out of his heart.

"I missed you!" Piper squealed, bounding toward the truck. Car doors slammed open and shut as Mr. and Mrs. Wallace emerged from the truck looking exhausted but happy.

"Parents!" Clara slipped from Jet's arms as she raced down the steps and into Mr. Wallace's hug. "You're three weeks late," she scolded.

The Wallace kids surrounded their parents, greeting them and exchanging news. Jet noticed Jackson pulling suitcases out of the truck bed. He skirted the family to help him.

"Jet!" Mrs. Wallace cried. "Let me look at you." His geography teacher took his arm and stilled him. "I think you've grown."

"Yes," Mr. Wallace said dryly. "He was only a few inches tall on the iPhone."

Piper groaned. "No one missed your bad jokes, Dad."

"I missed them," Jackson said.

Jet managed to say, "I missed your bad jokes, too, Mr. Wallace."

His former science teacher slapped him on the back. "I don't suppose it's any use telling you to call me Bob?"

"Nope," Jet said, wrapping an arm around Clara as they followed the noisy, cheerful family he'd always envied into the house.

"Did you guys hear Bowman's been named firefighter of the year?" Piper asked.

Bowman shrugged, mumbling, "It's no big deal."

Mrs. Wallace took his arm. "It is a big deal, and while I'd prefer you never scale another burning building, we're very proud of you."

Bowman didn't respond, but Jet noticed the glimmer of a smile as he hugged his mom.

"It smells fantastic," Mr. Wallace said. "Hunter, are you cooking?"

"I've got a welcome home feast for you. Unfortunately, it won't be ready until one o'clock," Hunter said. "I wish I'd gotten everything started earlier but I was stuck with the building inspector down at Eighty Local."

"The last seventy-two hours have been so

eventful, a few more hours will barely register," Mr. Wallace said.

Clara glanced at her watch. "Speaking of which, do you two want to take a rest?"

"Or, we could—" Jet gestured to the door, then took a deep breath and looked at Mr. Wallace. "Yeah, um. We could get your bags in?"

Mr. Wallace had not lost the ability to know when Jet needed to talk. He smiled through his exhaustion. "Great idea, Jet. Let's get the last of the luggage out of the truck."

"I'll get it, Grandpa," Jackson said.

"I got it." Jet jumped for the door.

Mr. Wallace stood and stretched. If he was tired after three days of travel, he didn't let it interfere with being there for Jet when he needed him.

"You are so right," Jet heard Piper say as they walked out the door. "He's a total parent hog."

"He does it on the phone all the time," Clara said as he stepped into the sunshine.

The screen door hit the frame behind them. The cool air energized Jet as he walked to the truck with Mr. Wallace.

"What's on your mind?" his old teacher asked with a smile, indicating he already knew.

JET CHECKED HIS phone as he waited on the front porch for Clara. No news from Michael yet.

"Anything interesting?"

Jet tucked his phone in his back pocket, then gave himself a minute to stare as Clara emerged from the farmhouse.

"Nothing as interesting as you." Clara rolled her eyes, but Jet hadn't meant to be cheesy. "I mean it, you look…" He faltered. How could he finish the sentence? There were no words to describe how beautiful, perfect, stunning, incredible she was. She was the most beautiful woman to ever slip into a sundress, which just meant she was Clara Wallace. Telling a woman she looked like herself didn't hold the level of romance Jet was going for. He pulled in a breath and leaned in to kiss her forehead. "You are the most beautiful woman I've ever seen."

She blushed as he wrapped his arms around her. He was getting better at this.

Now for the next step.

Jet placed a hand over his pocket to make sure the ring was still there and ran over the speech he'd prepared. Then he cleared his throat.

"Do you have time for a walk?"

"Dad dozed off the minute he hit the sofa and

Hunter's not going to have the meal ready for hours. I've got all the time in the world."

Jet's phone buzzed.

"Is Ken still calling?"

"Nope. I blocked him." Jet grinned down at her. His phone buzzed again, then twice more in quick succession.

"Don't you want to check it?" she asked.

Jet shook his head. "I'm not supposed to have my phone out on dates."

Clara laughed.

The phone buzzed once more with what Jet could only assume was Michael's good news. His friend had always been better than he was about rushing into things, but Jet would catch up, real soon.

Jet took Clara's hand, and they set out along the running path. Predictably, Shelby came trotting over and walked with them as far as he could. When the path branched away from the pasture, Shelby gave a snort and a toss of his mane, which Jet took as his blessing.

"I love this part of the path," Clara said. "I can't wait for you to see it in the fall, when all the leaves turn."

Jet cleared his throat. His heart hammered hard in his chest as he said, "This morning I started a running path on my property."

"Awesome! Can I come over and run on it with you?"

"Y-yes," Jet stammered. "Or..."

"Or?"

"Or you could just stay and run on it."

Jet stopped under an ancient Oregon white oak. He cleared his throat again and took both of Clara's hands in his. The words he'd practiced got tangled in his head but he pushed on. "You told me you thought I would fall in love once and hard. And I did. I know change is hard, and you..." Jet tried to reorder the words that were starting to scatter like marbles. *Focus.* "Clara, I will always be with you, steady when things get rough. You can depend on me." Her eyes shone as she took in his words. The practiced speech evaporated completely, and Jet was only able to say, "I love you. Please say *yes.*"

He dropped to one knee and reached into the pocket of his shirt. The diamond ring had been easy to pick out, bright and beautiful. But it was significantly more difficult to hold onto with shaking hands.

Jet then remembered he hadn't actually asked her to marry him yet.

He started to speak again, but his throat constricted, and nothing came out. Then he found himself opening his arms to accommodate Clara as she sat on his knee and leaned in to him. She laid a hand on his cheek and drew him into the sweetest kiss. The world narrowed into nothing more than the woman balanced on his knee.

"Yes," she said.

CLARA PUSHED OPEN the front door, her hand in Jet's, a permanent smile on her face. It wasn't just the ring on her own finger, but the picture Michael had texted of a ring on Joanna's finger, too. Apparently, her fiancé and her former client had spent the better part of the last two weeks planning a double proposal.

So much good.

"Hey, everybody!"

Jackson, Hunter and Piper sat in easy conversation. The opportunity to have her entire family all together to share the news sent her spirits humming.

Jet sat on the sofa and caught Clara's waist, pulling her down next to him.

"Are Mom and Dad up?" she asked. It was going to be so perfect to tell the whole family together.

"Yeah," Piper said, "Mom's in the kitchen." Piper stopped speaking and stared at Clara. She narrowed her right eye. In a sharp tone Clara wouldn't have expected, she asked, "Is that a ring?"

Too late to gather in all the troops now. Clara grinned and held up her hand.

"No!" Hunter said, obviously upset. He turned on Jet. "You already asked her to marry you?"

Clara could feel Jet tense beside her. This was not the reaction she expected. Hunter and Bowman loved Jet. They hung out all the time. Jet had been helping them build the events center for Eighty Local. Her brothers had even invited him on their annual climbing trip to Red Rocks.

Bowman came running in from the kitchen. Jet's hand clutched Clara's more tightly. Her brothers exchanged a glance, and then Bowman rolled his eyes.

"You couldn't have waited?" he demanded.

"I…" Jet started, then an expression of determination crossed his face. "No," he said, wrapping an arm around Clara, an edge to his voice. "I couldn't wait."

Clara stared at her siblings in horror.

Piper threw herself on the sofa next to Jet. "We were going to propose to you!" she wailed.

"We had it all planned," Hunter said. "We were going to ask you to marry Clara. I was going to cook a proposal dinner."

"I caught a steelhead," Bowman interrupted.

"We were going to give you Shelby," Piper said. "Like an engagement horse instead of a ring. Because we thought a ring would be weird."

Jet burst out laughing.

"But now that I'm saying it, an engagement horse sounds weird, too."

Jet laughed harder.

"I'm sorry." Jet wrapped his other arm around Clara. "I did wait an entire month, which was pretty tough."

"I get it," Hunter said. "And it's okay. End goal was to get you in the family."

"I figured it would take the fish dinner to convince you," Bowman said, "once you realized how bossy she can be."

Jet's gaze met Clara's. "I like her bossy."

"And we like you, Jet," Piper said. Clara's heart melted as her sister and best friend in the world gave her fiancé a hug. "We couldn't have hoped for a better man for Clara or a more perfect addition to our family."

Jet looked down and swallowed. He nodded.

"I never thought the family proposal was a good idea," Jackson said.

"You did, too," Hunter said.

"No, I thought Jet should propose at a football game."

"But then she wouldn't have been paying attention," Piper said.

Clara glanced up to see her parents entering the room.

"Congratulations, sweetheart." Her mom walked over to kiss her cheek.

"I am thrilled," her dad said. The smile he gave Jet suggested this wasn't much of a surprise.

Her mom took her hand and studied the diamond. "It certainly is enormous."

Clara glanced again at the ring. The round-cut diamond was lit with a fire within. She hadn't taken the time to learn much about diamonds, but she suspected there were several carats in this one.

"Oh, wow," Piper said, really looking at the ring for the first time. "Is it vintage? It's gorgeous. And massive."

Jet took her hand and studied the ring. "You know, Clara works with a lot of single men." No one responded. "I wanted a ring that people would notice right off, so there would be no questions."

"No questions?" Piper raised an eyebrow.

Hunter cut to the quick of the matter. "You wanted to broadcast that she's yours and everyone else better back off?"

"Well," Jet said and flushed, "I guess. In a completely nonsexist, woman-affirming, Clara-respecting way, uh, yeah."

"I'm not sure it's big enough," Bowman quipped.

"Right," Hunter agreed. "It's only visible from five hundred miles away. What about the single men on the other side of the Rocky Mountains?"

And then, in what Clara would remember as her favorite moment in a day full of wonderful memories, Jet grabbed a pillow off the end of the couch and threw it squarely in Hunter's face.

"Oh, I see how it is." Hunter pulled a pillow off a chair and hurled it at Jet. Bowman came at her fiancé from the other side with an armrest cover.

"I'm on Jet's team!" Dad yelled, flinging a pillow back at his boys.

"No hiding behind Clara's ring!" Piper cried, launching two more pillows at Jet.

"What's going on in here?"

The family froze as Ash entered through the front door.

"Jet and your sister are engaged," their dad said to his most serious child. "And we're celebrating with the traditional pillow fight."

Ash moved to Jet, hand extended. "Welcome to the family."

Clara watched as the two men connected.

"It's a nice ring," Ash said, giving Hunter and Bowman a warning look.

"You haven't even seen it yet," Clara said, holding up her hand.

Ash's lips twitched. "I could see it from out in the driveway," he said dryly.

Amid the laughter, Jet asked Clara, "Is it too big?"

"No!" Clara and Piper protested together.

"It was so sparkly and pretty," Jet said. "It made me think of you."

"I love it." Clara let her gaze travel from the ring to the man who had given it to her. "I love you."

"For the record," Bowman said, "I called it on the way back from Smith Rock. I told the guys at the fire station that Jet was going to marry my sister."

"Smith Rock?" Piper snorted. "I saw this coming when Jet was here for dinner."

"Why do you think I invited him for dinner in the first place?" Hunter said. "I called it when she roped you into the first group date."

"I hate to steal anyone's glory," their mom said, "but your father called it first, over ten years ago."

Clara looked at her dad.

"It was only a hope," he said. "I saw two extraordinary young people, working hard to overcome circumstances. I thought if the two of you, each with so much perseverance and resilience came together, it would be powerful."

"So we're bringing more beauty and joy into the world by falling in love?" Jet grinned down at her as he quoted the Love, Oregon mission statement.

"Go us!" Clara said, holding her hands up. "High five for love!"

Jet clapped her hands, his fingers curling around hers. He didn't let go this time. Clara let herself get lost in his warm brown eyes, then scanned the room. She took in Piper, her sophisticated city-girl sister. Hunter, a determined, passionate restaurateur. Bowman, the quiet daredevil firefighter. And Ash, her terse, grumbly oldest brother, with the weight of the world on his shoulders.

A spark of excitement ignited in her belly. "Okay, who's next?"

* * * * *

THE 2022 ROMANCE CHRISTMAS COLLECTION

NEW YORK TIMES BESTSELLING AUTHOR
RaeAnne THAYNE
ALL IS BRIGHT

MAISEY YATES
Merry Christmas Cowboy

JENNIFER SNOW
Alaska for Christmas

In this loveliest of seasons may you find many reasons for happiness, magic and love, and what better way to fill your heart with the magic of Christmas than with an unforgettable romance from our specially curated holiday collection.

YES! Please send me the first shipment of **The 2022 Romance Christmas Collection**. This collection begins with 1 FREE TRADE SIZE BOOK and 2 FREE gifts in the first shipment. Along with my free book, I'll also get 2 additional mass-market paperback books. If I do not cancel, I will continue to receive three books a month for five additional months. My first four shipments will be billed at the discount price of $19.98 U.S./$25.98 CAN., plus $1.99 U.S./$3.99 CAN. for shipping and handling*. My last two shipments will be billed at the discount price of $17.98 U.S./$23.98 CAN., plus $1.99 U.S./$3.99 CAN. for shipping and handling*. I understand that accepting the free books and gifts places me under no obligation to buy anything. I can always return a shipment and cancel at any time. My free books and gifts are mine to keep no matter what I decide.

☐ 269 HCK 1875   ☐ 469 HCK 1875

_____
Name (please print)

_____
Address   Apt. #

_____
City   State/Province   Zip/Postal Code

> Mail to the **Harlequin Reader Service:**
> **IN U.S.A.:** P.O. Box 1341, Buffalo, NY 14240-8531
> **IN CANADA:** P.O. Box 603, Fort Erie, ON L2A 5X3

#455 HOME WITH THE RODEO DAD
The Cowgirls of Larkspur Valley • by Jeannie Watt

Former rodeo rider Troy Mackay has given up risk-taking and wants to settle down with his baby. He only teams up with local farmer Kat Farley out of necessity—but now he's ready to take the greatest risk of all.

#456 HER VALENTINE COWBOY
Truly Texas • by Kit Hawthorne

With her horse-boarding business barely staying afloat, Susana Vrba offers newcomer Roque Fidalgo a deal—twenty hours of work a week *and* she'll even board his horse for free. But falling for the cowboy was never part of that deal!

#457 A MERRY LITTLE CHRISTMAS
Return to Christmas Island • by Amie Denman

When Hadley Pierce tells her good friend Mike Martin that she's pregnant—and he's the father—Mike can't propose quickly enough. But Hadley won't accept *any* proposal that isn't based on true love...no matter how much she wants to!

#458 A FAMILY FOR THE RANCHER
A Ranch to Call Home • by M. K. Stelmack

Mateo Pavlic intends to buy back his family's ranch land from onetime friend and neighbor Haley Jansson. But the cowboy hurt her once before. How can Haley trust him now with her land, her newborn son...and her heart?